The Lighthouse Keeper

JC Braswell

For my wife and daughter, never let the nightmares scare away your dream.

CONTENTS

ACKNOWLEDGMENTS

For their constant encouragement and friendship, I thank the greatest mentor an aspiring writer could ever have, Ronald Malfi, my tireless beta reader and constant source of sarcasm, Sir Ethan Grayson, and my friends and family. Without your support, I'm not sure how I would have made it this far. I would also like to thank others who have read my initial drafts, including Craig Reynolds, Paul Drgos, my 3rd Grade Teacher Miss Vicki Johnson, my sister Marcy Arnold, Steve Elville, and Christina Van Valkenburgh.

Lastly, thank you to C.S. Lewis.

JC.

THE LIGHTHOUSE ON MERMAID ROW

Davey McCrary stared at the obelisk spiraling upwards to the vast expanse of gray, its base anchored in an outcropping of rocks on the tip of the small peninsula. The red and white colors painted in the same pattern as a barbershop sign faded to muted tones from decades of weather and salt water. A thicket of weeds and flora sprouted around its base. Murderous vines clung to the side, curling around its cylinder form, ready to pull it free from the earth.

Most noticeable was the cracked windows that once protected the light, the lone vigil to help warn mariners of the dangers of running ashore. Some of them must've been pirates, Davey thought. On certain nights the moon reflected against the glass to give the illusion that the lighthouse was still operating, its flame reaching out across the whitecaps to contact those waylaid captains.

When he was seven, he thought the lighthouse was built to worship one of the ancient sea gods his mother used to show him in her picture books – a mastodon of a man with a swath of a white beard and a golden trident in his right hand, a snarl across his nose. But that was when he was younger and she was still around, before she dove into the Chesapeake from atop the structure. It saved others, but it couldn't save her.

His mother painted him a picture of the lighthouse before she passed.

1

Not of how it looked, but how it once stood decades ago when people still were nice to each other and not slaves to their computer. It hung above his old Ferrari bed his father refused to replace. His eleven-year-old legs reached over the foot of the bed, his ankles clipping the wooden frame, but he was small, and small meant his father didn't have to shell out more money.

It suited him just the same. Part of him didn't want to get rid of the bed. It reminded him of the way things used to be, just like the picture his mother painted, before the foreclosure sign appeared in front of their house, before the unkempt grass in their front yard grew to his knees, before their pier was taken by the hurricane, before his father descended into the madness of a bottle and rectangular yellow pills.

He stared at the lighthouse in the sea of high grass in his backyard, his feet sinking into the sponge-like earth, his hands in his pocket, listening to the angry waves crash and hiss along the Chesapeake shoreline. The cooled breeze sighed across the Bay and throughout his dusty hair, across his cheeks, massaging his anxiety. A slow rumble of thunder signaled the fast approaching summer storm, but he wanted to wait to see if her specter was real, to hear her whisper his name one last time before bed.

II.

The front door slammed hard enough to rattle the bay windows looking out over the waters. Lucky for Davey, he made it inside before his father arrived home from whatever odd job he worked or, even worse, from the bar he lived in until the sun began its descent. He knew his father hated it when Davey looked at the lighthouse, his discord emphasized by the scolding that followed.

From his perch atop the loft that doubled as his bedroom, Davey listened for the familiar rattle of keys on the kitchen counter. He listened for the refrigerator door to open, the usual clank of glass from the cardboard box where his father kept his liquid treasures. Then there was the pop of the bottle, the audible mumbling filled with hatred, followed by the sound of springs popping on the recliner as his father relaxed in his usual spot.

The ritual never changed as the old man drowned himself in self-pity.

"Davey," his father called, gravel in the back of his throat, a mild slur in his words.

"Up here," Davey hesitated at first, sitting on the highest step, arms hugging his knees. He never knew what kind of father he would get for the day.

"Yeah." His father sighed, clearing his throat after his sip. A quick *thwack* signaled his father reclining backwards. Soon he would bask in the warm oblivion of the television. "Homework?"

"It's done. Finished it earlier. Can see it if you want." Davey glanced over at the binders and math book spread across the floor. He didn't know if his calculations were correct, but at least he gave it his all. It was a far cry from his favorite subject – his mother's favorite subject – history. Numbers were never his friend.

"Only asking because I'm supposed to. Still saw the plate of leftovers in the fridge."

"Not hungry."

"Not hungry?" His father mocked him, kicking back the bottle, and with a couple gulps that sounded like Davey's humidifier bubbling, finished his beer – the first of many throughout the young night. It wouldn't take long for Mr. Hyde to make his appearance. "Boy's gotta eat. What, do you think I spend all that money on food for you to waste it?"

"Not feeling well. Stomach kind of sour." Davey lied. He didn't want to eat the two-day-old Salisbury steak TV dinner his father justified as a home-cooked meal.

"Ungrateful," his father mumbled just loud enough for Davey to hear, but the words only stung, barely registering in his gut. "Suppose you'll be wanting cereal later."

"I guess." Davey's eyes wandered through the bay window once more. The stone sanctuary lit up with a flash and rumble as the usual mid-summer thunderstorm released its fury. He wanted to see her, the pale silhouette of his mother, who promised she would never leave his side. She never appeared. Only in dreams.

"Boy can't grow with cereal."

"Don't like red meat. It tastes funny," Davey answered as he watched his father rock forward out of the chair and perform drunken acrobatics into the coffee table. Seconds later, he collapsed on their marlin-printed sofa. Davey's heart sank as he realized his father didn't work that day. Instead, he likely attended liquid church at Twain's Tavern. It was never a good sign, and likely spelled an early bedtime for both of them.

"You ok?'

"What do you mean I'm ok?" His father growled, pushing himself to back to his feet. His father took a moment to scan the room, appearing even more confused.

Davey's heart dropped when his father paused on the door leading out to the back deck. The golden knob underneath the handle remained angled to the right – unlocked. His dad would know. He always knew.

"I didn't—" Davey's preemptive strike would fall on deaf orders.

"You were outside again, weren't you?"

"No, I only opened the door because I thought I heard something. I didn't go outside."

"Why can't you listen? I thought I told you not to go outside?" His father stumbled towards the door.

"But I didn't go outside. I swear."

"Don't go on swearing to me. You understand? I don't like liars." His father flipped the knob to the left then cast the same menacing glare towards Davey like so many other workless evenings. His father's forearms bulged outside of his rolled up flannel shirt as he ascended the stairs, his dirtied fingertips holding tight around the railing. "Shouldn't be fibbing to your father."

Davey could already smell his father's body odor.

"I'm telling you the truth. I didn't go out back."

"I've seen that face too many times. You know you're lying to your old man, don't you?" The handrail rattled, supporting even more of his father's weight. "And you know how I feel about liars."

Davey couldn't move, paralyzed with fear. He hated when his father drank, especially from the amber bottle with the black label reading Jack Something. There was something particularly disturbing about the way his father ascended the stairs, his face twisting to resemble Mr. Malfi's half-starved pit bull.

"Dad, please." Davey rolled backwards, nearly backing into the TV tray converted to hold one of the two lamps in the room.

"Don't you please me." Davey smelled the pungent aroma of beer on his father's breath. The once proud man loomed over him. A far off gaze to distant times infested his eyes.

"Told you. I've been doing homework this entire time." Davey sprawled on the floor and frantically pointed over at his book bag and accompanying worksheets he finished.

"This you?" His father pointed at the pile of books.

"Yeah. Take a look at it. See, I'm not lying."

His father grumbled and grabbed the textbook with the grace of an elephant – his arm the nose, his swollen ears reddened from alcohol consumption. He rifled through the papers, his eyes darting back and forth as if he were reading Chinese.

"What's that bimbo for a teacher teaching you? Woman wouldn't know a hole in her head from one in the ground." His father continued with more misplaced words, some often repeated on the playground during a good game of tag. Davey didn't understand all the cursing, instead secluding himself to the small grove behind the middle school, searching for his Narnia books.

"Wait just a minute." His father squatted, his knees popping with old age. "What'd I tell you about getting into your mother's things?"

His father sifted underneath the loose-leaf pages, uncovering a baby blue hardcover decorated with the picture of a giant green sea creature with its mouth agape on cover: The Kraken.

"I asked you a question."

"I'm...I'm sorry, dad." How could he have been so careless? He found solace in the worn pages, hearing his mother's words brush against his earlobe, describing each creature in the book. And there was the mermaid.

"This was in her trunk." The broken man stared at his deceased wife's book with a hint of remorse, the suggestion of a single tear welling in his right eye before he shut the cover. He almost appeared human for once. "Why'd you go in her trunk? Told you not to go into my bedroom."

"I just thought—"

"You thought nothing. You understand? Nothing out there but memories."

"I know what I seen." Davey stiffened as he uttered the words. He knew better. He shouldn't challenge his dad, not after what happened before, not after seeing her spirit.

"What'd you say?"

"I said it's true. She's out there."

"No, no she's not. She ain't out there. You understand? No use in going on with that stupid theory of yours."

"But I saw her."

"Fine, then. Where'd you see her? Flying around, thinking she's some sort of angel?"

"Lighthouse." The words barely escaped Davey's lips when he realized his folly.

"You little bastard. I told you not to go up there."

"But I didn't. Never been up there." Davey didn't lie. He never went into the building, never finding the courage to explore.

"Then don't you ever say you saw her up there. You hear me? She's gone. She left us by her own choice," his father said, his voice reaching a fevered pitch. "She abandoned us. She left me to take care of you."

"You gotta believe me. I saw Ma up there... in my dreams."

"Don't start this on me again, boy. You don't know what kinda day I had." His father straightened his posture, clutching the hand across Davey's book.

"With the bottle." He heard his mother utter the same words repeatedly, especially during the last days before she threw herself over the edge.

"Boy," his father stammered, his eyes growing twice their size, a familiar glimpse into the past. "You been testing me too long. Like some devil brought to me, punish me for what happened to your mother."

"Dad." Davey couldn't hold it in any longer, releasing his emotion in a waterfall of tears, soaking his cheeks, wishing his mother would protect him from what was about to follow. "She's here with us. She's in the book."

"This book?" His father's eyebrows arched up. His father needed an outlet for his anger, for his misplaced part in this world, or so he was told. It was all Davey's fault. "You say your mother's in this book, right here?"

"Yes." Davey nodded, shying away from the old man.

"Where? What pages?" His father opened the book, ripping the first page from the binding, revealing Poseidon himself. "This guy, right here? Mr. Starkist Tuna?"

"No." Davey dug his heels into the carpet, shuffling backwards until his back touched the wall.

"Or maybe this one?" His father released a torrid of swears. Davey remembered those long nights where he sat up in his bed, fingers plugged into his ears, staying away his mother's pleas as his father exacted his "punishment." He was a good man, or so his mother told him with a bruised cheek or a cracked lip.

"No," Davey said, watching as the book's giant sea snake flutter to the ground, another of his mother's favorites from a place called Loch Ness.

"How about this one? Right here with the pretty lady? You think your Ma was pretty?"

And there she was, memorialized in the picture his dad held fast: flawless skin naked and unsullied from earthly pollutants, red hair braided with pastel sea shells and taken by the currents of the ocean. Her hazel gaze radiated both kindness and anger. Most recognizable in the myth that separated the creature from human – the green-blue scales replaced her legs, tapering off to a tail which would propel the mermaid through the depths of the sea.

He saw his mother in the picture, the mermaid's cheeks narrowing to a sculpted nose, her lips pursed but not overly plump, the same lips that sang Davey his bedtime stories before he lay his head down to sleep at night, and the way her eyes, a little bigger than most humans, massaged his worry from his repressed life. He didn't know how many nights he stared at the picture, its edges worn and faded from his constant handling. He didn't have a good picture of his mother, so the mermaid served him well.

He wanted to be in the ocean with his mother, swimming away from a downtrodden life.

"Davey," his father snapped him up by the arm, jerking him forward, his knees burning as they skimmed the carpet. "Stop your staring and answer me."

He didn't take his eyes off her. He couldn't.

"I see what this is. Disrespect me for everything I do for you." If everything meant a preloaded government card his father used to barter for liquor, then Davey couldn't argue with his old man.

"Let me go." Davey yanked back, and for the first time was able to muster enough strength to break free from his father's grip, slick from alcohol-induced perspiration. He lost his balance and flailed backwards into the TV-stand, the lamp toppling onto Davey's stomach. It hurt worse than any schoolyard bully punch.

Davey wanted to cry, burying his head into his hands, thinking of his mother and the lighthouse. All he could hear was his father's nervous panting. He felt his shadow through his eyelids, standing and staring in all of his drunken revelry, his other hand still affixed to his mother's mermaid.

"See what you made me do? This is what happens."

Davey widened his fingers just enough to see through them as his father tore his mermaid in half.

III.

Davey's stomach hurt for the better part of the night as he found refuge underneath his Ferrari bed covers, a flimsy shield he pretended would hold the monster at bay. But his father wasn't there. He was sprawled out on the living room sofa below, a "loaner" from his aunt after one of his father's rampage-filled nights when he shredded the old one, the same one his mother slept on for many nights.

Davey once again thought back to when he rested his head on his mother's lap, cajoling her to stroke his hair, helping Davey to find his sleep. It was another memory his father destroyed.

His father's snores seemed to vibrate the entire second floor, rattling the pieces of the broken lamp imbedded in the ratty carpet. Somewhere within his father's clutches, was Davey's treasure: the torn picture of his guardian angel.

He shouldn't have made his dad angry. It only made things worse for the two. His father always reminded him about their great misfortune. He blamed Davey for his mother's depression, for the black and blue welts that suddenly appeared on her back after a night filled with arguments, and eventually for her taking her own life.

When Davey brought up her fate, his father would release his disfavor with a forceful squeeze of the shoulder or a pinch to the back of the neck. He knew deep down his father hated him, but Davey served as another government check, another excuse for his father to self-medicate himself.

As Davey lay there, his fingers gliding along the raised welt on his stomach where the lamp hit, wondering when his father would finally flip out, he thought he heard something. The call sounded faint at first, a fingertip caressing his earlobe, barely audible underneath his makeshift fortress.

"Davey." It called him again, a silk voice surrounding him like the waves of Myrtle Beach, rushing in then bubbling out with the tide. For a minute, he felt his toes sift through the sand, its warmth massaging his heels. It was the last vacation he took with his mother, the last time he saw his family truly happy.

"What?" Dave whispered, his abdomen tightening with a stabbing pain in his ribs.

"Davey," she called again, a voice now more familiar, a voice from his dreams. It couldn't be.

"Mom?" The rush of excitement was too much, but he had to be careful.

He slipped out from underneath his covers, his feet soft against the floor, methodical in his movement as to not draw attention from below. His father's snoring undulated with a strong rhythm. Each step he took matched one of his father's breaths as to disguise his movement.

"Davey."

"Mom?" He whispered again, approaching the stairs. A wave of nausea overtook his senses as spotted his father's silhouette below, his right leg and arm hanging off the sofa, his hair blown out like a clown, the television reflecting off his bald spot like a kaleidoscope.

His fingers trembled. He swallowed with nerves in his throat as he grabbed the handrail. With a quick breath, just enough to fill his lungs, Davey braced himself and glided down the stairs, his feet moving fast with anticipation.

As he took his last step before his bare foot met carpet, he looked over at his father. His old man seemed to be truly at peace, possibly fighting whatever demons he harbored inside of his nightmares.

He was a good man once, long before alcohol became his crutch when he was a machinist proud to provide for his family. His once bright smile was now forever lost in old family portraits stored in their shed or forever discarded in a landfill. Davey watched him decline during the past three years, becoming more dependent on the cardboard box filled with bottles. Significant weight loss and an unshaven appearance made him look like a skeleton, particularly at night with the house lights turned off.

He wanted his father back more than anything, but for the time being he had to settle for a good book and the rare chocolate milkshake after a day's worth of mowing lawns.

But now was not the time to think about his father's condition.

"Davey," he heard the voice call for him again.

The back door opened without his help. The familiar scent of salt water and the soothing rush of waves overwhelmed his senses, pulling him outside to his forbidden backyard.

As he looked up, he saw the impossible luminescence, the lighthouse reawakening with its torch cast out to sea, tunneling through the heavy clock of fog and to the unknown.

He slipped through the door, watching as the lighthouse's torch shifted into something more familiar, a specter he'd seen several times before between closing his eyes at night and awakening in the morning.

IV.

Davey prepared his lunch just like any school morning. His usual routine consisted of spreading a thin layer of peanut butter across some Wonder Bread and maybe even adding some jelly, if he managed to fit any into his bicycle's basket. The long trip from the grocery store made every inch of real estate in his basket valuable, and sometimes jelly got the boot. His favorite flavor was grape, but the cupboard was devoid of the white-labeled jar with sugary goodness inside.

A quick stuff of a Twinkie into the thrice-used paper bag and Davey was off, leaving his father, who let his displeasure be known about the overabundance of alcohol consumption by moaning. The broken man thankfully didn't rise before Davey dressed himself and wrestled his schoolbooks together.

Part of Davey wanted to hug him, to find refugee in the monster's arms. He was part of him, and despite the sideways glances of Johnny Garrison's parents when Davey took of his shirt a Johnny's 10th birthday party to reveal to large bruises across his back, none of them would ever understand. His father was his only parent, the only reminder of his mother. He had to find protection somewhere.

He mounted the Huffy he recently purchased at Gary's Consignment Shop after saving up all summer from mowing lawns and dog walking. The other kids in the bayside community ridiculed Davey for the rusted state of the bike. He ignored them as his mother would have suggested.

With a circle of his legs, he sped off to middle school, up the side street covered with rocks, feral woods over his left shoulder, and the calming influence of the lolling waves of Chesapeake over his right. He cherished the ten-minute bike ride to and from school, through their lower class community, but it wouldn't always be like this, not when he became a doctor or a lawyer and moved far away from this place.

As the frowning porch of his father's home disappeared in the bicycle's mirror, the lighthouse appeared in the distance. He wanted last night to be real, to hold onto it like it wasn't a dream.

Davey knew better, though. It had to be a dream, an illusion of what could've been. He remembered racing through the high grass, the dew-soaked blades whipping against his ankles and knees, escaping under the cloak of darkness with only a waxing moon to guide his way. He remembered pushing his shoulder through the padlocked door, his frame just skinny enough to slip through, unveiling the spiraled staircase and the moss-covered floor.

There was a familiar smell about the place, citrus or vanilla, both of his mother's favorite scents.

He climbed the stairs, thankful that enough light filtered through the windows to illuminate his way as he raced upwards, his footfalls echoing in a metallic tone. It felt like an eternity, but he eventually reached the top where he expected to see her.

His heart sank after climbing through the trapdoor and discovered an empty platform, a rust-brown railing barely hanging on with a couple loose screws, almost falling victim to the breeze off the Chesapeake. Shards of glass flickering along the lighthouse floor like a shallow pond. It was just an illusion, a cruel joke played by God.

"Davey," she called for him below.

"Mom," he answered, his voice lost in the tide as he looked down. He saw a silhouette, a creature not of this world straddling a rock. It starred up at him, its emerald gaze catching the moon's reflection. Its fluid motion was unlike any other as it shimmied across the uneven surface. And with a splash and the gurgle of sea foam, the figure disappeared below the surface, forever out of memory and back into his harsh reality.

Removed from his thoughts, Davey peddled faster, building up a sweat and causing his t-shirt to stick to the welt on his stomach. His eyes stung with a yearning to see his mother as he turned off his barren side street and onto Mermaid Row. The constant jittering of tires against rock and the vibrating of his semi-numb arms surrendered to the paved road and a much smoother ride. More houses – old vacation beach cottages converted to fulltime housing – lined both sides of the road.

It also marked his halfway point to Queen Anne's Middle. A little further and he would lose himself in history and social studies before escaping to the back of the lunchroom, where he would think about how he woke up covered in sweat with his bed sheets curled around him, unaware of how he arrived back home from the lighthouse.

Today wouldn't afford him the opportunity to relax.

Preparing to make a sharp left onto Edgewood, Davey spotted the four of them – Gary Kimmel, Jason Bradley, Melvin Hoiles, and Bryan Ranstock – waiting for him in their usual spot. They'd been a tight bunch since elementary school, pretending to be some biker gang show they watched on television with their fathers. Each one mirrored those bearded bikers, hiding behind sunglasses, uttering curse words during recess. They'd been tormenting Davey his entire sixth grade year.

He wanted to take each one of them down, but knew better than to challenge them. He couldn't outrace them. The various dents on his handlebars and bicycle frame were a testament to their strength, their developed bodies.

"Davey," one of them yelled as a car *whooshed* by, serving as Davey's temporary savior, the passengers unaware of the torment Davey was about to experience. He wouldn't stick around to suffer their wrath, twisting the bike around and taking off without another thought.

"Davey," Melvin yelled. Their bikes were faster. They were stronger. But Davey knew his escape route, once again feeling the uneven pavement jitter his bike as he raced towards home.

"Tell us about your sea creatures," Bryan's voice moved from left to right.

"How about the Loch Ness, prick." Melvin parried Bryan's insult with one of his own.

They all laughed.

Davey's palms sweated, making his grip on the handlebars more difficult. His heart thumped against his ribs as the world flew by him in a swath of a green and brown.

"Come here, turd burger," Jason, their leader who Davey fantasized about disposing of in a toilet, called. The rattling of their bike chains, the sound of rubber tires grinding against and kicking back stone, approached fast.

Davey couldn't stop. His legs kept churning, spotting the tired cottage he called home that would serve as a refuge. He steered his bike over a portion of his fence taken by rot. He hoped they wouldn't follow, looking at his home as some sort of castle to keep the barbarians away. But the barbarians followed, still laughing and uttering obscenities reserved for the lunchroom.

"Ain't going to hide here," Bryan said. His voice was closer, cackling like a hyena ready to ravage the deceased.

"Don't matter to us. Worthless old man ain't going to do anything," Jason said.

Davey felt them not less than three bike-lengths behind. He thought he was a goner, victim to four eight-grade marauders who would make an "example" out of him.

In that instant, Davey knew where he could find escape. They were bigger than he was and couldn't squeeze through – at least he hoped.

Davey stood up on the bike and pumped his legs even faster, past the sting of lactic acid, his route taken by the thickening bay grass, which felt like quicksand as he targeted the obelisk. Everything burned. Oxygen left him, his body taken by fatigue.

"No, you don't," Jason yelled. Davey looked down to see Jason's shadow raise some sort of stick overhead.

Seconds later, the world tumbled as Davey felt himself weightless, rolling over top of his handlebar, his feet overhead, and towards the ground below. The sun blinked as he watched his bike sail to the right, its wheels spinning in the air until it disappeared over the cliff. But Davey didn't stop, ignoring the pain, sucking in wind, and rolling to his feet without missing a beat. Five strides later, he was upon the lighthouse door and the mangled padlock.

"Kid like Spiderman," Melvin said, jumping off his bike. The other three followed.

Davey didn't wait to be the victim of their ill intentions. He sucked in his chest and stomach. His nose clipped the sharp edge of the metal door, summoning a fountain of blood, but Davey ignored it, collapsing to the unforgiving floor, watching as four silhouettes blotted out the sun's rays, their features hidden by shadow.

"Get him," Jason ordered his cohorts forward.

Gary was the first to try, sticking his arm through the door. In those seconds, Davey imagined what would happen to him, the beating he would take with no adults to save him. They would introduce his face to every hard surface in the lighthouse. Fueled by an animal instinct to survive, Davey planted his foot on the door and shoved backwards.

A crack followed then a *thunk*.

Gary cried out in pain as he withdrew his arm, allowing the door to slam shut.

"You prick," Jason's muffled voice called from the other side. Gary still cried out.

Davey sprung to his feet and fixed his back against the door, sucking in air, and digging his heels into the small rivulets of the concrete floor. He needed to survive.

"Get him," Jason yelled.

The door jarred forward, nearly sending Davey off his feet. He pushed back, shutting it just as fast. The others wouldn't dare put their arms through.

"It's too heavy," Melvin said.

"We try, he's going to slam the door on us like Gary," Bryan followed, blunting out Gary's cries.

"You're all chickens."

The duel lasted a few more minutes, but to Davey it seemed like hours. They would kick the door, sending Davey into a moment of panic, before he recovered and pressed his back into the metal slab, digging his heels into the ground again, ignoring the pinch in his lower back and neck as the door snapped shut.

"Fine. Just stop," Jason ordered. Gary's cries had dulled. "You in there, Davey? You hear me?"

"Go away," Davey answered, about the dumbest thing he could think of saying.

"We ain't going away. We're going to wait here until you get out here. You hear me? Tired of you trying to make us fools."

"And miss school?" Davey asked, realizing it would be the first day he missed as well, all but disappointed the memory of his mother, who preached the virtues of perfect attendance.

"Don't matter to us. You ain't going to get away with what you did to Gary."

"I can wait it out. My dad will be out here soon." Davey feigned strength.

"Your dad. He says it like he can do something." Melvin chuckled with all the sensitivity of a sea urchin.

"We all know about your dad," Jason's voice cracked with puberty. "Probably at my dad's bar last night. He spending all that money you don't have."

"He's…he's not." Davey wanted to run and hide. There would be no savior, no angel to protect him. He might as slip back out and let the four release whatever mislaid anger they held within.

"Davey," her voice called from above. It couldn't be.

"Did you…did you hear that?" Melvin asked.

"Heard what?" Jason asked.

"Someone called Davey's name," Bryan added, his response laced with uncertainty. "I heard it, too. Think it's his dad?"

"Davey," she called again, her voice more pronounced.

"See, there," Melvin said.

"I don't…I don't see anybody." A hint of terror betrayed Bryan's statement.

The pressure against the door stopped. Davey looked up, transfixed by her again. It wasn't a dream last night. It couldn't be. After all, it was daylight.

"I didn't hear anything. Don't tell me you guys are chickening out on me. Are you?" Jason wrangled them in. They wouldn't cross him.

"It's just that…Gary," Melvin pleaded.

"Gary's fine."

Then it happened. Davey heard the rush of water outside joined by the force of a hurricane crashing into the shoreline. A menacing wind howled underneath the doorway, clanging the railing and the crooked flagpole above. It suddenly became dark.

"Holy…no," Melvin pleaded.

"Davey," the voice called from above. Without another thought and curious as to what was happening outside, Davey abandoned his post and ran up the old metal stairs, each step swaying below, listening to the unknown occur outside.

"Gary," Jason yelled.

"Run," Melvin followed.

Half way up, Davey reached the point where he could see outside the two windows. He expected to see angry whitecaps and a large expanse of gray, but instead, he could only see a deep green blotting out the sun. He blinked and looked again, focusing on what appeared to be scale-covered skin twist and brush against the lighthouse, its weight buckling the structure.

More screams followed, distant in their call except for one, more terrified, begging and pleading.

Davey didn't stop. His fatigued legs barely responded to his commands, listening to the chorus of pleas for help until he reached the ladder and climbed towards the plateau.

He didn't know what to expect. But as he opened the trapdoor, pulling himself up into the circular interior chamber, the morning sun bristled against his cheeks. Their screams stopped. Silence.

It took him a moment to gain his bearings, his mind spinning around from the unknown, his imagination taking control. He first spotted three silhouettes racing away on their bicycles, tiny ants heading back to their sand pile, but not a fourth.

Another rush of water pulled Davey's attention towards the shoreline.

"What?" His breath escaped him at the sight of a massive shadow, maybe the length of one of those sailboats at Baltimore's Inner Harbor, glide underneath the waters and out towards the deep waters of the Chesapeake. The large blue outline moved fast, swimming effortlessly, a beast that could not be.

And all was silent as Davey backed away, keeping his attention towards the unknown until it disappeared from sight, sending a small wave back to shore.

"Can't...be." Davey's swallowed. Maybe his father slapped him too hard one time. Maybe he was just tired, and his imagination caught up with him. Whatever the case, Davey, although youthful, fell victim to exhaustion as adrenaline left him drained. He slumped to the ground where he caught the sight of a fourth bicycle, not his, but one that belonged to Jason.

"Davey. What-did-I-tell-you?" It was a voice Davey didn't want to hear.

V.

The unpleasant march through his backyard felt like hours. His father, still taken by his hangover, barked at him the entire way to their house, blaming Davey for losing his bike, for instigating a fight with neighborhood kids, and for skipping school.

His father refused to listen to Davey's accounts of what happened. It didn't matter, though. Davey took a seat on the same couch his father used as a bed, his teeth chattering, and his entire body cold from fear as the verbal tirade continued.

In that moment, Davey made a horrible mistake by glancing towards the lighthouse, reliving the last thirty minutes in his head.

"What...what do you think you're doing? I'm here, not over there." His father emphasized by pointing over to the lighthouse.

"Nothing, I'm just—"

"Just what? Going down the same road as your mom? You want to leave me too? Give up?" His father paced, a tiger eyeing its prey.

"What are you talking about?"

"What am I talking about?" He scoffed, crossing his arms muttering something underneath his thick caterpillar for a moustache. "I'll tell you what I'm doing. I'm raising my son as best I can, and my son don't give a good god damn about anything, about me."

"But they chased me. Wasn't my fault."

"Here we go again. It's not your fault? We going to start that again? Nothing is ever your fault, is it? Not your fault you didn't go to school. Not your fault you didn't make friends with those kids. Starting to sound like your mother more and more every day."

"I'm telling you the truth. I got no reason to lie." Davey's voice cracked. There was no getting through to his father.

"Oh, you've got plenty of reason to lie." His father's eyebrow curled up like the devil's arch. "Always wanting to avoid trouble, just like your mother."

"No."

"Yes." His father crept closer, his hands balled to fists at his side, his breathing heavy, deliberate in its purpose.

"I'm telling you, no. It was them. They chased me." Davey scooted back on the couch. He wished he could disappear under the cushions, to fade away to some distant world where his father couldn't touch him.

"You're just making excuses. Trying...trying to miss school so they'll take you from me. Blame me for not raising you right."

"Dad, please," Davey begged.

"Ain't no pleasing. No more." The scent of stale beer and body odor wafted over Davey. His father had already been drinking.

"Please," Davey pleaded one more time, lifting his arms up over his head, ready for the blow that would follow. He looked once more to his lighthouse. Maybe he could escape. But it was just a maybe when he felt the first blow.

VI.

Davey hid under his covers for the better part of the day, reliving the morning in his head. He heard the inevitable phone call from the school, which went to an answering machine with his mother's voice. She sounded happy and sincere in her greeting. He wondered why his father never

15

deleted the message. Maybe his father was reliving happier times. Maybe.

His arms and legs throbbed from his father's anger, but there wasn't a bruise to be found. It was par for the course. His father never left a mark. Even during his father's inebriated stupors, he knew better than to wind up in handcuffs.

Davey often thought about telling his guidance counselor Ms. Lewis about his home life. But it would only lead to his father being arrested. Davey heard horror stories about foster kids becoming wards of the state. He'd seen the shows on television where kids would go to juvy hall because there was no hope for their future.

And in his own twisted way, Davey thought by losing his dad that he would lose his last connection to his mother. Some nameless social worker would force him out of their home, far away from the lighthouse, to some family he didn't know. He'd be court record, not a person.

Davey suffered through it all, using his mom's old makeup case to hide any bruises that might appear by mistake, and losing himself in his schoolwork and books. It wasn't ideal, but at least he wasn't a starving kid in Africa – a fact his father made sure to remind him of whenever Davey complained about the lack of food in the house.

He kept his eyes closed until he heard the screen door slap close, the sound of the old Ford pickup's engine grumble to life, and rocks kicking up on the gravel road as his father navigated to whatever sanctuary he would find for the day. He wasn't going to find work. He might not even come home until the next morning. It wouldn't be the first time.

Davey pulled his sheets down over his face swollen, his cheeks chaffed and reddened from wiping too much. He slipped out of his bed and walked over to the bay window, his right leg limping slightly from the first strike.

Jason's bike peaked out of the tall grass, its wheel spokes shining in the high noon sky. Davey wasn't concerned about the bike. It was the flash of blue-green scale outside the lighthouse window followed by a loud splash. His father denied hearing it, but how?

"Davey," her voice called, but not from outside.

"Mom?"

"Davey." Her ethereal whisper prompted Davey to turn around where he noticed movement where it should not be. His painting, *her* painting, rattled against the wall. The painted lighthouse flashed with light as the distinct rumble of thunder resounded within the frame, causing it to shake even more.

"Mom?" Davey blinked, expecting it to be a trick of the mind, but there would be no trick.

The distinct sound of water breaking against rock, the marauding black sky cracking with electricity, and the howls of a forlorn wind ushered in the tempest within his mother's painting. He moved forward without thinking, mesmerized by the supernatural. He'd seen the movie called Poltergeist, but this wasn't a haunting. There was no Indian burial ground or history of ghosts.

"Davey," she whispered. Unlike before when she beckoned him outside, her voice came from within the tempest. Then he saw her: a bright silhouette atop the lighthouse, her familiar hair flowing, captured by the storm.

"Mom." His lips trembled as he jumped on his bed and grabbed both sides of the frame. He expected to feel weight, but it was weightless, lighter than a sheet of paper.

He looked past the oil strokes, ignoring the impossible storm and the flash of painted clouds whirling around, concentrating on the specter. Though minute in stature, every detail of his mother's spectral form came into focus, even her hazel eyes – a beacon of her love for Davey.

"Davey." She extended her transparent arm towards him, as if reaching out of the painting itself. He wanted nothing more than to dive into the art, be lost with his mom in whatever world waited for him inside.

"What do I do?" Davey's voice trembled, panicking as he looked inside, grabbing the frame hard enough to expose the whites of his knuckles. "How do I get inside?"

"Davey." His ear tickled as she called him again. She turned around, her face disappearing within the apparition, hazel eyes turning white as she approached the edge of lighthouse.

"Mom."

"Follow me."

"Mom, please. How do I come in?" Davey shouted and stood, his feet sinking into the mattress as he watched his mother cast herself off the edge and into the Chesapeake, disappearing below the black waters.

"No." Dave collapsed to the floor, tears streaming down his cheeks as emotion took hold. The picture frame shattered beside him, but he didn't care, pushing himself to all fours, watching as droplets fell from his eyes, plucking the floor in tiny geysers of helplessness.

"Mom," he said with a mouthful of mucous. When he opened his eyes, he did not see the storm, instead the painting remained calm, serene just like his mother intended.

Maybe it was all an illusion, a cruel joke by the world that already forsook him. He rocked backwards, thumping his back against his Ferrari bed and thought about times past.

He would do anything to be with his mother again.

VII.

Davey sat by the bay window for the remainder of the day, watching as the sun made its descent, as summer clouds fueled by humidity gathered overhead. It wouldn't take long for another late afternoon storm to ignite the sky with energy, and it was energy Davey lacked, his legs dangling over the edge of his loft, his forehead resting against the railing, too tired to move, too emotionally drained to care.

He tried to put the pieces of the puzzle together, to wonder how the world could be so cruel. He never did anybody wrong. Never. Whether it was by helping Allison Smith with her science homework or bringing the widow Ms. Gilmore's trash inside every Monday morning, he always looked out for other people, but nobody looked out for him.

Every so often, he glanced over at his mother's ruined painting, wondering it would come to life again. He wished he could see her again, to discover away to find inside the picture and embrace his mother, even if it was one last time.

As distant yellows along the horizon turned orange and red, Davey expected his father to arrive home fresh off an all-day bender and stumble inside, somehow eluding the Eastern Shore police and another DWI.

He feared what would follow. His father would find the painting on the ground, its custom frame shattered, one that his father shelled out one hundred dollars to purchase – a princely sum for the old man.

He imagined his father's face turning beat red and twisting to look like some Halloween mask. The answering machine message from school would only compound the matter, reminding his father about Davey's "disobedience." Another uncomfortable confrontation would follow. More smacks. More reminders.

Maybe this would be the night his father finally lost it. Maybe this would be the day the both of them would lose everything.

All Davey could do was grin and bear it. So he resolved to sit atop his loft, waiting for the inevitable as the sun disappeared behind the clouds, the bright blue sky surrendering to the silver horizon. But he couldn't wait any longer. He wanted to find his father's treasure, to find solace in something.

Against his better judgment, Davey headed for his father's bedroom, ignoring the crick in his neck and the swelling around his right knee and thigh. As he ran through the kitchen, he glanced outside the window and checked the front yard: No two-tone truck. His father was still out.

Perspiration built along his hairline. He ran past the barren walls once filled with pictures of the three of them at the beach. Faint outlines marked where the frames once hung.

His father hated when Davey went into the bedroom without his permission, permission his father never granted. But he needed to take the chance. It's where he discovered the last of his mother's memories secreted away in the closet, underneath a pile of unwashed clothes, buried for none to find.

But he needed to find her, to find hope, so he glanced over his shoulder one last time then cast his luck forward, pushing aside the bedroom door fresh with a new hole the size of his father's fist.

It was dark inside, a musty caveman's lair compared to how his mom used to decorate it with vibrant colors. Gone were the intricate figures of Disney princesses, replaced by empty prescription bottles, a thick layer of dust absent any sense of joy. It smelled like the usual – body odor and fetid beers. The air was thick and stale, likely from his father sweating out alcohol after a night filled with bottles. Davey was surprised his father could even locate his bed.

Davey navigated his way over the landmines of dirty t-shirts and jeans until he came upon the closet.

A sudden strike of thunder shook the foundation of their home, causing an already excited Davey to jump. The storm came faster than expected, but it didn't stop him from his purpose as he spotted his mother's trunk, faded pink with a painting of a butterfly. Davey smiled at the sight, knowing his mother had it since her childhood.

He opened it up to the smell of pine and discovered the unexpected – his mother's sea creature book, the same one his father took from Davey the night before. He hesitated to retrieve it, wondering if it would produce more tears from his already depleted supply.

As his fingers traced the cover, he felt a slick substance of tape over the ridges where his father tore it the previous day. Upon closer inspection, Davey noticed clear packing tape curled around the edges of the book and to the binding, the tape's wrinkles pronounced and uneven, revealing a hasty application.

Davey flipped open the first page.

Another rumble outside shook the windowpanes, followed by the first plucks of the storm against the aluminum siding. The storm arrived.

Davey didn't care, taken by the picture of the muscular man breaking through the surface of the water, a trident in his right hand, the same stark white beard flowing around his wide frame. And across the torso of Poseidon, a piece of packing tape fixed the once torn picture together.

He also felt a few raised portions no bigger than an M&M, likely swollen from water...or tears. No other person could've fastened the book together other than his father. He imagined his father secreting himself away in the room, lining up the pictures, and applying the tape. Maybe somewhere in the deep recesses of his father's mind he thought of his mother in a positive light. It would be the first time Davey could remember such an occurrence, and his heart ached for the old man. His father might've cared for his wife once, maybe even seeing her resemblance in the mermaid.

Another rumble of thunder rattled the house, followed by a vengeful lighting strike lighting up the window with strobe like effect, this one more pronounced. The sky unleashed its fury as the rain plucked the house with the consistency of a machine gun. Wind blew outside, whistling through the windows, popping Davey's ears.

Davey flipped the page to the Loch Ness Monster, its uncanny appearance restored with two more bandages fastened by packing tape. He fingers perspired as he flipped to the next page, anticipation building as he would see the mermaid resembling his mother.

As his eyes rested on the oceanic scene where an artist's palette of undersea life swam about the coral, something was missing. Davey took in a breath. It couldn't be. The mermaid and her emerald eyes, the same ones that provided Davey comfort since his mother took her life was gone, replaced by the uncaring void of deep blue sea.

"What?" Another lighting strike cracked outside, more intense, resonating with the energy of a Fourth of July firework.

"Davey," his father's voice pierced the storm.

Davey jumped up from his Indian style seated position, the book toppling off his lap as he spotted the silhouette fill the doorway.

"What do you think you're doing?" His father's words slurred from his lips with the consistency of pudding.

"I was just...I was just."

"Somewhere you weren't supposed to be." His father backhanded the doorframe, shattering his bottle and puncturing the drywall. "I told you not to come in here."

Another flash of lightning illuminated his father's twisted visage, his eyes that of a beast knowing no boundaries, his lips curling, and his nostrils flaring with a diabolical purpose. Davey knew he couldn't be there any longer, not with the shattered man he knew as his father falling off the cliff of sanity.

The same man who shouted, "Merry Christmas" up the stairs, the same man who encouraged Davey to take his first few pedals of the bike, the same man how saw him off on his first day of kindergarten was no more, replaced by the demon in the doorway, a demon taken by remorse and alcohol.

"Just too curious." His father stumbled forward and caught his balance on the bed with the remnants of the broken beer bottle still clenched in his hand.

"Please...please don't." Davey held his hands up, but he knew better.

"Tired of you disrespecting me. I try my hardest by you. Do hear me?" His father took another step. Another flash of lightning. Another scornful gaze. But this time, Davey didn't wait to feel the brunt of his father's anger.

His muscles tingled. Adrenaline pumped through Davey's body as he darted forward in a last ditch effort to save himself.

"Davey," his father shouted.

Calloused fingers and untrimmed fingernails scratched Davey's shoulder, but he muscled past his father, running out into the kitchen and into the living room. Davey tossed aside a barstool in an attempt to throw obstacles in his father's way.

He didn't know his ultimate destination, but he knew where could find sanctuary. Maybe he could stay there until his father passed out for the night and then plan his next move, or so he hoped.

"You little bastard," his father yelled, uttering obscenities as he pinballed around the furniture. Davey escaped through the forbidden porch door and out into the tempest where he saw the same vision that took his mother's painting: funneling clouds, white caps spitting up onto the peninsula, a storm unlike any other he'd experienced.

"Davey," his father called from behind, crashing through the door.

Davey ran. He ran faster than he ever ran before. His legs pumped like pistons on one of those old cars his father bragged about fixing. His arms rocked back and forth, willing him forward. He tightened his fingers hard enough to draw blood. All he could hear was the sound of his own breathing amplified in his head.

"Davey, stop." He could barely hear his father's voice in the torrential rainstorm.

He feared knowing how far he was in front of his father, but Davey glanced over his shoulder, watching as the old man zigzagged forward, panting, and gasping for air. The old man's lifestyle finally caught up with him. In the end, it would be Davey's savior, or so he thought.

He felt his ankle catch Jason's abandoned bicycle, sending him toppling to the ground. The world came upon Davey fast as his face snapped against the moist earth. The intense pain coursed around his ankle and down to his toes. Davey rolled to his back and grabbed his leg. He couldn't run. Not in this condition.

"That's right, boy," his father's malevolent call struck him.

With no other choice, Davey pushed himself to his feet, grinding his teeth together, summoning the last of his willpower. He'd been here before, from the schoolyard bullies to his father's abuse, but he wouldn't surrender, not this time.

Before he could run, he felt the old man's hand grab him by the collar and snap backwards, nearly choking him.

"Always causing trouble. It was you who took your mother."

Davey's head whipped back against the ground, sending his vision to a tunneling cloud of stars amidst the fat raindrops. His father's silhouette loomed overhead – an uncaged animal ready to devour its prey.

21

"Dad...please." Davey's head throbbed as his father lowered his knee into Davey's stomach, pressing against his bruised chest. Davey let out a whimper.

"Enough pleasing. Enough disobeying."

Davey blinked, trying to hold onto consciousness as his father raised his arm, preparing to strike his only son.

"No." Davey closed his eyes and wished it all away, preparing for the impact. None would follow, not with a creature born of imagination and ancient origin, an odd guardian angel.

Davey heard the rush break the Chesapeake's surface, sounding like an elephant blowing out water from its snout. Gray became black against his eyelids. Its presence loomed above, a giant veil wrapping around them.

He cracked his right eyelid just enough to see the shimmering blue-green creature above. The plague of the ancient Mediterranean sailor now made its presence known in the Chesapeake.

"What the—?" His father said, lifting his knee off Davey and falling backwards in a comical way.

Davey wouldn't wait around. He spider crawled backwards as the Kraken crashed back down below the surface. Davey embraced the pain and ran off.

"Help," his father called, his voice a pathetic squeak of a cornered mouse ready to meet its end. And he was just that – a pitiful mouse deserving no less a fate.

Davey pumped his legs faster, more pistons firing off. Lactic acid burned his quads, causing him to stumble, jarring his knee into the ground, but he didn't notice. He steadied himself as a wave large enough to blot out the sky crashed against the rocks to his right, spraying the ground surrounding the lighthouse, the impact sending Davey back to the floor.

It hurt worse than before. His ears rung. His vision seesawed from the natural colors of the storm to shades of red. He didn't know where he was for a moment, only that he had to run.

"Davey," she called. Davey blinked then rolled his head to the right where he saw the ominous shadow glide beneath the surface. The Kraken turned abruptly, another funnel of water blowing up to the sky as it prepared to strike again.

"Ain't going to escape me," his father called, having recovered from his fall. "Not meant to escape me."

His head still ringing, Davey looked up to top of the lighthouse, past the curtain of rain, to see the first light of her figure, his mother's figure.

"Mom," Dave whispered.

"Yes," she answered unlike before.

Davey's eyes opened wider, her body becoming corporeal, more of a reality. It had to be her. There was no other answer. It gave him a renewed purpose, more of a reason for him to will the strength to roll to his stomach and push himself off the ground.

The lighthouse stood no less than fifteen feet away..

"I'm coming." Davey hobbled forward, his lifeless right leg acting like an anchor as he approached the lighthouse.

His heart sank when he noticed the remnants of the broken padlock and chain discarded within the high grass. The electric yellow "Keep Out" sign lay against the wall before another gust of wind caught it, sending it out to the sea with the monster. It was no longer a sanctuary, instead an open door for his father to pass through.

It didn't matter. Davey willed himself through the mariner's doorway and lunged for the staircase guardrail, a mountain of an obstacle he would have to climb. The rusted metal bit deep into his palm as he shifted his wait onto the structure and climbed. The stabbing in his ankle grew worse as bone separated from tendon, feeling the snap of a rubber band against his skin.

Another lightning strike caused the circular corridor to flash with energy, igniting the old bones of the lighthouse. Davey braced himself with each step, grinding his teeth together even harder, wondering if he would pass out from pain.

He almost lost himself in his imagination of her nurturing smile, when his father's voice boomed from below, swirling around and beating against his eardrums like a bad grade on his report card.

"You get your butt down here right now," he said. The staircase shook as his father started his own ascent, forcing Davey to move faster.

"Just…leave me alone."

"I said stop it."

Davey reached the trapdoor's ladder. It seemed like a sheer cliff as he grabbed the first rung his body refusing, but his mind willing to escape.

His back tightened with every rung as he pulled himself upwards until he reached the platform. It kicked back a rouge gust of wind circled around his malnourished frame, lifting him through and nearly sending him outside of the circular room where the lighthouse once held its beacon. In a last ditch effort, Davey hooked his arm underneath an interior railing until the wind subsided.

"Davey," she said, her waiflike voice captured his attention. Her figure, her deep crimson locks that made other mothers jealous, her slender arms reaching forward, and her hazel eyes shimmered into existence. This time she wasn't a specter or a dream, rather his mother exuding the same calming influence as she did during her previous time on earth.

"Mom." He started forward, his entire body numb with anticipation. "Mom."

Another lightning strike branched out along the horizon, a spider's web racing along the Chesapeake. His mother didn't react, instead casting her gaze over Davey's shoulder.

The trapdoor slammed back down as his father emerged like a turtle through its shell. His ravenous eyes locked on him, ready to exact its toll.

"I'm only going to tell you one more time…" His father stopped. "Helen?" Anger lost itself upon his words. His sneer relaxed. His eyes dropped along with his shoulders.

For that split second, Davey felt his family together once more, if only for a moment.

"You left us," his father yelled, anger returning. There would be no escape.

Davey turned back around, but his mother was gone.

Another crack of lightning, another flash of light danced along the sky, this time with enough strength to cause the lighthouse to buckle a little, the plateau shaking below.

"Davey," her ethereal voice called again.

"Mom?" He gasped, his heart beating faster, his ankle swelling around his shoe as his father approached.

"Davey," her voice drew his attention towards the rocky shoreline where he saw her: the mermaid from the picture book. Her legs, now aquiline and covered with scales, splashed in the waters. She extended her arm upwards. "Come to me. No more pain."

"Mom?" His voice trembled, studying the rocks. Would he jump? Would he leave this life?

"Boy, you better stop right there," his father demanded.

Davey ignored his father's threat, taking one step onto the railing and shifting his weight forward.

"Davey, you stop it right there."

"It's me. Come with me." The mermaid said, his mother's face – her hazel eyes – as clear as ever before she dove into the waves.

It had to be her. She came to take him away, the entire time directing him to find his escape and to be a family once more.

"I said stop what you're doing." His father's baritone voice joined the thunderous chorus of the tempest.

"Making it easy on all of us." Davey threw himself over the railing, towards the end of his nightmare.

JC Romero

THE MERMAID AND THE KRAKEN

Davey imagined his brains oozing out as his head collided with the rocks, followed by blood, lots of blood. That's how his father described his mother's fall during one of his drunken ramblings. But it would not end that way for Davey.

It happened so fast. He listened as the waves crashed and popped with a fizz against the shoreline, the slime-green algae coating each rock as he spiraled down, his arms flailing to the sides like a duckling, his father's please from atop the lighthouse. He didn't want his fall to stop, rather, he wanted to join his mother, to see her again in whatever afterlife the sea gods would grant him.

He knew suicide was wrong, but he didn't care. His mother called for him, and he wanted to follow.

Then it happened. The waters rushed up around him as he twisted and slammed into the angry Chesapeake Bay. His lungs tightened as his back broke the surface, exhaling what he thought would be his final breath.

Everything went black as weightlessness took over. Warm became cold. Bubbles gurgled. Light replaced dark against his eyelids. He felt no pain, no anger, only peace for those brief moments, alone in his world without a worry. Maybe he died. Maybe this was it.

His right eye opened first, followed by his left to see the beauty nature provided. The surface rippled with the appearance of the sun, its rays sweeping away the storm, dancing along each wave.

Davey imagined that living underwater was like the inside a mirror: everything appeared the same, except slower and protected from the evils of the world, including his father. He enjoyed the muffled serenity – his friends' distorted laughter as they dove into the bay, free from the pain of their parents.

As he floated further down, he spotted the lighthouse's outline wavering above, the red and whites blending into one. He thought he heard his dad call for him. Maybe he his father would follow. Maybe he would hit the rocks instead. And for the brief second, he felt remorse.

How did I miss the rocks?, Davey thought, the waters becoming darker the further he descended. He didn't remember it being this deep along the coastline.

Then the first hint of fear crept into his thoughts like a wolf spider crawling into his sleeping back during a camping trip. His fingertips and toes tingled, desperate for oxygen. It dawned on him he needed to breath. He was alive, not dead. He didn't want to die, not like this, not by drowning.

He remembered the story of George Haslett drowning in fifth grade. They say he fell into the Chesapeake when his mother was watching her soaps. He thought about George's mother dressed in black for a year, the way his father left town, never to be heard from again. Maybe George was escaping from something, too.

The water shifted around him, tugging at his hips. He looked down in time to see the ominous shadow glide under his feet, the beast's oblong shape masked by the abyss that shouldn't be.

"Mom," Davey said, spilling out more bubbles from his mouth. A naturally strong swimmer, he righted himself in a last ditch effort to reach the surface, but he couldn't move. He was trapped, a prisoner to a paralyzed body refusing to live.

More sinister thoughts invaded his mind. He imagined the water washing into his lungs, the pain and fear that would follow. He only wanted to be with his mom, for it to end quickly and without pain.

It wouldn't be easy for him. It never was.

Blowing his cheeks out, he held in his breath until he felt like his lungs would explode, struggling to keep focus as his vision faded.

Another shadow darted across the deep blue expanse of the Chesapeake, out in the nether regions where it was blacker than any night sky. It was only a glimpse, a second before it disappeared.

Davey looked up again. The lighthouse appeared like the miniature wood carving his mother kept beside her nightstand. Color left his sight, save only blue and black.

His fingers went numb. His toes and legs followed. He couldn't hold it in any longer, opening his lungs and closing his eyes, imagining the best time in his life – the Christmas morning where his mother told his father about the pregnancy, a baby boy that would never come.

He was going to die like this: alone, left to the sandy floors of the Chesapeake.

Davey drifted down, his arms reaching out. He let go. Water filled the back of his nose and his throat, suffocating him in an instant.

Blue faded to black.

II.

Warmth against lips massaged Davey's mouth open. A quick burst of oxygen filled his throat and lungs, forcing water through his nose in a burning stream.

"Davey," she said, "you need to wake up. Your end is not now. There is more work to be done."

Davey saw a distorted vision at first, a blur of a face hovering before him. It came upon him again, the foreign feeling of lips against his, much like when Amanda Walker innocently pecked him – his only kiss, one much like his mother's – last year at the church BBQ.

With another burst of warmth, air entered his lungs, expanding his chest and sweeping away the cold. His savior pulled back, revealing a vision more distinct against the obscure waters of the Chesapeake.

She appeared beautiful by all accounts, staring back at him through round eyes accented by an emerald green powerful enough to penetrate the darkness. Her hair blazed orange and red like the trees reflecting against the Chesapeake during high autumn, framing her narrow face.

He saw his mom for a moment.

"Mom," he said, regaining use of his arms and legs.

"No, I'm not your mother," she said, her fluid voice soothed even his frailest of his nerves.

"No?" Excitement left him as the girl's features became more distinct.

"I'm sorry." The girl's right lip curled up in a smile as she shied away. "You will forgive me."

"For what?"

"For fooling you."

"I don't...understand."

"In time you will, but it was the only way. Our time is short, and we need you, Keeper."

"But, what? I don't—" Davey stopped short as the current shifted underneath, the long shadow once again emerged below, its massive tail propelling it forward.

"He means you no harm." Again, the sound of her voice calmed him.

"What…is it? Did it take my mom? I saw her, I know I did just before I jumped."

"As I said, I needed you. *We* needed you." Her large eyes circled down below. He followed her movement, noticing his descent into the abyss stopped. They floated, weightless.

"I don't understand. Am I dead? Did I die?" Davey whipped his head around then up. There was nothing, No lighthouse. No rocky shoreline. Not even the mirror of the surface, only placid ice blue stretching into an endless landscape.

"There are few like you. You are one, one who can open themselves. It must be you," she answered, unblinking.

"Who are you?"

"A friend." She circled around, finally revealing her true self, an impossible creature reserved for his mother's book. Blue-green scales glimmered where legs should be, flanked by hair flowing with her movement, conjuring a whirlpool of energy as her tail whipped back and forth, propelling her faster until she circled back around.

"The picture." He would've gasped if he could. "It was you…the entire time it was you calling me. You caused me to—"

"Please."

"No." He hated her in that instant. "You fooled me. I jumped because, because." He tightened his hands into a fist in a way he never had before, staring through the mermaid with all the anger. His eyes stung but could not cry.

"It was for the better. Your father would've hurt you."

"He's not a bad man. Just misguided. You shouldn't have."

Something tugged at his legs, followed by another force. The hulking behemoth surged upwards, its intent obviously on protecting the mermaid, her companion. Davey first saw the glint of gold, a sphere rising from the depths, revealing another until its green form blotted out the calm blueness of the Chesapeake.

"What?" Davey said as the Kraken stopped thirty feet below, wading, waiting to strike.

"Relax. He will not harm you. He is just a protective sort, always careful when I face anger." She traced her fingernails along the length of Davey's forearms. The touch tingled, causing his skin to pimple with goose flesh, his mind to retreat to a place of serenity. It reminded him of the gas he received while his dentist pulled his wisdom teeth.

"O…ok."

"He's a friend. He's here to protect us."

"You sure about that?"

"Oh, I'm quite positive, despite his attitude." She smiled again.

"I don't know if I can trust you. I mean, I don't know you."

"I don't expect you to. Not now, but soon."

"Then you can answer me. Am I dead?"

"No, you are very much alive for the first time in your life. And what you are about to discover will help those like you in similar positions."

"This…this is all making no sense. I mean, how can I breath underwater?"

"Nor should you understand right now. In time, all things will be revealed to you, but not now, Lighthouse Keeper. We must depart these waters." She tugged on his arm to follow, but Davey resisted, noticing their destination being a horizon of nothingness, dark waters he dare not explore.

"Wait."

"What is it?'

"My…father." The warm rush of embarrassment filled his cheeks. She must've known about their relationship.

"What about him?" Her tail whipped around, again moving the water surrounding Davey, the current pulling at his hips. Davey remembered reading about a mermaid's temper in the book, the way they lured corrupted sailor's to their doom. Part of him thought she had the same intentions.

"Is he…will he be ok?"

"The Keeper still cares. I'm not surprised about this."

"I just want to…know. He'll be all alone."

Water churned below with even more bubbles as the Kraken stirred, followed by a hollow groan.

"Relax." She giggled, shaking her head a tad. "He doesn't care for types like your father. Call it a mutual understanding."

"Yeah, most people don't like him."

"I think we both know why."

"He won't eat him, like he ate Jason, will he?"

"Jason?"

"Yeah, Jason. He's one of those kids that followed me earlier today. Think your friend, well." Davey swallowed, thinking of the abandoned bicycle at the edge of the peninsula.

"You mean the boy who tormented you much in the same way as your father?"

"Yes."

"Well." The mermaid closed her eyes, again another playful grin reaching across her face. "He's quite ok. Maybe we'll meet him in our travels."

"He's alive?" Whatever small amount of guilt Davey felt subsided.

"Um, for the most part he is. But we needn't worry about that. The day has gone long. It's best we leave this place."

She tugged on him again. Davey kicked his legs back, resisting. He needed to know.

"He was a good man at one time," Davey said, his mind lingering to times past.

"Who is that?"

"My father. He's not all that bad."

"You are quite concerned." Her face grew softer, less hurried as she looked over him.

"He's just…lost himself since he lost my mother. That's all. I know he's good inside. He'll come around." Davey looked back up, hoping to see the lighthouse and his father, the last connection to his mother.

The mermaid waded backwards, less energetic in her movements as her grin faded to a somber line. It was as if she knew his pain, experiencing the same.

"You mustn't let your mind be poisoned by things you cannot control."

"But he's my father."

"Everything will be ok, I promise." She caressed Davey's cheek with a long stroke of her hands, cajoling him to close his eyes. It was a familiar touch, one reminiscent of his mother combing his hair, the way she lulled him to sleep during those nights his father lost himself. And for that moment, Davey lost himself as well, somewhere between a new reality and the world he once understood.

"You'll be ok. I promise," her voice, his mother's, called just as it did before. "You need to trust her."

"Mom." His eyes popped open to see the mermaid still wading before him, waiting for him to answer.

"It's time to go Davey. Your mother is right."

"But," Davey hesitated but did not pull back. "I need to know something."

"What's that?"

"Your name."

"The Keeper asks the mermaid's name?"

"Yes, I need to know, so I can trust. They say you can't trust someone until you know their name."

"Of course." She tilted her head up, her hair, capturing the flickering light from some unknown source spread out around her expressionless face, highlighting her calmness. "Gwen."

"Gwen?" He bit down on his lower lip. He knew the name, but didn't know how.

"Yes, but we need to go. The moon is about to rise, and with it, the lost ship."

III.

They swam faster than Davey could ever imagine. Water rushed across his face and cheeks, pulling it backwards as they went high and low, right and left through the current. The Chesapeake's bottom served as a graveyard for abandoned crab pots taken by rust and the occasional license plate or empty turtle shell half-poked out of the sand.

It was a world Davey could never have known before, one captured by picture books and his one trip to Baltimore's Aquarium. He always thought the undersea life was a world of quiet majesty, one he was drawn to since his early years, those days when they first arrived at the shore house, when fishing off their pier and grilling their bounty was a routine for his family.

Gwen pointed out all manner of sea creatures, even waving to a few during their journey. The fish seemed ambivalent to his presence, carrying about their usual activities as if he weren't even there.

She remained by his side entire time, her hand clasped around his wrist, guiding him forward, pulling whenever Davey felt the slightest bit of hesitance. In the background, the Kraken's bibulous shadow loomed, the beast who saved Davey from his father's drunken rage.

"Are you quite alright?" She said several times, still keeping forward as they coasted atop of an old crab trolley, its paint chipped and weathered from its time spent slumbering underneath the Chesapeake.

"What?" He said as they drifted to a stop.

"I said are you quite ok?" Gwen whirled him around in a playful sort of way.

"I suppose." A school of silver fish huddled together in cloud formation, their skin capturing the moonlight filtering through the waves above before swimming off in the distance. "Don't you think I should know where we're going?"

"To know where you're going?" She looked down like a child being scolded, holding a secret within.

"Yeah, I still don't know everything. It's like I'm in a dream world."

"I'm sorry, then. It isn't my intentions to keep things from you. But it is for your safety."

"I don't feel safe, if that's what you're asking. Everything is happening so fast."

"As it should," she answered then looked up. The Chesapeake's surface reappeared, shimmering above them, waves lolling back and forth in a lazy effort. The remnants of the storm subsided as the water turned to a crystal sheet. "You will understand in due time, but it's best you don't know for now, for what you're about to see may scare you."

"What?"

"They're here." Her eyes darted open, growing even wider. Gwen turned to the Kraken, who still kept himself at a distance "We must be quick. Be precise."

"What? I don't understand." Davey's heart thumped twice as the Kraken swam off until it was a mere pinpoint in the distance.

"Promise me you'll be careful up there," Gwen said.

"Careful? About what? Why won't you tell me anything?"

"You must be quiet. Pretend you are a ninja like you always do."

"Hey...wait a minute. How did you know?"

"If he's here, we must be careful to escape him. He would do terrible things if he discovered us." Gwen spoke at a rapid pace, her tail darting back and forth, her movements more rigid. "Are you ready?"

"For?" His imagination worked overtime as he thought about her warning.

"It will only take a second. It might feel like you're drowning again, but this time with air." Without another word, Davey felt Gwen wrap her arms around his torso and swim upwards.

Davey noticed the distinct round pearl of the moon during the rapid ascent taken by a column of bubbles. Seconds later, they broke through the surface. The air felt dry to his mouth and nose, almost foreign as his lungs exploding, expelling water. His chest constricted twice, squeezing his ribs, before he acclimated himself to the atmosphere, the world he thought he left.

He immediately looked around, noticing the Chesapeake's placid appearance, a black expanse sweeping as far as he could see. There was no storm, only calm.

With the exception of the rolling waves that nipped at his neck, undulating up and down in their movements towards the shore, everything remained quiet. A Christmas Light string dotted the distance, homes of the wealthy who could afford such land, away from the ruffians of life.

As he squinted and looked further, Davey swore he could see the tip of a lighthouse. A jolt of energy captured him at the thought of swimming back to find his false safety, but he didn't know if it was his or another's, its light lost along the haunted waters.

"It's not what you think it is. Not at all." Gwen said. Her porcelain doll complexion glowed in the moon's pearl luminescence. But her hair remained aflame, brilliant, matted against her head. He then noticed her ears peak out of her hair, pointy ears like an elf.

"I wouldn't make it anyway." Davey spit out the salt water, its contents pruning his tongue. "That light is lost."

"Maybe. Maybe not."

"What are we even doing here?" Davey bobbed up and down, the swells blinding him then carrying forward so he could see the dark outline of the Eastern Shore. He would normally be afraid that his muscles would tire, but he wasn't. Not with her.

"We're escaping."

"Escaping what?"

"This world."

"What? Where?" Davey circled his arms around at a frantic pace. He wanted to be brave, feigning courage in the face of the unknown. After all, everyone fears the unknown.

A distant toll resounded in the distance, carrying across the waves with no impediment. Davey though it a buoy marker at first, but then it rang again, more purposeful in its call.

"He's here," Gwen gasped then plunged underneath.

"Gwen," Davey called. "Gwen."

He was alone again, forsaken in the middle of the Chesapeake, a fear he'd had since he lost his footing and fell off his family's pier. He remembered flailing about, his fingers outstretched, reaching for something solid only to find water. His parents were inside arguing.

He waded around to see the silhouette of the lighthouse in the distance. Maybe Gwen lied. Maybe it was his home. They didn't swim that far, or did they? Despite his earlier assessment, it was his only hope at this point after Gwen abandoned him.

With a fresh lungful of air and the likelihood of facing exhaustion, Davey kicked forward. He knew he would battle the current, so he angled himself just to the left. Maybe he would be lucky. Maybe he would reach it before he drowned.

As he kicked forward, a whirlpool emerged to his left, just outside his reach. He prayed it was a friend.

"Gwen?" He choked out the words.

Something nicked his foot, something solid and strong, the consistency of sandpaper against skin. He tried to stay calm, not moving his feet or legs. Seconds later, it bumped into him again, more forceful in its purpose.

"Be still," Gwen whispered for his attention, her desperate words pulling him from behind.

"What?" He swallowed more of the salt water and guided himself around to see her pale silhouette, a specter in a sea of glass.

"I said be still. They mean you no harm if you show no fear."

"Sharks?" Davey's lips trembled, unsure if it was prompted by fear or the cold.

"Not in this world. In the others, maybe. But not this one."

"I've seen the movies." Davey's chin dipped into the waters, their unnerving presence making it all the more difficult for him to concentrate.

"And those movies are in another world."

"What...what are you saying?" The dorsal menace glided next to him yet again, maybe ten feet away, zigzagging back and forth, churning the water.

"Remain calm. They will leave us within minutes."

"I don't understand. You disappeared—"

"You need to be quiet."

With a subtle splash and fizz, Gwen disappeared, the moon catching the last of her tail as she submerged into the depths, once again leaving Davey alone with the sound of the tolling bell in the background.

"Need to get out of here." Talking aloud was the only thing that calmed him. He righted himself and kicked forward once again, lying on his side like he was taught in Boy Scouts. Somewhere beneath the black veil, the sharks took notice of him. He half expected to be eaten at any moment.

After taking a few strokes, he noticed a mist seep from the Chesapeake's surface as if the water itself were set ablaze. It grew thicker with each second, smelling of his fireplace back home. Another toll of the bell sounded, this time without a direction. His heart beat at the same pace.

They would smell him – sharks smelled fear.

She's left me, he thought, remaining steadfast in spite of his lips going numb, his face cold enough where he couldn't feel to the touch. He'd been through worse. He suffered his dad's wrath.

The water churned next to him. With a quick gasp, he stopped cold and looked for the dorsal fin, but the mist thickened and shrouding the entire area in a curtain of uncertainty.

He imagined this is how all sailors died in World War II, how those men his grandfather told him about were abandoned after a Japanese torpedo took them out, left to the sharks as supper.

"Gwen," he stuttered. The desperate cold crept down his forearms and to his elbows, from his toes to his knees.

Another swirl to his right caused him to whip around. A solid object bumped his chest, moving him sideways for a bit.

Davey expected sting of teeth to come at any second, digging into his skin and the warmness of blood. He couldn't survive, or could he?

A soft burn permeated through the fog, like headlights through an April rainstorm. It was indistinct at first, a simple light bathing the mist in its radiance.

The water continued to bubble, this time more purposeful, stronger in its arrival that no animal could conjure, save Gwen's Kraken.

"What?" Davey couldn't feel his lower jaw as he spoke, watching the carved masthead harkening back to the time of pirates pierce the fog, revealing a vessel's presence with the help of a dozen or so lamps lining each side.

It didn't take long for Davey to identify it as a frigate, an old pirate style ship his grandfather kept in his model case. It also had no earthly reason for being in the modern world, a relic from the past usually reserved for ship shows in Baltimore.

Its movements were deliberate, the lazy waves sloshing against its hull as it cut through the fog-covered waters, its wooden frame dipping down then back up again, kicking up whitecaps.

Davey forgot himself in the moment, tilting his head up as far as he could see, his jaw agape in the marvel. He spotted the two large masts reaching towards the heavens with sails whipping back and forth through stagnant air.

The mist danced and circled the relic of a ship as if it following the frigate's commands – a monkey to an organ grinder – morphing along the sides into figures resembling various sea legends Davey recalled from the book.

The bell tolled again, louder and dissipating some of the mist.

"Hel-lo?" Davey could barely speak, spitting out more water, realizing it may be his only chance for rescue. The frigate answered with the sound of ropes slapping against the hull, nary a mention of the boy's existence.

Maybe they couldn't see him? Davey thought, abandoning all fear of the shark's reprisal. He didn't leave it to chance, swimming as fast as he could towards the boat.

With each stroke, the water kicked back against his eyesight, blinding him with a slight sting. But it didn't matter. He needed to get there or be eaten by sharks.

He caught a glimpse of wooden hull, following by the unknown depths of water and the amplified sound underneath its waves. He repeated the exercise, lifting his head every so often as the boat sailed towards an unknown destination.

Determination became panic. No matter how hard he swam, the boat drifted further way, trailed only by the mists.

"Please, no. Stop" Davey gasped, reaching forward as he stopped to catch his breath. He couldn't have expected what followed.

What sounded like a whip cracking in the wind startled him. Seconds later, Davey watched as what appeared to be a snake jumped out from the ship's side, its black length twisting in the vapor for a moment before bowing downwards and plunging to the water next to Davey.

Davey jerked backwards, fearing for the worse when he realized it wasn't a snake at all, but a rope. Someone had listened to his plea. Someone wanted to help. But who?

With no other choice, Davey grabbed hold of the rope, feeling every fiber bite into his pruned and soft hands – a natural reaction of the human body to get a better grip in the water, a fact Davey learned in class. As his fingers wrapped around his would-be savior, the rope pulled backwards, guiding Davey to the vessel.

He was safe, somehow.

"Hello?" His voice echoing up into nothingness. Was there even a crew at all? He looked around only to see his faint reflection staring back up at him from the Chesapeake. "Fine, then."

He swung forward until his feet planted against the hull. The wood felt covered with something the consistency of slime, making his footing more difficult. He looked up the ship's side. It could've been Mount Everest, but he couldn't stop. He had to go forward. With a quick breath, he hoisted himself up.

One after another, Davey found the strength to scale the side, and he was never one to excel in gym class. Maybe it was motivated by fear. Maybe it was motivated by the reality his friends would not attend his funeral if he was lost at sea. Or maybe it was something else, a force that would see him live, the possibility of seeing his mother as Gwen, who he hadn't forgotten abandoned him, said would come to pass.

Davey ignored the exhaustion, guiding himself up, his hands feeling like they would rub off at any second. The aged wood itself appeared to flake with a white substance, a smattering of old sea growth chipping off with each step. Certainly it wasn't a seaworthy vessel, and if so, it wouldn't last much longer.

But he didn't have the time to study the intricacies of construction. He had to get to safety, his legs, now numb, dragged behind, until he came upon the railing and flipped himself over, unaware of what dangers the ship might hold.

Davey landed back first with a thud, sprawled out like a spread eagle and looking to the foreign heavens. His legs and arms were of no use, tired to the point he'd never felt before. He lay there, listening to his lungs expand and contract in a fast cadence until the bell tolled again, over and over until he found the courage to lift his head.

IV.

"Hello?" Davey pushed himself up to a sitting position. "Anybody...anybody there?" He stuttered from the sudden cold only damp cloth could provide. His words resounded across the empty deck. He half expected to see a ship filled with skeletons like the one movie, but there would be no skeletons, only the mist.

"Hello?"

Again, no one answered, save the sound of the water dripping in heavy drops from his hair, the snapping of the sails, and the groan of the wooden frame.

"Alone. I'm alone."

Davey wiped his face clean of salt water and looked over the railing to see two murky fuselages rubbing against the boat, their dorsal fins cutting through the mist. His heart skipped a beat.

"Big. Too big," he expelled the stale, fearful air from his lungs.

"Davey," Gwen called.

Davey surveyed the waters but didn't see a sign her. Was it his mind playing tricks on him?

"Davey," she called again, prompting Davey to look up.

And there she was, a banshee within the mists. Her red hair set the ship on fire, her round emerald eyes staring back at him opposite the galley. A white gown, as white as any he'd ever seen, hung from her shoulders, making her appear as if she were floating.

"Gwen?" He couldn't' be sure, but it had to be her.

"Yes." She *stepped* forward. No scales. No wild look. Just Gwen.

"Whoa, wait." He held his arm out in an effort to stop her movement. "You can't…you can't just do those things."

"Don't go on telling me he's going to be making the rules around here," another called, a boy's voice a little older than Davey's said, a little rough in the delivery.

"What? I'm not taking over anything." Davey noticed a boy sitting atop the railing in front of the ship's wheel, one leg dangling off, covered by tattered trousers, the other tucked underneath his leg. He wore a sort of doo rag, covering his long hair, which appeared the oft-color of seaweed. He reminded Davey of the schoolyard bullies for a moment.

"I told you, Didn't I?" He spoke with an accent Davey couldn't place. "Boy has no spine. It can't be him."

"Relax. It's him. He's the Keeper."

"Enough," Davey said, "yeah, so, I may not be the bravest or anything, but it doesn't mean y'all can push me around. Just tell me what's going on? And what's this Keeper stuff?" Davey steadied himself, his head throbbing, his world canting to the right.

"You've been patient enough," Gwen said, her head moving in an arc as she looked to the sky. "Crossover his happening. Time for you to know."

"I don't even know if I can trust you. I mean, you trick me into thinking I was seeing my mom. Then you drag me out in to the middle of the Chesapeake, where you abandon me. Then there's the sharks." As he spoke, Davey realized his voice had changed, lower in tone with a little more bass. Gone was the high-pitch squeal, an albatross whenever he held a conversation with an eight grader.

"I know you're mad, but we needed to see." The boy atop the railing masked his laughter by placing his hand over his mouth. It didn't faze Davey. He'd been the victim one too many times.

"See what?" Davey said.

"To be sure you're the one." The boy answered. "To be sure you were indeed the Keeper. And it appears you might be, I mean, are the Keeper." He hopped down, nary making a sound as he landed from nearly ten feet up. "And I suppose I should respect that, though I was expecting someone a bit more…brave."

"And…who are you to say that?" Davey asked, finding the courage to walk forward.

"Your guardian angel." The boy bowed like one of those old Victorian dancers, chuckling the entire time. "You know, he don't look much like a Keeper to me, does he?"

"It's been awhile. Then again, looks aren't everything." Her eyes became brighter, more welcoming.

"Glad to see someone has finally accepted me." Davey rung out his shirt, hoping it would provide a little warmth.

"I'm sorry we had to put you through that," the boy said.

"We?"

"Who else do you think was down there with you?" The boy smiled in a knowing way, revealing his true nature. He was the beast transformed, though a little more drastic from his former self, like Gwen.

"It was you. The entire time it was you." Davey pointed several times.

"The Kraken. That's right, mate. Here in the flesh. The one and only." He bowed again. "Sorry about being so rough back there. Seemed to have gotten yourself in a lot of trouble in a hurry."

"My life in a nutshell. What can I say?"

"Not much, apparently, mate."

"The name's Davey. I mean, well, you know."

"Davey the Keeper. Has a bit of a sound to it. You know, the sound of someone who don't know what he's getting into."

"And that's your name? The Kraken?"

"Only name I've gone by since I could think of it."

"Simple as that?"

"Simpler. You can just call me Kraky for short." The Kraken laughed.

"That's just…weird."

"Didn't really have a name. Was too young, just born when they threw me to the sea."

"Threw you to the sea?"

"Yeah." The Kraken shrugged. "Parents didn't see much in me. Webbed fingers and all." The Kraken held out his hand and spread his fingers, revealing translucent webbing much like one of his grandfather's old horror movies: Something about a Black Lagoon.

"I see. And you were born that way?"

"Sure as much as I was." The Kraken clicked his tongue. "What can I say, though? Parents thought I was some sort of…mistake. So, they threw me out to see, and, well, I became the Kraken. Long story. Would sure like to tell it to you some other time." The Kraken sauntered over to the boat's railing and looked over. Davey could tell there was something more on Kraken's mind.

"Suppose I should thank you, too." Davey followed the Kraken's lead, his head swirling with a million ideas, a millions thoughts he couldn't place.

"You'll thank me later." The Kraken looked back at Gwen, something hidden within his intentions Davey noticed. "For now, you do your job, and we'll do ours."

The Kraken patted Davey on the back with a little force, revealing the boy's strength. Davey noted it and made sure he wouldn't cross the Kraken in the future.

"A mermaid and a...sea monster, or whatever." Davey glanced back down to the brackish waters. Mist still swirled much like clouds on a lazy summer afternoon at the park. Beyond the mist, Davey noticed the first hints of white caps, waves displaying a little more emotion than before, heralding another storm. Then again, what did it matter? He had no idea where he was or who he was anymore.

"It must be a lot to take in right now. And for that, you're braver than you give yourself credit for," Gwen said, tugging on one of the ropes connected to the sail before joining Davey at his side. "But we need to prepare. We have a long journey ahead of us."

"Because of me?" Davey spun around, nose curling just a bit with anger. "Is it because I'm this Keeper you keep mentioning? Can you at least tell me that? Or why I'm here?"

"Right, then. You're here because—" The Kraken said, but Gwen silenced him before he could finish.

"On second thought, we need to prepare." She answered with a stern voice and even tighter expression. Davey knew there was a secret he'd have to pry out of her, but for now, he only wanted to have some semblance of where he was at in the world.

"More secrets." He glanced over Gwen's shoulder at a dismissive Kraken, who simply continued staring overboard. Waves smacking against the ship's hull grew more distinct with every passing second.

"No, no more secrets. You want to know what the Lighthouse Keeper is, don't you?" Kraken said. Gwen shook her head in objection.

"Yeah, if you keep calling me that."

"It may not mean much to you now, but you play an important role in the future of mankind. You always have," Gwen said, reluctance laced in her words.

"Put it this way, you're like some great protector, you know." The Kraken snapped his fingers and pointed at Davey with a little emphasis. "Someone who can lead people to shore safely, like a lighthouse. But instead of being a building, you are its keeper, and you can turn on the light."

"So I can turn on a light in a lighthouse? That's why I'm here?" Davey's forehead furrowed in a bit of confusion. "Doesn't sound all that impressive…"

The boat rocked to the side, much deeper and diagonal as before, revealing churning waters below. Wind hollered with a brutal gust, blowing by Davey's ears and lifting Gwen's hair.

"It's not any lighthouse. It's *the* lighthouse." The Kraken smiled and shook his head, looking at Davey as if he had a third eye. "Are you sure it's him?"

"It's him. Trust me. His humbleness is all I needed to see." Gwen nodded. "The lighthouse. It's—" Again, the wind howled, this time angrier in it presence, whipping the sails back and forth with a snap. The boat teetered opposite, high enough to cause Davey to brace himself against the splintered railing, his feet sliding along the floorboards. "He's here. He must've followed," Gwen said, a little more panic in her voice.

"Did you want me to?" The Kraken pointed to the waters.

"No, you might get lost in the crossover. Once we cross, I don't know if you'll be able to find us."

"What's going on?" Davey balanced himself, holding his arms out much like the way the surfers did at Ocean City, hoping beyond hope he wouldn't slide against the deck. He saw himself for a split second falling back over the rails, causing Davey to tighten his grip a little more.

"You just need to stick with us." The Kraken yelled, his words almost lost in the approaching tempest.

Lightning surged overhead in a white-purple blaze, highlighting the popcorn cloud cover. But unlike a normal storm, the clouds churned with a purpose. With each flash of lightning and crack of thunder, the clouds thickened, billowing out like a volcano eruption. The pungent aroma of ash swept over the galley.

Then came the rain, a sheet of water descending from the sky with fat drops splashing against the deck in tiny geysers, plucking Davey's ears with machine gun rapidness.

An even more powerful gust of wind took the ship, this time shifting old trunks and barrels, splintering the railings and sending them to the depths. The captain's quarter doors flew open then slammed back shut. The Chesapeake gushed up over the sides, pulling at the wooden planks, which groaned with each rock.

"Go inside before he sees him." The Kraken yelled before running towards the ship's wheel, his eyes wide and full of urgency.

"Let's go," Gwen hollered and grabbed Davey by the arm.

The orchestra of lightning strikes cast its blue-white light in the background, revealed the silhouette of another ship out of time, its masts taller, its sails wider, rocking back and forth roughly one hundred yards away within the storm's fury,

Davey paused as another tentacle of lightning struck, this time revealing a black hole spinning over the rogue boat – the storm's genesis.

"We need to go. He can't see you, not yet," Gwen said.

"Who can't see me?"

Another crack of thunder, its energy arcing around the rogue ship's hull, revealing a silhouette hovering at its bow, a figure Davey couldn't see, its details covered in shadow, but one he knew by its presence.

"Dad?" Davey said, pulling his hand free from Gwen.

"You mustn't let him see you."

"That's…my father. I don't know how I can tell, but that's him."

"It's not him. It's not what you think it is."

"But it's him. I can tell." Davey refused, focusing on the other ship. His dad was coming for him.

"He'll take you back. You can't go back."

"Home?" His father's specter jumped down from its position and grabbed onto one of the ropes, slicing through the air with ease.

"You need to tell me. You need to tell me now," Davey wiped his face clear of water, his vision distorted by the barrage of rainfall. He kept his attention fixed on the figure the entire time.

"We're in crossover right now. Your father…his anger found us."

"His anger?"

"That's what I'm trying to tell you. It's not him. It's not your father. It's something more evil. It's the rage he holds inside, the rage all humans hold inside."

"None of this makes sense. None of it." Davey wrenched back again. This wasn't a place for him. He needed to be back home, maybe even take care of his father, and make him see the error of his ways.

"Davey, please."

The tempest opened up, its fury twisting the boat around and tearing one of the sails clean off – a ghost in the sky – sending it into the oblivion, where it slipped into the clouds lost forever. They were no longer in control of their destination, a mere prisoner to the Chesapeake's will.

"I can do this. I can talk to him, tell him he can't hurt you." Davey rounded his shoulders back.

His father's silhouette swung forward like a bat through the air, and landed on Davey's ship near the stern, making no sound as he landed.

He expected to see his father's age lines, the deep resentment set in his lost eyes from alcohol abuse. Instead, he saw nothing, a void lost in a wisp-like smoke that disguised the figure. Red-blazing orbs flickered where his eyes should rest, a specter ready to see Davey's end.

"Should I?" The Kraken yelled.

"You can't. Just steer us forward." Gwen said, answering through the fury.

"Gwen," the shadow hissed, "this is not our place."

Another branch of lighting struck the middle of the deck, splitting off chunks of wood across the deck in a puff of smoke.

"The boy is mine." The figure swirled about, losing its human form in a cloud of ink as it floated forward, cutting off Davey from Gwen before reforming once again.

Gwen was right. It wasn't his father, but something far more sinister, more diabolical.

"Where's my father?" Davey asked.

"Don't listen to him." Gwen's voice filtered through the storm, the rest of her words lost. "His words will poison you."

"I'm your past. I'm your future. You will step no further towards the Nether." Its words snapped like a snake, filled with venom and malice. "Do you understand me?"

"You're not my father…then you can't tell me what to do." Davey dared challenge him, taking one step back, his heel clipping one of the lose boards, causing him to fall on his butt.

"Son." The specter grew in height, expanding outwards, its words echoing with a million different voices. "You *are* mine."

It reached out with what appeared to be a hand, fingers stretching out in wispy lines, fluttering in and out as if formed by moths.

"No," The Kraken yelled as he jumped down and threw itself at the specter, but he would not find his mark, cutting through the physical rage of Davey's father. The Kraken tumbled to the ground with a *thwack*, then silence.

"Fool of a fish. No wonder your parents disowned you." The specter cackled, throwing its head back, its hair snapping, a hundred little strands each with its own life.

"He's going to kill us all." Gwen said as the Kraken curled into a ball. "Davey, you need to summon your light."

"What?" The rain picked up even more, coming down in buckets. Innocent splashes grew to piercing stings with each drop.

"There will be no crossover." The disemboweled voice said, pulling down on Davey, his will to go further. "There will be no savior."

Another plume of broken wood and sawdust filled the sky as lightning struck again, a massive pop sounding off in their midst. The boat wouldn't last much longer, sending them all below the Bay to be feasted upon by Gwen's "guardian" sharks.

"Take my hand, boy, and I assure you this will all be over. You can save these new friends of yours if you simply follow my lead." His father's hand reached out once more, tentacles spiraling forward.

Davey stared at the rage. He'd seen it before, the night his mother took her life.

"You aren't my father." Dave kicked backwards and sprang to his feet.

"Much more than your father. I am what you left him as, a broken man who knew no love." The body circled like a tornado, forming and reforming its human body still lost with blackness.

"No. My father was good once."

"Liar," The specter brought both arms down by its side like a sledgehammer, hammering away at the boat. Gwen screamed. Her high-pitched shrill lost in the typhoon as Davey watched her listless body smack against the mast and crumpled to the floor. Both the Kraken and Gwen were out, leaving Davey to fend for himself.

"I would ask once again, and that is it," the specter hissed.

"Summon...the light." The Kraken coughed, rolling over to his back.

"What, what light?"

"The light is gone. Your mother lost the light." The specter whirled to the side, manifesting into something bigger, its physical body a floating inkblot ready to send Davey from the ship.

"No," Gwen called. "You have it. The light is within, you"

"Don't listen to them. You come home with me." Lightning cracked again, its spider-like pulses emanating within his father's ethereal form, which hugged the ship, tearing at its structure, peeling away all particles and objects not tied down.

Lighthouse Keeper? Davey thought about the words from before. To light the lighthouse?

The ship buckled, sending Davey sliding from the railing and closer to the specter. A blanket of smoke poured over the railings, almost following his father's lead. They were helpless as the ship spun out of control.

"Just reach your hand out, and we'll take you home. Promise I won't go back to drinking. Promise I won't punish you that bad."

"I told you you're not my father," Davey said, fighting back the tears, searching for any weapon as the black mass grew, engulfing the smoke pouring up from the sides. The tempest's lightning surged within the heart of the dark form.

"You lie. Father doesn't like liars."

"I don't...want to repeat myself." Davey closed his eyes, concentrating as much as he could past the popping in his ears from the torrid wind, and tried to think about what they meant by him being the Keeper.

He saw his grandfather – his mother's father – on his usual post of a tattered recliner, one with floral designs. The old man would station himself on the back porch and stare out to the distant waters for hours on end. He found peace there, and for good reason. His mother's entire side of the family grew up on the Chesapeake, former fishermen who lived in the area since the settlers arrived.

They had an affinity for the Bay, all of them, including his mother. His grandfather would stroke his feathered white beard, taking puffs of his angled pipe (which he hand-carved) and told ghost stories about pirates and treasures, about mermaids and beasts of the deep, and most of all, the importance of lighthouses and the way they brought ships safely to shore.

He'd tell them while Davey was on his lap and they looked as the burnt orange of a late summer sun turned the Chesapeake alive, almost setting the waves ablaze with its brilliance.

He lost himself in those days before his grandfather contracted cancer, a victim from his time spent at Sparrows Point after his fishing business dried up. "Asbestos" they said. It was the first time Davey experienced death, the start of his mother's sadness.

At least he could lose himself in his imagination, a sanctuary from whatever the usual torment of the day. He watched as his grandfather studied him, those kind baby blue eyes displaying genuine care as he gave Davey something he carved – an old lighthouse no bigger than a PEZ dispenser.

Davey remembered the intricate design, a perfect replica for the lighthouse on the peninsula in his backyard, even down to the off-center shape. But it wasn't the details Davey remembered, it was his grandfather's words, the same words his mother recited during those nighttime prayers.

"When all hope is lost, when you are lost, just remembered the lighthouse and its light will guide you to shore. You are the lighthouse keeper, Davey. It's in our blood. Never let your nightmares scare away your dreams," his grandfather's voice boomed in his head as Davey's eyes snapped open

"When all hope is lost," Davey repeated the words as he watched both the Kraken and Gwen struggle on the ground. His father's specter grew to twice its size, abandoning his human figure in favor of a black mass.

Davey thought about his grandfather, his mother, and the tiny wooden lighthouse. It would protect him; it would pull him to shore.

Somehow, somewhere, he found the strength, the courage to look into the black mass where he saw a vision of his father's visage painted in muted grays and black. He saw the anger, the fire-like rage. He saw the schoolyard bullies tormenting him every day. He saw the sadness of waking up every morning, wishing it would just all go away.

But most of all, he saw the hope is grandfather and mother spoke of during their time on earth, and it was within that hope that set the lighthouse's candle aflame and guide him to shore.

"No," Davey whispered, balling his hands into a fist, rolling his shoulder back and standing defiantly against his father's rage. "We will go to shore."

What sounded like a firecracker going off or the firing-up of an old locomotive engine rumbling to life, reverberated through the storm and across the ship.

Then, beyond all hope, beyond all reason if reason even existed in the crossover, a beam of light brighter than anything Davey had every seen struck the heart of the storm.

In an instant, a million high-pitched screams cried in a chorus of pain as the light engulfed the ship, penetrating the swirling black mass of rage, casting it backwards. With one final scream, the mass exploded in a rainbow of colors, shining outwards, its remnants spilling to the brackish waters below.

And just as the tempest arrived, the wind stopped. The rain faded to a relaxing drizzle as clouds spiraled upwards in a dozen columns, retreating to their natural position. The beam faded until it became a dull yellow light, then to nothing.

"Gwen," Davey collapsed to one knee, looking at his waterlogged friends, who pushed themselves up off the disaster area of a ship deck, which looked worse than Davey's room before it was cleaned.

"Here," she looked around dazed at first, her emerald eyes tired. "You did it."

"Can't believe it." The Kraken groaned. "You were right."

"Told you." A smile crept across Gwen's face, one of satisfaction.

"It'd sure be nice if you told me what it all means." Davey took several deep breaths, filling his lungs in an effort to find himself. "I mean, not trying to be forceful and all."

"Maybe you would believe us now," Gwen whipped her hair back, water spraying behind her. She brought it around her shoulder, and with one ringing motion, the water left her hair, leaving it dry and brilliant as ever.

"I suppose I'm up to believe anything." Davey sat back and let his muscles relax, his mind stop racing. He bowed his head and buried his face in his hands. "It's all happening too fast. I just want to know. Maybe I should just go home." The fear of his father crept into his mind again.

"We can't now. There's no way. We've already crossed over." Gwen joined Davey at his side, squeezing his shoulder in a comforting manner.

"What do you mean?" Davey looked up to see Gwen surveying the destruction. Davey followed suit, and what he saw was the last thing he expected.

"You're the Keeper. We need you here."

V.

Davey braced himself against the captain's wheel and looked over the alien landscape. Water stretched as far as he could see, holding a crimson tinge to it as it lapped along their beleaguered ship. Deep purple transitioned to light along the horizon where a smattering of rock outcroppings bobbed in the distance.

The sky glowed dark with odd stars that seemed to hover around like

June bugs would in his grandfather's backyard. He tried to reach out and grab one, only to realize they were somewhere within the deep regions of outer space.

Kraken nursed himself along the bow, legs crossed over, his head ducked in quiet contemplation. Gwen kept as his side, a wry grin on her face, one filled with confidence Davey wished he could have.

Davey saw nothing he recognized around him. Gone were the Bay Bridge, the various crab houses and party decks dotting the both shores of the Chesapeake. The usual sounds of motor boats rumbling in the distance, the wealthy yachts sailing up and down, were mere ghosts, replaced by a couple mastheads in the distance, too far away to be concerned with at the moment.

Davey bit his lower lip. His stomach felt empty and low. The bitterness of his new reality loomed in the background as he gazed along the majestic landscape – a rare beauty in his otherwise depressed world he could not deny.

"Can you tell me now. Was that my father?"

"Yes and no," Gwen said.

"I don't understand."

The boat creaked in the background, a miracle it survived the storm, staying afloat amidst his father's rage.

"We were in crossover, the time spent between your world and ours."

"Your world? What do you mean?"

"It's difficult to explain, more difficult for you to understand. Scary at first, I know."

"You can give me a try. I get good grades in school."

"There's no doubt about your intelligence." She ruffled his hair.

"Then tell me."

"This is the world where innocent children go if they are taken too early from your world. It is, how should I say, a sort of escape, one where they will know no pain until the time is right."

"Like a dream?" He asked, but Gwen's words "taken to early" stuck with him. Did she mean if they died? Did he really kill himself?

"Sort of." Gwen pursed her lips, obviously lost in though. "It's…well, difficult to say really, because adults and older kids have tarnished the world with so much pain. Look at this world as…where your dreams come from, where all imagination is born."

"Ok, and say this isn't a dream. Then why am I here?"

"Because you're the Keeper." The Kraken snickered, rocking his head back. "Thought we made that quite clear."

"You are here because others need you," Gwen followed up.

"And my dad?"

"Proof that others need you."

"You know this doesn't make a good bit of sense to anyone."

"Look at it this way, lad." Kraken hopped up, obviously cured from his run-in with his father. "We can't very well have kids who go too early sitting in the darkness. So they come here and live out their dreams with, well, people like Gwen and I. Problem is, as your race became more dependent on things, they lost themselves. Greed and all that unnecessary stuff, you know, started poisoning your world...and ours."

"It may be hard to understand, but your world is dying, and now it's affecting ours," Gwen followed up.

"And that's how your father, or his rage, was able to find you here." Kraken joined the three at the wheel. "It knows we brought you here, and it will do everything it can to scare you away."

"Who's that?" Davey asked. "Did I do something to somebody?"

"No, you didn't." Gwen titled the wheel to the right just a little to some destination lost upon Davey. "You are perfectly fine. Stronger than you think."

"Are we not meant to scare the boy? He's going to have to find the strength soon," Kraken said.

"What do you mean by that? I've just been through whatever that mess was with my father."

"It wasn't your father. Just his anger manifested in the physical form. Know that. Adults cannot cross here, but now their souls can, which is why we must be cautious. I fear he may return."

"Didn't we just defeat him?" Davey knelt down again, more confused than ever.

"Sorta. Nothing's dead with him around," Kraken said.

"It's why I didn't want to say anything, because it would only confuse you," Gwen followed.

"You said...you said I would see my mother again. Is that still true?" Davey grasped for any hope in their words.

"Yes," Gwen said, her lips turned to a frown.

"Why...why did you just do that?" Davey asked. "I saw that."

"What you need to be thinking about is your role in all of this. You wanted to know, and we're going to tell you."

"So be it then." Davey focused on the purple horizon. "Not like I can go back home. Not like I have any friends."

"You have us." Kraken slapped Davey on the back. He must've had something for slapping others, Davey thought.

"There are others like you here, others who have come from your world who are still alive. They are going to try to stop him, and when they do, they'll need someone to guide them back to their world."

"The light," Davey's words spilled out of his mouth. For some odd reason, it all made sense to him.

"Yes, the light you command will guide them all back. That's why we needed you here. You need to bring them back after their task is complete."

"You said they were like me? Kids and all?"

"Quite right. It's only children who can come here, or so we thought." Kraken jumped down to the bottom deck and scanned the area. "But we'll be needing to find a way to make repairs if we're going to find them."

"We need to get to them," Gwen added. "And it won't be an easy task."

"Why do you say that?" Davey asked.

"Your father's specter was just the beginning. There will be others who find their way here, the machinations of adults who would see stories and legends told to each other. And they have already manifested themselves in our world."

"Like?" Davey asked.

"I don't know." Gwen looked down, again appearing to hide something. "All I know is we need to stick together if we're going to make it through this, to find a port of sorts."

"What...what kind of port?" Davey asked.

"I could've answered that before, but I don't know. Everything is changing so fast. We see images from your world here, creatures not meant to be here. So we are lost just like you are in a way."

"Ok." Davey heard the trepidation within Gwen's voice. He needed to find strength for her too. "But we all stick together, am I right?"

"As right as you can be." Kraken tugged on a rope, shaking his head at the same time. "We need to find a port soon."

"You need to stand by me. Not going to pretend I'm strong or nothing. I just need to know someone will be there for me," Davey said.

"And I will." Davey felt Gwen's fingers intertwine with his as she clasped his hands around his. "We'll be there for each other."

THE MERMAID'S TIDE

Suffering from a swollen tongue and parched throat, Davey McCrary leaned over the ship's railing and poured the contents of the wooden cup down the back of his neck. The salt water served as a tonic of sorts, soothing his sunburned skin, a temporary reprieve from the familiar bite. The high sun – an albatross in the cloudless horizon – would turn the droplets atop his neck into tiny prisms, bubbling his skin even more.

From his time growing up along the Chesapeake, he was a veteran of such mistakes but didn't care. He needed the relief, especially while they toiled in the doldrums of an endless platinum sea that held the wayward ship hostage. The winds grew stagnant, surrendering to the soup of humidity surrounding the hapless vessel.

"A crossover," Gwen, his mermaid companion, said multiple times, the last time being seconds before she dove into the lapping waves, her shadow gone for what must've been an hour. That is, if time still held meaning in the land called The Nether.

"Well," Kraken looked up, his head tilted to the side, one eye closed. "Not really supposed to be telling you."

"Why not?" Davey asked, trying to muster enough spit to swallow.

"Simple." Kraken stretched his arms out and cracked his knuckles. "Cause she don't want you to be anymore scared. She's real protective of you. Her decision was all with none of my input of course."

"Still don't see how this makes much sense."

"You got quite the task ahead of you. Afraid if you knew, you might think twice about your decision."

"We talking about bringing those other kids back? The ones I don't know?" Davey recalled their conversation about him being something called the "Lighthouse Keeper."

"I'd say you're right."

"Then I'm not scared. If it's what I'm meant to do, then it's what I'm meant to do." Davey's voice trembled with contradiction.

"Understand, but she's in charge, and she says we have to toughen you up at first."

"I'm tough right now." Davey feigned strength, sitting up straight and puffing his chest out.

"One step at a time, mate." Kraken hoped down with an eager grin, his feet landing with a squish-like noise. With each step, the boy left a footprint of some odd slimy substance that caused Davey's stomach to turn in the same way when he smelled Chinese food. "But I think you'll be tough enough when we reach where we're going. Be ready to learn more."

"So you do know where we're going? I mean, is there even any place to go?"

"Why wouldn't I?" Kraken shrugged. "Problem is, we aren't getting very far without fixing the one sail on this ship. Looks like Swiss cheese."

"You think it really matters?" Davey found his laughter for a moment, the only thing that felt real.

"What's that supposed to mean?"

"Not sure if you've noticed, but look around you. There's nothing here. Like we're out in the middle of nowhere."

"Really?" A smirk reached Kraken's right ear. "Could've pulled me for a loop."

As Davey looked back down at the jigsaw puzzle of a broken deck, a swift breeze swept over his blistering neck. The shadow – large and pointed at the top – engulfed the entire boat within seconds as the distinct sound of waves crashing against shore pulled his attention to the right.

"Impossible."

Davey stared at the shadow's genesis: an island reaching out of the golden waters with a mountain peak shrouded by clouds at its center. A smattering of ramshackle hovels, all white in color and reminiscent of Greek architecture, lined the beach. It was from the remote village where Davey heard the first sounds of civilization in a day's time, the sound of commerce, of a chorus, and of yelling something about a fish market.

"It's about time. Never know when the Endless Ocean will give you something." Kraken took hold of the wheel, his emerald gaze fixed on the hodgepodge of piers reaching out from shore, most of them already occupied by a variety of sea vessels dating to various historical ages. "Yeah, this should be interesting."

"Why'd you sound like that?"

"Say what?"

"Say it should be interesting. Nothing ever good comes from that."

"Oh, it's nothing. Always say that."

"It's because you haven't visited it before," Gwen said. "And you know what danger's in that. Can't expect anyone to be friendly during these times."

"You're back." Davey smiled, watching as Gwen placed a small net on the ground, its scaled contents flopping with the last of its energy.

"Told you I wouldn't be long," she answered.

"I'd normally agree with you." Kraken interrupted, slapping the boat's wheel. "But I don't think we can afford to wait. She's on her last legs. And you never know when we'll run into another one of—" Kraken sucked in his lips and narrowed his eyes.

"Suppose you're right." Gwen kept her gaze locked on the fishing village. "But something doesn't sit right."

"Chance we have to take. Let's just hope it's not full of uglies. Still exhausted from crossing over." Kraken directed the wheel, allowing the wind to take the tattered sails. "Hopefully he hasn't showed up yet."

"My father? I know you're talking about him. He could be here?" Davey was quick to notice Kraken's not-so-subtle comment, particularly after an earlier conversation about his father's potential reappearance. He joined Gwen in investigating every alabaster building of the seaside hamlet, hoping his father wasn't on land.

"He can't be here. Not yet at least," Gwen said.

"Unless," Kraken said.

"Unless nothing," Gwen fired back at the Kraken, a side of her Davey hadn't seen. "If we're going to make these repairs, we need to be quick. No lollygagging."

"Finally, you speak my language."

"So, we sail into this harbor and repair the ship, get back on the ship, and do whatever it is you need to me to do. Do I have that right?" Davey asked.

"More or less." Kraken answered, nodding in his usual flippant way. The sails yawned as another gust of wind pushed them closer to port. "At least it will feel like home…for a bit. Nice architecture."

"Don't get too cozy, ok? Need to leave before he finds out we're here."

"My father?" Davey asked. "You bringing him up again."

"Not just your father, mate. We're talking about someone much worse, someone who could set our whole plan to fail. Pop's just one piece of the puzzle." The ship's wheel twirled as the Kraken pulled back, making his course.

"The Dark Guardian," Gwen said. Her lips spread to a thin line, her eyes a little duller as she spoke its name.

II.

The harbor's bell tolled thirteen times, at least that's what Davey counted in his head during their approach. Kraken took point, tossing a rope towards one of the long silhouettes standing guard along the pier. Minutes later, and another few bell tolls to follow, the ship crawled along side the ramshackle structure of rotting wood fashioned to look like a dock.

"Still don't feel good about this," Gwen sighed, her attention focused on the olive-skinned man assisting Kraken in fastening a rope around a pylon. "This shouldn't be. This must be happening."

"What do you mean?" Davey asked.

"They shouldn't be here." Gwen pulled her fiery red hair back into a ponytail, almost like preparing for battle…or the unknown. "Stay close to me. We don't know what we're getting in to."

"All secure." Kraken joined them after securing the last line.

"Did you notice?" Gwen asked.

"What? Think anything would get past me?" Kraken glanced over his shoulder in a terrible effort to keep his intentions hidden at the three men dressed in tattered cloth, their complexion marred from spending countless hours in the sun. "How couldn't I?"

"They're looking at us, you know," Davey said.

"And they can continue to look at us until we figure out a plan," Gwen whispered.

"Since when did we need a plan? We go in there, find some lumber, and leave. Best we make quick work. Looks like a tempest is gathering again." Kraken nodded opposite the town where the Endless Ocean reached out.

Curiosity's lure got the best of Davey, who noticed the orange horizon of approaching dusk meet ink sky igniting with electricity. It had to be him, his father calling his name along the wind.

"That didn't take long. Two days at most until he catches us," Kraken said.

"And who knows if he's communicated with…" Her eyes shifted to Davey, who wondered if Gwen and Kraken were indeed his friends or held other intentions. It wouldn't be the first time someone used him. "Doesn't matter. We get in and we get out. Longer we wait, the more of a chance he has to catch us. At least we know he's not here."

"Are the three of you just about done over there? Be needing any more assistance?" The darkest man, one wearing a red bandanna and a golden necklace as thick as beef jerky called over from the pier after wrestling with the last rope and pylon.

"We're ok, mate. Just talking amongst friends." Kraken waved at him.

"Ok, then. Harbormaster will be by to check you in. Old guy. Scary looking. Can't miss him."

"Thanks."

"And if I may offer a word of warning. I wouldn't be wandering around here at high moon. Strange things afoot." The shorter deckhand, one with a trident for a beard and a sinewy frame, waved back and sauntered down the maze of piers. The two others followed, meandering off without a clue.

"Something odd about the lot of them," Kraken said. "We both know they don't belong here, being adults and all."

"Maybe lost souls? If so, we won't know until nightfall, and I don't think we intend to stick around for that. Maybe that's why they warned us," Gwen said, glancing back at the tempest then back to Davey. "You stay close to us. No wandering off. Not yet at least."

"That's like the third time you told me. The both of you are making as much sense as a Rubrics Cube."

"Remember what I said about this world being reserved for imagination, creatures born of an innocent's mind?" Gwen asked. Davey noticed a hint of uneasiness in her words, her attention volleying between their conversation and the deckhands wearing the same forlorn look, carrying about their business.

"Won't make much a sense what she's telling you right now, but give it time and you'll grasp it. But like Gwen said, stay close. They find out what you are and they're likely to report you," Kraken followed.

"To that Dark Guardian character?"

"Quiet. That name will only set off some nerves. Best to get the ship corrected and our efforts off." Kraken revealed his jagged teeth once again and squeezed Davey's shoulder. "And we all heard him. Don't want to be wandering around here after nightfall."

"No argument here."

"Speaking of which, have you thought of a name for her?"

"A name for what?"

"Your ship, of course. What else would I be talking about now?" Kraken raised his arm once again, but Davey sidestepped him in a subtle way in hopes of not offending. He couldn't withstand another slap on the shoulder.

"You want me to name the ship?"

"It's yours. Always has been."

"Not much for thinking of names." A dozen ideas, ranging from Fox to Speedy, raced through his mind, but nothing that set of fireworks. He thought back to Gwen, who remained eerily silent, preoccupied about something.

"Give it a try. You'll be surprised what your imagination can do for you."

Davey shut his eyes, begging his mind to conjure a suitable name. "The Mermaid's Tide," Davey blurted out.

"Mermaid's Tide." Kraken scratched his chin and puckered his lips in satisfaction. "Think I like it. What do you say? Might have some affection for you."

"We need to move along. I don't much like it here," she answered without acknowledging the name.

"Guess that answers that," Kraken said. "Shall we?"

The two stepped up to the side of the frigate now known as The Mermaid's Tide where a two feet or so gap existed between the pier and the ship. The dock's wooden pylons, much like Davey's pier back home, were covered with barnacles and sludge. It provided a little relief knowing maybe things weren't all that different in the two worlds, including the need to upkeep the wharf.

Negotiating the distance to jump over the golden water below, foaming and sloshing against the hull, he noticed a shadow glide back and forth in a lazy manner, much too large to be a fish.

He looked up to see Gwen standing with her hands on her hips in an impatient sort of way. Davey glanced back down but not in time to see where the shadow disappeared.

Suddenly, Davey felt his body jerk forward. His heart beat in his throat as he imagined falling between the pier and the boat to the unknown waters below, only for his momentum to be stopped by a tug of his Captain America shirt.

He swallowed hard, his fingers tingling as he looked back to see Kraken with a satisfactory grin mixed with diabolical intentions. It wasn't by mistake he held a fistful of Captain America's shield.

"What'd you do that for?" Davey said, righting himself.

"Testing your meddle. Need to make your spine strong," Kraken answered, close enough for Davey to smell his putrid breath – a scent that reminded Davey of the local fish monger – before jumping across to the pier and landing with another squish. "You going to jump or not."

I'll make you jump, Davey thought, waiting for the ship to rock closer to the pier. Kraken's back and forth personality didn't make much sense either.

Counting in his head to five, Davey launched himself off with a bit of a prayer, thinking the entire time he would find his end at the bottom, disappearing below the waters. If anyone would fall, it would be him. That's how his life went.

Davey proved his premonition wrong as he landed, stepping a couple feet to the edge of the pier before stopping his momentum. Again, he averted disaster.

"There we go. Wasn't much, was it?" Kraken slung his arm around Davey, who reoriented himself to the false land below.

"I could kill you, you know."

"You wouldn't hurt a friend. That's just nonsense."

"Hold up there, lads." A gruff voice reminding Davey of his father called. Davey stopped in his tracks, wondering if the black spirit found its way back. Instead, a skeleton of a man adorned in a loose fitting white shirt sprouting equally white hairs from his chest stood in their way. Like Kraken, he too held the distinct smell of fish.

"Yes, my friend?" Kraken asked, jumping up to attention like a soldier.

"Ya' haven't introduced yourself. Must get permission from the harbormaster before you can keep your ship here." The man nodded to the ship.

"The ship?" Kraken answered.

"Yes, your ship right here. The one with all the holes in the sail. Not really much of a vessel, is it?" he muttered. "Should expect it by now. People always bringing in ships about to sink."

"Oh, that ship? She's a beaut."

"If you're a blind rat maybe."

"Then I would like cheese."

"Well, while you're admiring your beaut, could you at least state your business?" The skeleton flipped through some parchment. "And I'll see to it you can stay, but we need your business…and your names."

"Business? Well, yes, we came to make repairs. And we report this to the harbormaster, you say? Who's that?" Kraken's game of verbal sparring made Davey shift back and forth in his stance.

"Me." The man folded his bones for arms around his chest and harrumphed.

"We're not wanting any trouble," Davey interjected. His voice already mirrored the Kraken-speak.

"Not wanting any trouble?" The weight of the harbormaster's lazy eye bore down on Davey, causing him to slink backwards. Something in particular about the gruff man's investigation plucked his nerves. "I didn't say we were going to have trouble. Only making sure there aren't any riff-raff coming into my ports. Strange times are ahead for us."

"Strange times, indeed." Kraken nodded, exposing his teeth with a wide, relaxed grin. "And with strange times come strange answers."

"What?" The harbormaster furrowed his caterpillar eyebrows.

"Nothing. Nothing at all. She's called The Mermaid's Tide, and she's bound to save the world."

"I suppose the holes in the sails have something to do with saving this world of yours?" The harbormaster's right eyebrow peaked in a triangular arch.

"Had a bit of a struggle out in sea." Kraken played his part perfectly. Davey hated himself for being such a stiff. "Ran into a few marauders. Thought were must've been traders."

"Marauders? Around these parts? Troubling. Very troubling." The harbormaster scratched something down on his dried piece of parchment.

"Yes, sir. Said it yourself. Strange things are afoot. We managed to survive, though, and we're here, so we'd appreciate us showing a little hospitality."

"Hospitality? Here?" The harbormaster harrumphed, his salamander for a tongue slipped out of his mouth and licked his cracked lips. "You sure you're from around here?"

"Forget I said anything. Put it this way. Promise won't stay long. Will pay whatever tariffs and fees we need."

"Ain't be needing no tariffs. Only be wanting information." The harbormaster combed his beard with his dirtied fingers. "Supplies are with the quartermaster down by the beach."

"And would be happen to know proper routes in this area?" Kraken chuckled.

"A route to?"

"Uh, well, hard to say at this point."

"As it should be. Only route you'll be finding out here is luck. This is the Island with No Name, a farce in a sea of mistakes appearin' only to those it calls a home. The only way out is to sail straight then sail back. But you won't be concerned about that now. You best get your supplies and find yourself out of here by dusk. Don't want to be finding yourself all liquored up during high moon."

High moon again, Davey could only think of his encounter with his father's rage.

"Mind if you tell me why we can't go wandering?" Kraken asked.

"Because," the harbormaster grunted. "The lost souls of the Endless Ocean come here to commiserate when their time is spent. You won't wanting to be caught with them when you depart your homes."

"If you put it that way," Kraken said, "we'll find ourselves off."

"Yes, thank you." Davey followed Kraken, shouldering past the harbormaster, his footfalls heavy along the wooden planks. It was then he noticed the absence of their third companion. "Where's Gwen?"

"She'll pop up. Trust me. For now, we need to find a good place for cheap supplies…and to get in the shade. Skin's drying."

III.

Of all the places Davey didn't want to end up, the back of a tavern was one of them. He'd been there too many times before, standing in the corner of his father's old watering hole, its walls lined with wood paneling, while watching his father drown in the spirits of those with no hope He remembered the parade of men who sauntered in and out, abandoning their once fruitful dreams at the bar, playing Keno with pocket change, and uttering a string of obscenities while some multimillion-dollar ballplayer struck out.

This tavern was a lot livelier than back home. Its bright interior didn't smell of mildew and dirty rags, replaced by salted fish and coffee beans. Islanders and their common jet black hair gathered within the ivory walls, tilting their oversized mugs back, lost in private conversations.

Then there was the occasional odd glance in their direction. It didn't seem to bother Kraken, who downed some odd-looking three-tailed fish platter. Davey, however, remained unnerved to the point he kept his head down, shielding his face with his hands.

"The Tavern with No Name." Kraken licked his fingers and surveyed the crowd. "A sordid bunch if you ever seen one. Still odd given the circumstances."

"Almost as odd as us being here while Gwen is somewhere else."

"Gwen can take care of herself. Better believe me with that." Kraken finished off his entrée, sucking down the last tail like a piece of spaghetti. Davey would've hurled if his stomach held anything.

"Still wouldn't been nice for her to tell us where she went off to."

"Maybe it was on purpose." Kraken rocked back, wiping his hands on his thigh.

"What do you mean?"

"Look around you. Notice anything suspicious."

"Besides a bunch of adults you said couldn't exist here."

"No. Not quite it. Take another look."

"I don't," Davey looked over the ragged bunch, their words lost in the bustle. "Don't see anything."

"Might be too young to care. But look. No girls. No women."

"Think you're right." Davey hated himself for not noticing.

"Only saw a few lasses on the beach before we entered. Kept their heads down like you're doing right now. Looked guilty, almost ashamed. Thinking Gwen might've felt uncomfortable, went for a swim or something."

"Think it has something to do about her turning?" He pointed to his feet, hoping Kraken would notice the clue. "How can she—"

"Hush. We don't need any prying ears finding out who we are, or *what* we are."

"Sorry, didn't mean to say anything."

"You best be learning the art of picking your battles. Be smart about saying your thoughts out loud here." Kraken stood, almost dismissive of Davey. "Have other things to do, including finding the quartermaster so he can direct us towards some good wood."

"You two," haughty words preceded a bull of man heading in their direction. A sullied tunic hung off his bowling ball sized shoulders, matching the rag for a hat wrapped around his swollen head. "The two new arrivals. Would like to have a word with you fellas."

"Would love to, but we're short on time," Kraken answered, cutting off the bull from getting to Davey. "Have a ship to repair."

"Which is why I must have words."

"Unless you're willing to help us fix it, not sure if I have the time." Kraken attempted to bypass the man, but was cut short by a deliberate hand. "Suggest you go about taking your hand off my chest, friend." Kraken stared at the hand, his gaze narrowing on the man before him. Nothing good could from that stare. "Don't mean any harm to these people."

"Hold on for a second." Davey interjected in spite of his apprehension. "Doesn't have to be like this."

"The boy speaks. And who are you?"

"I'm the..." Davey stuttered, glancing at an already preoccupied Kraken for directions that wouldn't come. "Captain." He regretted the words as he spoke.

"Good, then. Maybe you could tell me how you came into possession of it."

"Davey," Kraken said.

"It's my ship," Davey once again lost his thoughts before he spoke. "That's all you need to know."

"No, I think I'd like to know a little more." The bull bent down, his purpose still carrying no meaning to Davey.

"Nothing to know. We just...found it." Davey shirked back, realizing his folly.

"Found it? You can't just find *that* ship. It comes to you. It searches. They may not know." He pointed at the patrons, all of whom kept to themselves, seeming to pay no mind. "But I do."

"And what is it that you know...friend?" Kraken grunted.

"Well, then." The bull grunted, his breathing heavy on Davey's head, who continued to feign strength despite a tingling feeling in his toes and fingers. "I know it's the Keeper's ship, and I would certainly would offer my services to be part of its crew, as I once was at one time."

"I don't..." Davey pulled back, watching as the antagonistic lines defacing the bull's face relax, decreasing the tension in the air. "Understand."

"We ain't no Keeper, if that's what you're getting at." Kraken remained steadfast, curling his fingers around the brute's wrist.

"Ain't no use in fibbing with me. You both have the smell about you, the familiar smell of adventure and innocence. And you know full well that the both of you can't do it alone."

"What do you know about our purpose?" Kraken asked as Davey pondered the bull's cautious approach with his line of questions. How he could know who they were unless he was the Dark Guardian that Kraken mentioned?

"I know I served under this one's grandfather." The brute's beard covered his chapped but genuine smile.

"You knew my grandfather?" Davey blurted out against his better judgment.

"Oh, no," Kraken muttered.

"Relax, young man. Like you, I mean him no harm." He extended his giant maw towards Davey, his fingers, calloused and worn like that of a pier worker, twice the size of a microwave morning sausage. "Name's Gregor, and I'm at your service, if you are who you claim to be."

"Should I?" Davey looked at Kraken for direction, but his little known companion apparently disagreed, shaking his head just slightly.

"I understand your friend's grievance." Gregor straightened himself, his back cracking the entire way. "I was the same way when your grandfather was about your age. Always wanting to protect him."

"Fantastic, mate. Now that we've all but blown our cover, what's your purpose here?" Kraken sat back down, scratching the chair's legs along the floor.

"A good one, or so I hope."

"Great. How about you try answering my question."

"No need to get upset. It's quite simple really. Never thought I'd see her again. She carries many memories between your grandfather and I. They were memories I hoped were buried forever." Davey stared at Gregor as he spoke. Gregor's eyes twinkled with the same memories Davey's grandfather once held, the same reverence for the past. He scratched his peppered beard, looked at the seat next too him, but shook his head in disapproval. "But I suppose the signs were all there. The Nether is reacting. The silver tide is rolling in to shore."

"I would pretend to understand what you mean." Three more figures meandered into the bar, the last holding the same lost gaze as the others who inhabited the fishing village. He hoped one would turn out to be Gwen. But it wasn't to be. "But I don't."

"And how much have you told him, especially of his role? The boy seems green." Gregor's stern expression reappeared, his emotion directed to a bothered Kraken, who propped his feet up on the table, his hands intertwined behind his head.

"As much as he needs to know right now."

"To withhold the truth?" Gregor shook his head. "Would not be a wise choice."

"He's innocent. He'll know soon enough."

"Best we tell him as soon as we can. He should know what his grandfather knew."

"We?" Kraken scoffed. "Who says you're even invited? Just because you claim you knew his grandfather doesn't mean you know him. I mean, do we look like fools? What if you're an agent for—"

"Never." Gregor grumbled.

"Wait just a second." Kraken kicked his legs off the table. "What are you anyway? We both know the rules here."

"In time, my friend. For now, I believe it's up to who the Keeper selects who may attend to the ship."

"My ship?" The very idea of the Mermaid's Tide being Davey's ship never sunk in, nor did even seem important. "How did it become my ship?"

"Now that is a question that I can answer." Gregor reached into his pocket, pulling out a sheet of paper, golden in color, thin but strong. As subtle as Gregor attempted to be, holding it close to his chest, Davey noticed one of the patrons, one wearing a three pointed pirate hat, look over with the same foreboding look his father displayed before a whooping.

"Where'd you get that?" Not being one for subtlety. Kraken sat up, nearly kicking the chair over. His already abnormally sized eyes grew even wider.

"I thought you didn't believe me?" Gregor smiled, even cajoling Davey to chuckle. At least he had a sense of humor.

"Never said that. Just didn't trust you. That's all. How could you expect me to trust someone from around here?" Kraken's jaw opened even wider.

"Yeah, where'd you get that?" Davey read over the golden parchment holding a language both foreign but eerily familiar. What started out as different shapes and lines spread apart, pulsing in and out, reformed to legible words in front of him. "I'll be."

"I think your grandfather would very much like for you to read this."

To Davey,

I have been told by those who can see that you will pass through this world at a time when both need you. I am only your age when I write this, or maybe just a little older. You must understand, it is quite difficult to write something when I am not yet myself an adult, whatever that's supposed to mean.

But that's for a later day, I suppose.

If Gregor has found you, either by his own blind luck (which he seems to possess plenty of) or by your calling, then you should know my ship is yours to help you claim victory. She is a sturdy ship. Took a long time to build her from the fairy wood, but good wood, though near impossible to find. She holds together even through the fiercest of storms. And you can name her what you like. I prefer the name Mermaid's Tide, and I'm sure you'll think of one just as good.

A warm rush washed through Davey's body at his father's humor. He knew...somehow.

Now you might ask, as did I, what do you mean by victory? I wish it was that easy to explain, but it never is. I, myself, even had trouble understanding how a child, a kid who plays with Tinker Toys and a Red Ryder BB gun, could help save the world we know.

Much like I did on my journey, you must learn to find your strength. What I saw was a terrible life I would never want for our family and friends (except for Janie Leatherwood. I don't much care for her). It is strength that you will find when there is none to be thought, strength that will guide you through the Nether and help those who will need it the most.

Listen to Gregor. He will make a wonderful first mate. Listen to the wonderful friends you will meet along the way, for they will provide you courage when you need it the most. And most of all, listen to the mermaid. Though I've had my terrible run-ins with mermaids in this world, she is close to you, as she is close to me. Trust her with everything.

You are the Keeper, my boy. My ship is at your disposal, as it will carry you to and through the Nether just like it carried me. And do not fret, for fear is a terrible enemy. You are never alone, a mere footstep away from the world you once knew if you turn the light on.

But don't do it too soon, for you might not experience the wonderment nobody else will in your lifetime.

Love,

Pa (Richard is my name)

"He even wrote it like his name." Davey's attention lingered on the golden sheet as Gregor slipped it back into his pocket.

"What'd it say?" Kraken asked.

"Said to fillet you and eat you for dinner." Davey said, his grandfather's alleged letter helping him find his humor. Kraken scowled then harrumphed.

"This place isn't safe for us," Gregor whispered. "I overheard your conversation, and I understand the Tide is in needing of some repairs.

Fortunate for you, the wood needed is along the opposite shore of this island, but it's a half day's travel by foot."

"Wonderful. The Tide isn't in any seaworthy condition to sail around the coast," Kraken said.

"Right, which brings me to my next point." Gregor rolled his shoulders, his mastodon-sized neck cracking with the slight maneuver. His confident stare vanished, replaced by downturned uncertainty. "I've only arrived two nightfall ago. Strange thing are afoot when the three moons rise."

"Davey's had his fill of strange things," Kraken said.

"Is that so?"

"Let's just say he's already received a healthy dose of what our world can offer, of how shadows in the other world can reach into ours," Kraken said. Davey knew the Kraken referred their encounter with his father's specter.

"So, another has followed him into this world." Gregor bit his lower lip and shook his head.

"That would be the short of it, yes." Kraken stared at his fingernails.

"Then best we move along with more haste. We don't be needing the Dark Guardian to catch you...or that shadow of yours. But you'll be needing to invite you to your crew first."

"Yes, a friend of my grandfather's is a friend of mine." Davey didn't hesitate. After all, there wasn't any use in waiting, not with a proper warning.

"Honored, my boy." Gregor scuffed Davey's hair. Davey couldn't help but begin to feel a kinship towards the bull, almost feeling like he was Mr. Sanders – his old fifth grade Sunday School teacher, a kind man who know no boundaries with his generosity. And for that, Davey was thankful he had a father figure in this unknown world.

"He don't like that." Kraken said, ever protective.

"My apologies." Gregory removed his hand, then immediately combed his hand through Davey's fingers again. "But back to what I was saying, we need to repair the Tide then sail towards the second sun. Should take us right to her shores."

"The second sun?" Kraken said. "Thought it died?"

"It'll reappear this eve. For now, we be needed to worry about what we can control." Gregor peeked out the open window where a single sun carried overhead. "Our time is short. Maybe a half a day, then we must find shelter and keep to ourselves."

"Not without Gwen," Davey said.

"She's a big girl. Can take care of herself." Kraken said.

"Don't be so certain about that. You told me already there's—"

"Strange things afoot. That hasn't been lost on me." Kraken stood, slamming the rest of his drink down. "But you said it yourself. We need to go. She'll pop up."

"Hope so," Davey said.

"We'll stop by my quarters to collect my belongings. Just follow my lead," Gregor barreled off, his movements purposeful.

"You really trust this guy?" Kraken asked.

"He knew my grandfather, and my grandfather was a good man."

"Could be a trick." Kraken cut him off. "I just don't like the smell of him."

"Stay close. If he knows how to repair the ship, we follow."

"And if he stabs us in the back."

"I guess that's where you come in." Davey slapped Kraken on the shoulder, finding a small bit of delight in playful retribution.

IV.

The sun reached its zenith, the usual indicator for school time lunch or a dockside swimming party during the weekend. The three of them snaked through the labyrinth of crooked docks, vaulting the occasional loose board, and past shirtless men carrying sacks upon shoulder. The islanders grunted every so often, the thick smell of liquor as their perfume.

Gregor acted as a battering ram, his shadow even bigger, clearing a proper path for them to follow. And as Davey kept close behind, he looked at each man, trying to find some hint of happiness, some sense of emotion. But there was none, save the same destined look of failure about them. Then there was the occasional hateful glare Davey first encountered in the school hallways where an errant backpack would clip him on the calf.

Davey secured those thoughts in the back of his mind. There wasn't time to reminiscence, only time to look forward. With Gwen's assurance that he would somehow meet his mom again and with his grandfather's letter, he stepped with a renewed purpose, a will to see whatever task they assigned to him completed.

"You say she had red hair?" Gregor said, his bulbous head towering over the would-be fishermen, acting as a periscope.

"Real red. Like a fire," Kraken answered, still displaying little concern for Gwen's well being. "Shouldn't be hard to miss."

"If you say so." Gregor's beard glistened with sweat.

"You can't see her?" Davey shielded his eyes while looking up. The pier made from mismatched boards shook as one of the fisherman, about as thick as Gregor but much shorter, dropped a potato sack. A purple shimmer slipped out of the opening, and upon closer inspection, Davey noticed it wasn't potatoes, but a skin of sorts complete with a tail. The laborer gathered it up as fast as he dropped it.

"Only a bunch of soured faces." Gregor's face soured like a cartoon. "Explains the stink. And here I thought it was me." He bellowed out a laugh, the only hint of happiness Davey experienced since landing on the rock.

"Can't say I see anything that even resembles her." Kraken looked over the edge of the pier.

"That's because you don't. No women around here." Gregor shrugged.

Suddenly, Davey's shoulder bumped with enough force to spin him around, his right sneaker barely maintaining its grip on the pier before stopping his forward momentum by windmilling his arms back. He turned in time to see another sinewy frame tossing down a sac without any intention of hiding its contents. Just like the other one, it was filled with large dark gray fish tails, flimsy and devoid of meat.

"Pardon you, sir," Gregor said, but the man said nothing. Instead, the dockworker cast a sideways glare towards Davey, his eyes belonging to that of a shark – dead and hungry – before shoveling the skins back into the sac with one hand.

"Not much for manners around here, are they?" Gregor opened one eye bigger than the other, his skeptical expression returning. Kraken shouldered up next to Gregor, but had a less of a subtle look of disgust. His green skin turned a slight shade of red, almost like Davey's sunburned flesh.

"What do—"

"Hold your tongue," Gregor said, cupping his hand over Kraken's mouth. "Let the man move along. I'm sure he didn't mean to do it."

"Nonsense."

"Let it go," Gregor insisted even more. The three of them watched the dockworker hoist the sac on his shoulders, giving one last glance before tunneling through the crowd. Davey waited until they disappeared into the confines of a wooden shack to satisfy his curiosity.

"What was that about?"

"Not sure we want to know." Gregor's attention lingered on the shack.

"Something ain't right here. Telling you. Don't like the looks of them." Kraken shifted in his stance.

"Keep focused. Best we find ourselves a quick escape."

"You know what they were, don't you?" Kraken looked back at Davey, again with insistence.

"I don't...I don't know anything of what they are."

"Wasn't talking to you," Kraken answered, nodding to Gregor. The distrust was rampant between the two.

"Place is getting to both of you. Suggest we keep our heads straight and make haste." Gregor reached his harms around both of them, and despite Kraken's resistance, ushered them towards the beach, leaving Davey's mind racing with different theories until they reached the golden shores.

"Where is everyone?" Davey asked, noticing the alabaster homes devoid of light or life. Not even a market remained open. It could've been a ghost town if not for the heavy footfalls along the pier as men were trafficked from ship to ship. The rickety setup reminded Davey of the board game Mouse Trap.

"Empty. The beach is completely empty," Kraken said.

"Let's keep our voices down, shall we?" Gregor said, kneeling to pick up a handful of sand. He rubbed it between his hands then held it to this nose. "No needing to call attention our way."

"I don't like this. Don't like this one bit." Kraken's jovial demeanor plummeted faster than an anchor.

Davey quivered. The tone of their voices didn't sit well. He looked back at the maze of piers where the occasional silhouette darkened by the high sun's position would stop. Even though he couldn't see, he felt their attention turn towards the shipmates of The Mermaid's Tide.

"They could have Gwen you know," Kraken said.

"We don't know that." Gregor said. "But it isn't in our best interest to be questioning. Our ship still holds port, and we wouldn't anything to be happening to it while we make ourselves some trouble, now would we?"

"But if they have Gwen?"

"We'll get our companion back. I promise you that." The more Gregor spoke, the more Davey relaxed, almost like his mom was there beside him. "It won't do us any good by sitting around here. Island is big. Best we make our way around."

V.

The three walked the better part of the never-ending day. As the otherworldly sun descended, its hue changing from yellow to gold, another the horizon birthed another – bigger in size but duller in color. The soil turned from sand to rock as they traversed further around the island and into the mountain's shadow, where the waves crashed angrier into the shore, the waters blacker, more ominous.

And it was a lighthouse Davey spotted in the distance, jutting upwards from a peninsula with no beginning, that caused him pause. The narrow structure held the same faded red and white colors, the slightly off center construction, and broken windows capturing the light from the new sun as the one along Mermaid Row. No matter how far they walked, the lighthouse never seemed to get any closer, rather a ghost in the background.

"You can still see it, can't you? It provides the hope you must hang onto." Gregor asked with a knowing smile during their journey, but made no mention of it again. At least it provided Davey with a sense of comfort, a warmness he held with every step.

After what felt like his first day of wrestling practice, the three came upon a particular grove of trees glistening with same golden reverence as the platinum ocean. Leaves fanned out like a palm tree but thicker and with the distinct smell of maple syrup.

Davey didn't know how they would carry them back, their height that of a basketball hoop, but Gregory didn't miss a stride, keeping quiet and uprooting them one by one. The small roots shriveled to dust when exposed to the environment, dust lost in the wind.

Gregor insisted the both of them try, and even though they appeared heavy, the trees weighed no more than the lightest of bamboo, maybe even lighter. And it was because of their weight that the giant Gregory was able to carry them on his shoulders on their way back to port.

The return journey felt longer. Davey wiped away the sweat stinging his eyes as the second sun descended, fading to crimson red until it dipped into the golden sea, illuminating the waters in a fiery wave. Davey swore that right before the sun cast its final rays upon the sea, he saw the familiar lights of the Chesapeake reflect off the surface.

He smelled the spice of Old Bay, heard the wooden crack of an Orioles bat, and the familiar toll of the harbor bell. Part of him wanted to go back home, but the other part wanted to find Gwen and continue this adventure. After all, his grandfather had been here. He wanted to make him proud.

Three moons soon appeared in the sky, each one the same size, pearl and bright like a full moon back home. They radiated a fantastic brilliance, turning the sands from golden to silver, and highlighting the pier village up ahead like a strand of fireflies.

"We're here," Gregor set down the trees and stretched his arms.

"Hear that?" Kraken stepped out from the three, his mind obviously preoccupied with finding Gwen. He'd been mentioning her every hour or so. "Sounds like splashing."

"And singing," Davey added, hearing the first of the voices: a female nipping at his ear as if she stood next to him. A second one joined, not loud, but soft and caring, longing for something more than the words of the melody Davey didn't know how, but he knew, and it caused him to look backwards to see the light – the light from his lighthouse far off in the distance, too weak to reach them.

"I hear it, too," Gregor said.

"It's beautiful," Kraken said.

"Aye."

"Up there. You see it?"

"What am I supposed to see?" Davey joined the two.

"Flames, but no movement. I don't even hear a footstep. Just singing and splashing."

"You think its Gwen singing?" Davey asked with an ounce of hope.

"No, she doesn't sing." Kraken said, taking a few more steps as the rocky shores gave way to the beach's silver sands. It was then Davey noticed the first glimmer of candlelight within the alabaster village.

"There. It's coming from in there." Davey pointed out. "The singing."

"Selkies," Gregor said with a hint of disappointment. "Has to be."

"Has to be what?" Davey asked. He'd never heard of Selkie's before.

"Half-seal. Half-female. Beautiful as any creature, and with voices to match. Innocent as the day is long. But why are they here?" Kraken asked.

"How do you know they're Selkies?" Davey asked.

"The skins you saw that fell out of the dockworker's bag. Belong to them ladies," Gregor said.

"You noticed?" Davey asked.

"Notice everything. Let that be a lesson to you. Notice everything," Gregor said.

"And they can't go back home?"

"No, that's not how it works. You see, when one of those lasses visits land to see a man who might've fallen in love with her, she sheds her skin to appear human. Wouldn't go over well if a seafarer found himself in love with a myth. Now would it?"

"Suppose not." Davey recalled the one time Jason and the rest of his gang shoved Margaret Baggins into the locker. The poor girl who loved My Little Pony wasn't the same afterwards, even having to transfer to another school after elementary school.

"That's right. So, they shed their skin, but they have to put it somewhere, hide it, so they could return to the waters." Gregor's words captured the remorseful hymns of the Selkies less than a hundred yards away. "And if they don't return to the water, they become lost, sickly, and eventually die."

"So, they're like Gwen."

"Not mermaids. Different." Kraken turned to Gregor. "They don't shed their skins. No barrier to them returning home."

"That's what it is. They're keeping them prisoner here," Gregor said, snapping his fingers. "They can't return home without their skins."

"I can end this, you know." Kraken said with the rush of the sea behind him, an energy matching his words. "Doesn't make sense." Kraken paused, kicking a loose rock

"Don't let your anger get the best," Gregor said. "Won't do us any good out here."

"Tell that to them, the girls." Kraken kept his attention forward, refusing to look at either of them. "We need them to get them back home, back to the ocean. Not right what they're doing." Kraken growled.

"Hold on to yourself, lad. The Mermaid's Tale is still on the dock. They would try to sink it if you would release what you are."

"Fine, then." Kraken grunted and kicked another rock.

"What'd I tell you about that anger of yours? We both know times are changing as the end of all things approaches. Would be fruitful to save that energy for later."

"Easier to say when we're free and they're not." Kraken pointed towards the white homes by the shore. "Would be useful to know why they're keeping them prisoner."

"There's another way," Gregor answered.

"But the Selkies, the Mermaids, I don't get it." Davey slumped back, more confused than ever.

"What didn't you tell him?" Gregor said in Kraken's direction. "He doesn't know much, does he?"

"She thought it best for him to find out for himself." Kraken switched his attention between the waves foaming along the rocks and the singing. "Said he needed to find strength on his own."

"When we get out of here, I'll tell you all you need to know about this world." Gregor's eyes flashed with the blackness of anger as he glanced at Kraken before turning his attention to Davey. "You should know what you're up against. But for now, we need to get the Mermaid's Tide repaired and get these poor creatures back home. The quandary lies in the identify of their captors."

"So, then?" Davey asked. "Do we just storm them like soldiers?"

"No we don't. Not without knowing what they really are," Gregor said. "Have an idea?"

"Not a clue," Kraken said. "Those islanders had an odd look about them, so they could be anything."

"Do you think it has anything to do with them not coming to land?" Davey asked, studying the silhouettes walking on the planks, still heaving bags around, going about their business in the midst of nightfall. One silhouette seemed to dive into the waters, its form narrowing during its decent.

"Could have," Kraken maintained his posture. "You know, you might be onto something."

"Mermen?" Gregor asked.

"Couldn't be them. Would never align themselves to the Dark Guardian."

There was the name again, a name that caused Davey pause, sending the same shiver down his spine that his old man could conjure during one of his drunken benders.

"Suppose you're right. What about Vodyanoy?"

"No, unless they're true shape shifters. And they're not, so we can toss that theory out."

"Possibly Adora." Gregor scratched his head. "But they didn't have the look about them as well, the smell either."

"They smell?"

"Yes." Gregor nodded and scowled. "Particularly during the day. I've run into my fair share of them, and they're not known to visit the land, but it's not them. They're much more wicked creatures."

"We could argue all day about their origins, but the fact is we need to get going." Kraken paced, obviously agitated, his concern for Gwen more prevalent than ever.

"I could sneak in there. See what the singing is about?" Davey feigned courage, his mind drawn more to the sound of their voices. "Ain't doing us any good to be waiting on anything."

"No, I want you to stay close to me."

"Then we all sneak in together," Kraken insisted, rolling up his cuffs as if he were going to be a prizefighter like Matt Murdock.

"Suppose it's the only idea we can come up with." Gregor sighed. "We must be careful, though. Careful and swift."

"We're the small ones. You're the one we should be worrying about." Kraken jabbed.

"You'll be surprised how fast I can move." Gregor said with a staunch expression. "See if you can keep up."

"We'll see." Kraken smiled, his yellowed teeth glowing white.

A low rumble echoed through the sky, its origins emanating from the distant storm – his father's storm. Davey looked up as did the other two, each with a bewildered look, an unknown fear that captured Davey. He didn't want to meet his father's specter again. Not now. Not ever.

"Time is now. We stay close." Gregor started forward.

Davey followed the two as they cut through the shoreline, keeping low to the ground, their movements heavier when the waves crashed along shore, soft when the tide took it out.

As they ran, the songs became distinct, a melon-collie chorus of some of the most soothing voices, like those he heard during Catholic mass on Christmas Eve, the songs of angels long forgotten. Their words drifted in and out of Davey's mind, relaxing him, numbing him.

His arms and legs tingled with adrenaline. The lolling of the waves pulled at him, begging him to dive into the ocean. The songs called his name just like this mother. They called for him to take a bath on the silver sea, to dive underneath and find him lost in her majesty.

The soft crunch of sand underneath transformed to splashes as Davey veered into the tide. It wasn't until he felt the squeeze of his shoulder that he was pulled from his imagination, his young desires.

"You ok?" Kraken whispered jogging up beside Davey.

"What? Yeah?" The warmness in Davey's head subsided as the world shook in front of him. The singing, the song, drifted back to beautiful voices, but none that begged him out to sea.

"Stay focused. Ain't going to do any of us a bean of good if you tire yourself." Kraken steered Davey to the side of the first shack. Davey's attention still drew towards the haze, looking back towards the open waters, to the silhouette of the Mermaid's Tide.

"Lost myself there for a moment." Davey exhaled.

"You ok?" Gregor followed, his breath suffering as well.

"Fine." Davey looked towards the piers where the silhouettes moved like robots, their actions deliberate and slow. He thought back to the songs, the calling of their names. What could've called him like that?

"Good, then. Looks like we haven't called attention to ourselves quite yet." Gregor pointed towards the dock.

"And still nobody on land," Kraken said.

"Here," Gregor twisted his barrel chest around to the side of the building facing the island's interior where shadow prevailed. "Think I hear something inside. Only way to find an entrance that's a bit more discreet."

"That window," Davey said.

"Can't fit into the window," Gregor answered.

"We can," Kraken said.

"Sure." Davey nodded, but remained uncertain, his mind still a fog from the singing.

"I see. Suppose we have no choice." Gregor swallowed. "Both of you be careful. Set no alarms. And keep your voices low. Do you hear me?"

"Let's hope Gwen is among them," Kraken said.

"I thought you said she'd be ok?" Davey asked.

"I'd be lying if I said I didn't know anymore." Kraken nudged Davey forward. "But never now than ever."

Kraken disappeared around the corner before Davey could react. Though fear wanted to misguide him, Davey followed in time to see Kraken's legs and feet slip through the square opening. There wasn't even so much as a thud from the other side.

"Kraken?" Davey whispered, looking up at the makeshift entrance. He could reach with a strong jump, but he was never quite good at high jumps, always the boy who couldn't accomplish a chin-up in gym class. "Kraken," he asked once more.

Again, no answer.

"You can do this." Davey blew into his hands, hoping it would dry the perspiration enough so he could maintain a grip. He sized up the window once more, an obstacle he would never dare try to climb out of fear of failure and humiliation, and jumped up, spreading his fingers.

He was never this lucky. Never. But his fingers grasped the cold plaster. Every ounce of energy, of courage, coursed through his body as his arms and shoulders squeezed tight. And with the rest of his luck, Davey pulled himself up and over, finding a dark room waiting for him inside.

Momentum was not his friend as it carried him through the window.

His grip slipped, his arms flailing about to grab something, but his body went weightless as he plummeted into the room, fully expecting to feel the harsh sting of concrete. Instead, he landed on something soft with a slight rustle.

It didn't take long to recognize the distinct smell of fish and straw, and odd combination by any stretch of the imagination. He pushed himself off the ground, ignoring the slight swell of pain along his elbow, and looked around, waiting for his eyes to adjust to the darkness.

Then he listened. At first there was only one whimper, followed by another, then another.

"Kraken?" Davey asked, expecting the worst.

His eyesight adjusted. Black became purple. Purple revealed contour and detail, the first being Kraken's form standing in front of him, back turned, and silent as he'd ever seen the brash creature.

"Kraken?" Davey asked again. Kraken didn't move, a statute by all accounts.

Another whimper, this one more urgent cajoled Davey's attention. He looked to see the first set of golden orbs no bigger than marbles cutting through the darkness. Just like the whimpers, more sets of golden orbs, followed by the first hints of angelic faces, both innocent and lost in their youth, staring back him.

"What?" Davey whispered.

No words were spoken. They didn't need to be. Davey felt their sadness, their pain, and anxiety. It was the same pain Davey felt so many nights after his mother passed. He wanted to heal them, to get them away.

"Kraken?" Davey pushed himself off the pile of hay.

"Quiet," Kraken answered then exhaled.

"What happened here?" Davey looked around. There might've been twelve of them total all sitting along the wall: famished legs curled in a fetal position, eyes devoid of meaning and as hollow as the deepest of wells cast in their direction.

"Evil. Evil happened here. And who knows for how long."

"Why?"

"Because he wants to take everything pure from your world's imagination and tarnish it. He wants to rid hope, rid happiness. It's what he feeds on." Kraken kneeled beside the smallest, who recoiled and shivered from the approach. "This is the work of the Dark Guardian."

"I don't know...who." Davey couldn't find the worlds, kneeling beside another, one whose ribs jutted out from her torso, with sunken eyes and an open mouth covered with blisters.

"We need to find their skins."

"How? How can we help? There's more of them. Not enough of us." Davey reached out to caress the Selkie, but she recoiled, pulling her legs closer to her chest and let out a squeak, shivering as if suffering from the coldest of winters. Davey wondered how they could've sung to call out for help. They couldn't in their current state.

"There's a way. There's definitely a way." Kraken's eyes flashed red in the darkness as he rose, fists balled at his side.

"We should ask about Gwen."

"They're not speaking. Will's been taken from them. Taken by force, mate. This is what we're up against."

"Davey?" Gregor called, causing a wave of whimpering and squeaking from the malnourished Selkies. More disturbing, Gregor's voice came from the front and not the back.

"What's he doing out there?" Kraken asked, facing the doorway.

"Gregor?" Davey whispered.

"Yes, boys. I don't know what to say."

"That doesn't sound good." Kraken darted through the front door, his movements filled with rage. Davey glanced at the downtrodden Selkies, each one a shade of their former self.

"I'll be back. Promise." Davey swallowed, unsure if he should stay to act as a protector – if that was even feasible – or join his two companions.

One of them reached up, an arm of only skin and bone, allowing Davey to easily slip past. He knew they didn't want him to forsake them, but he had no other choice in the matter. He was never one to abandon his friends, particularly when facing bullies.

"Seriously, I'll be back." With his words, Davey gave one reassuring glance at each of them and left. As soon as he did, he wished he didn't.

Gregor and Kraken stood shoulder-to-shoulder, facing forward with the only the sound of the tide breaking the otherwise eerie silence.

"Guys?" Davey asked. But he didn't need to. There was a reason for the silence, for Kraken and Gregor's stance.

A procession of skeletal figures lined the piers, tall slits of malevolence staring in their direction, each one swaying slightly among hushed murmurs. They appeared as a pack of wolves sizing up their prey, faceless creatures taken by shadow, toying with those who intruded in their territory.

"Just what we need," Kraken said, his head volleying through the small army of unknowns.

"I should've known, but I thought they'd retreat," Gregory said. Whatever he meant, it couldn't be good.

"What's that?" Davey watched the statuesque creatures bathe in the silence, nary a movement out of any of them.

"Finfolk," Gregor said, the light capturing his downturned face, his eyes lost in the overwhelming odds.

"Finfolk," Davey repeated the words, recalling the story he read maybe once or twice in the underwater mythology book that belonged to his mom.

Though he didn't read the entry much, finding it boring and not as mystical as the others, he recalled something about an underwater realm and human-like creatures who kidnapped humans to take as a spouse. But most disturbing of all is they were evil, not good at all. "I know them."

"How so?" Gregor whispered.

"In my mother's book. They're not good, are they?"

"Furthest thing from it. Black hearts. Black souls. A creature of vile imagination."

"And why would they take Selkies in this realm?" Kraken asked. "Doesn't make sense."

"Does anything make sense here anymore?" Gregor answered. "He's distorted everything here. Poisoned their minds."

"Do you think they made a pact?" Kraken asked.

"Yeah, they most certainly did. More to add to the Dark Guardian's army. Should've known, though. Davey's grandfather warned me."

"About?" Davey asked, watching as the lanky figures shifted, regimented footfalls shifting across the pier towards their direction in a somber cadence.

"That these days would be darker than most."

"They have her. They must have Gwen," Kraken muttered something more under his breath, pacing about. "How could she be so foolish?"

"Then we get her." Davey swallowed.

"Hold yourselves, lads. Looks like we be having some visitors." Gregor crossed his oak-like arm across Davey's chest, preventing him from moving forward.

"Why? Why can't I help? Look what they did to them?" Davey pointed back at the homes where the Selkie's remained captive.

"This world cannot afford to lose its Keeper quite yet. Not—"

Before Gregor could finish his thought, three waterspouts erupted from the silver tide, giving birth to three lanky figures who flew into their air, arms and legs long like those of a stork, arching upwards then down.

With little more than the displacement of the sand, the three landed, faces revealed by the three moons to be gloomy and sunken with nary a hint of happiness. Black locks hung like shrouds over their faces.

"Looks like they be bringing the fight to us." Gregor bowed his head.

The three Finfolk wore a cloak, tattered and waving from the sea breeze, exposing their sinewy frames. Dead eyes cast in their direction as they fanned out and hissed. Davey knew it wouldn't end well for them.

"Take this." Gregor unbuckled an elongated object from his belt and pushed it into Davey's hands. Something solid extended within the tightly wrapped cloth, slipping off as Davey handled it, first revealing a pommel so silver that it almost appeared blue, followed by the thinnest of blades, glowing blue-silver as well.

"What...what am I supposed to do with it?" Davey wrapped his fingers tight around the sword, expecting to feel its weight, but there was nothing, almost like air. Even Kraken paused at the sword's revealing.

"Belonged to your grandfather." Gregor kept his back to Davey as the three Finmen swiped and hissed again, wolves ready to pounce. "You'll know what to do with it. Believe me. It's in your blood, Keeper."

"I've never even handled a sword. Only my light saber, and that's plastic." Davey waved the sword in front of him in a slow sweep, its metal almost singing as it moved past his face.

"You see to protecting the girls. Kraken and I will take care of them." Another hiss and a swipe caused Gregor to counterattack, an effort to keep the Finmen at bay.

"I can help." Davey held the sword out, the blade shaking from anxiety. How could he know how to use a sword? Let along defend the Selkie's from an army of Finmen? But yet he couldn't help but smile at the adventure, a reprieve from his terrible life and the terrible man whose rage sailed towards them.

"I'll take care of those on the pier." Kraken said through gritted teeth.

"You can't. The Tale is still in in dock. You destroy the pier, you take a chance with sinking the ship. And you know Finmen carry a reputation for sinking ships."

"I'm not as good of a fighter on land," Kraken said, removing a small dagger from his belt.

"Learn to be."

"Fine, then." Kraken juggled the dagger between two hands and spit. "Won't let me have some fun."

Another of the Finmen leapt into the air, his cloak whipping back, fingers extended to talons. Unlike before, Davey watched the Finman meet Gregor head on, but Gregor parried with a knee to the Finman's stomach, bending the menace in half with a sickening crack.

The other two charged as Gregor dispatched the first, pressing him over head and throwing the limp body back into the ocean, one hundred or so yards in the air in an impressive display of strength.

"Stay back, Davey." Gregor said, parrying the second, who tore into Gregor's arm. Gregor yelled, but kept on the Finman, picking him up and slamming him back to the beach.

Kraken held his own as Davey backed away, keeping his sword steady, following Gregor's instructions: Guard the Selkies.

As he positioned himself before the doorway leading to the Selkie's prison, he watched the shadows along the pier – the Finfolk silhouettes – move at a hurried pace. They were coming for them, coming for the three.

"Gregor," Davey yelled, pointing his sword to the small platoon of Finmen jumping off the wooden structures and racing towards them, their frames cutting through the ocean wind with little effort.

"Remain steadfast, boys. Keep cool." Gregor said, thick in his breath as five more Finmen leapt from the waves like bats in the air, swooping down atop Gregor and Kraken. The odds mounted fast against them as Gregor absorbed their blows, moving a little slower with each assailant.

Kraken, on the other hand, used his agility to dance through the attackers, moving through the cavalcade of cloaks, biting with his dagger like a cornered dog.

Davey held fast, watching as Gregor and Kraken edged closer to the building as more Finmen emerged from the waters. He knew they couldn't hold out much longer, their purpose lost to the vast legion.

"Enough," a voice boomed through the chaos, emanating from the approaching Finmen. "Enough of this." He sounded throaty, a guttural sound which seemed to bubble from the ocean itself.

The ensuing Finmen seized their attack, displaying their contempt with a few more hisses.

"Wretches," Kraken cursed and spit again.

"How did I know it was you when they told me of a gruff man?" The Finfolk's apparent leader, who stood nearly a foot taller than the others, cut through the crowd, his legs the length of stilts, his skin pale, almost translucent in the night air. His hood hid his eyes and the remainder of his lost visage.

Davey adjusted his fingers, numb and taken by sweat, along the hilt as the Finfolk army gathered around, dominoes of misfortune seeing to their downfall. One of them snapped at Davey, but Davey refused to give in to their threats.

"Malent, leader of the Finfolk, how did I know you were here?" Gregor barreled through the two Finmen in front of him, shoving them aside until he was face to face with the Finfolk known as Malent.

"I smelled you from my arrival." Malent's words faded in and out. "They were right that the Wild Beast of the Black Forest made himself known here. And here I thought you were still in prison."

"Pardoned," Gregor answered.

"Pardoned? Weren't you serving him after that favor of yours?"

"You know nothing."

"Now, now." Malent turned away, pulling his hood down as he swept over his troops. "We don't need to jump to false conclusions. We both know who you would serve. There is only one leader."

"Where is she?" Kraken interrupted, still holding his dagger.

"The castoff from the Isles. What are you doing here?" Malent laughed. "Oh, looking for her, your companion, I suppose."

"I said, where is she."

"In the depths for your crime of trespass. You know this island is mine and not yours."

"Just like the Selkies." Gregor joined Kraken.

"Those rats of the Endless Ocean? Please. Call it necessary. Ever since his arrival, the two worlds haven't been providing us with enough of an opportunity to find suitable slaves, so they serve us now. And they will continue to serve us until this grand war is over."

"As a sacrifice to the Dark Guardian?" Gregor asked.

"What would you know about sacrifice?" Malent didn't back down. "Moment you see the tide turn, you run."

"I've served my punishment. How will you serve yours to the Dark Guardian."

"Awfully bold with throwing his name around, aren't you?" Malent whipped his cloak around. "But to answer your questions, they might be, and they also might not be. Depends on the outcome."

"I don't care about outcomes. I just want to know where she is." Kraken jumped up again.

"Careful what you wish for." Malent didn't seem fazed. "You will get what you want, if I get what I want."

"And what is that?" Gregor asked.

"A beauty. A thoughtful prize. One that may be sold for a fortune of silver, silver to replace that which was grinded as punishment and spread across these very shores."

"You're not making any sense."

"Why, I would want the vessel you bring. I would want the Mermaid's Tide," Malent said, extending his arm, which resembled a decaying tree limb, towards the prize.

"Impossible," Gregor said.

"Without the Keeper, it's not impossible unless he's here to claim his prize."

"Doesn't matter." Gregor didn't reveal Davey's truth. "You'll have to think of something else. And just so you know, we take the Selkies with us. They don't deserve to meet a fate you would see them have."

"I'm not quite sure you should be the one making the rules. You did find *my* island. Rather, you did *invade* my island. Why don't I simply take your ship and leave with my newest prize as my bride? I could use another one." Malent spoke with no emotion. Hollow. Empty.

"You will give her to us, or I will take down your entire army, this island of yours," Kraken said, his words poignant and angry.

"Which requires you to go into the ocean." Malent smiled, his black teeth dripping with malice. "Tell me, monster, could you control such emotion? Or would you lose yourself again? Cause your parent's village to fall into the sea itself?"

"Not again." Kraken brought up his dagger.

"Don't." Gregor jumped on Kraken quick, pushing his dagger back to the floor. "Not now."

"I see that we're at a stalemate," Malent's solders grew restless behind him, each one shifting with more excitement, some shuffling closer to Davey. Davey drew up his grandfather's sword, but with a palm slicked with sweat, the blade betrayed him, falling to the ground with the slightest of twangs.

"What was that?" Malent's eyes grew wide and red underneath his cloak. Davey felt the Finman's attention zero in on him much like Mr. Malfi's pit bull would do to the postman. Davey swallowed even harder, squatting to take up the sword once again.

"Davey," Gregor whispered, looking towards Davey with obvious disappointment.

"And who do we have here?" Malent recoiled as did the others. "It can't be."

"He's not who you think he is," Gregor said, words more hurried, less confident in response.

"No," Malent hissed. He sniffed the air, arching his gangly head up to the heavens. "The Keeper."

"The Keeper," was muttered among the others, drifting over the Finfolk's position. "Who brought him here?"

Malent moved towards Davey, his cloak billowing out with each step, revealing his gaunt face, transparent skin sinking into cheeks, forming more lines with each passing second. He could've been a raven or a bat in another world, and Davey loathed birds.

"This isn't the one I remembered." Malent growled between each word, his depressed eyes penetrating Davey's being. "Does he not speak?"

"It's of no concern to you," Gregor again shifted position, drawing more of Malent's guard in front of him.

"Stop." Malent held his arm up in disapproval, prompting his guard to stop. "This isn't him, but it is the Keeper."

"I told you—"

"Who are you?" Malent cut off Gregor. Davey swallowed, readjusting his fingers once again around the sword, the weightless blade suddenly substantial. He pretended it was his favorite toy from time's past – a plastic sword from one of those pirate shows on ice.

"Don't answer him," Gregor said.

"He will answer me."

Davey licked his lips – dry and chapped from nerves. He studied the length of his grandfather's blade and then the approaching Malent, who brought with him the fetid smell of Cambridge's fish market on a warm afternoon.

"It's true. The Keeper's Sword." Malent blurted out a laugh. "He'll be delighted to learn of your presence. Gafor, send news to—"

"Wait." Once again, Gregor displayed his courage, a trait Davey wished his father possessed.

"And how so?" Malent's lips curled into a grin with mischievous intentions.

"He's just a boy, yet. He's not like his grandfather."

"He will grow to be dangerous like his grandfather." Malent flashed Davey a sideways glance, a teacher catching a student cheating. "Or did you forget my previous run in? I owe the Keeper much for past transgressions."

"Enough of this nonsense." Kraken dared once again to challenge Malent, running forward. But his rebellion would be short-lived. Several of Malent's soldiers seized Kraken from behind. Kicks and obscenities followed but ignored by the others.

"You best hold your tongue, boy. We all know you're nothing until those feet hit the waves. Take him to the stockade with the wenches."

Davey watched as they wrestled Kraken to the ground, wrapping rope fashioned from underwater vegetation around his ankles, preventing any more kicking, and then dragged Kraken over the sand. Davey could only watch, helpless in whatever efforts he would use to save him.

"No," Davey said, bringing his grandfather's sword up once again. "Let him go."

"The boy speaks again, this time with disagreement." Malent titled his head to the side with the same condescending gesture he'd seen many times before from the know-it-all high school kids.

"You can't hurt them. None of you can hurt them."

"Brave boy. He's just like his grandfather," Malent said. "So tell me, why can't I hurt him? They did intrude on my land, my island. They did try to free my prisoners."

"Because…because it ain't right."

"Then you have a lot to learn if that's your grievance." Malent turned towards those holding Kraken. "Take him, but do not let him touch the water. His trial will be here tomorrow."

"A trial?"

"As are the ways of our people."

"Then, then it's not fair. I know how this works. Jamey Marks told me herself. Said the deck was stacked against her father after that boating accident. Said people already made up their mind before trial." Davey mentioned anything that would cause Malent pause, even if it was a long shot.

"You don't make the rules here. These are those handed down by my people."

"Which don't seem right." Davey didn't know where he found the courage. Maybe it was the Selkies, each one looking upon him like some hero he always wanted to be. Or maybe it was the Kraken's sarcastic nature and his drive to find Gwen. Regardless, the Finman named Malent would have his own way unless challenged. And his grandfather always spoke of standing up for what was right. "Must be another way."

"Other ways?" Malent smiled even brighter than before. "And what would you propose?"

"Well," Davey stuttered. His forehead and armpits stung with perspiration. His mind whirled, searching for any ideas. He looked up at Gregor, who had been standing beside him the entire time lost in thought.

"Speak up. If you are indeed the Keeper, I suggest you grasp the role. What do you propose?"

"Don't say it, lad," Gregor said.

"Silence. Let him make up his mind," Malent said.

Davey eyed up his sword once more. Seconds later, the idea, though odd and quite impossible, hit him. He'd even seen it in movies about pirates and the way they handled things. At least it would be worth a shot.

"A duel. With swords." The unwelcome tinge of regret stung Davey as soon he spoke. He didn't want to set Gregor up for failure.

"A duel you say? Maybe he has a little Keeper in him after all."

"Not today," Gregor said, holding his ground.

"Why wouldn't he? It wouldn't have allowed him here if he wasn't ready. And with the offer being on the table, I accept. We will have our duel. But first we must lay out the rules."

"Rules. Yes, rules. And rewards."

"Naturally."

"Then I would have Kraken and Gwen set free if Gregor were to win. And you will release the Tide from port."

"A natural negotiator. Such is the position for a Keeper, but also false in one of his suggestions." Malent whipped his cloak back, exposing an ivory hilt, bigger and thicker than Davey's. A carved fish head from ivory – one of those Chinese fishes with the large mouth – fastened atop the pommel. Malent's obsidian talons removed the sword from his sheath.

"Don't do this. You push the boundaries of the Code," Gregor said. There was something unsettling about Gregor's warning.

"What? What are you doing?" Davey asked.

"You issued a challenge for your companion's lives as well as your ship. I accept that challenge," Malent's sword sliced through the air in a display of advanced swordsmanship.

"Wait, I didn't mean." Davey held his sword up, a puppy to Malent's wolf.

"Words have meaning here. And Gregor is not the one who challenged me."

"Gregor?" Davey looked to his newfound friend for help, but he remained still, almost reserved to Davey's fate. Kraken, on the other hand, still kicked and thrashed about.

"Get him. He's old and decrepit. And you're the Keeper," Kraken shouted before being tossed back down to the ground like a sack of spoiled potatoes. His escorts weren't kind at all, following up with kicks and punches to the ribs.

"Yes, he's the Keeper." Malent's stared down.

"Keep steady. Have your mind about you. You are his grandson," Gregor said.

"Yes. More truths. But before we begin, we shall discuss my prize. If I win, I take your ship, your sword, and you, along with your companions." Malent sneered.

"No, that's not what I meant," Davey said.

"You've challenged me. I am allowed to propose my judgment. Such are the rules." Malent snarled then without warning swung his sword down.

"Davey!" Gregor shouted.

Davey allowed instinct to take over, raising the sword in time to meet Malent's. The two blades clashed in a display of lights and sparks, the impact so hard that Davey's ears popped with a deafening ring, sending his vision into a spin.

"Boy," Malent said, readying again with a coy grin. "Just like his lineage. Everyone is lucky." The Finfolk clicked their tongues, a possible display of encouragement, Davey thought. It wouldn't be his first go round with the odds stacked against him.

Malent struck again, and Davey met him once more. The swords clanged together, sending a shockwave of energy throughout Davey's body, numbing his arms and fingers. It took every bit of strength for Davey to maintain his grip.

"The boy holds court. You may be right. Has the movements of a Keeper. But this ends here." Malent stepped back, juggling his sword to the other hand, unfazed by Davey's lucky defense.

"No," Davey looked at his sword, praying beyond hope that something would help him. He saw Malent's shadow outlined by the moon's luminescence shift along the silver sands. He was no different than the others who would see him fall, who would mock and make fun of him during recess.

As the midnight waves rushed in, Davey was taken back to the last August morning with his grandfather, a repressed memory long thought forgotten. He watched as his grandfather slumped further in his weathered rocking chair with a small pile of shavings at his feet, the sound of blade against wood, carving out the last of the silo.

Davey remained silent as his grandfather hummed an old tune he couldn't place. He felt the morning sunrise, the way its welcoming rays greeted Davey with by warming his cheeks.

"Davey," his grandfather's ethereal voice said, a voice pulling him from Malent's discord. "Don't forget yourself or else you will not be able to remember. You're meant to be something in this world. Your favor never returned, but one of the greatest gifts ever given," his grandfather's words dissipated as Malent's form emerged from the vision with a sword hoisted in the air, meant to cut Davey down.

"No." Davey whipped his sword in the air, his movement swift, faster than Malent could react. He didn't know how, but it guided him, his thoughts overcome with his grandfather's words. The blade met Malent before the Finman could react, sending him off balance to the right.

Again, Davey's fluid motions continued, circling down with his blade until it met Malent's torso, slicing through fabric, exposing pasted white flesh more akin to scales. Malent screamed with a deafening shriek, recoiling back, his sword to his side, his left arm disappearing into his cloak.

"Insolent fool," Malent grunted.

"Leave us," Davey answered with an unsteady voice, letting out a stream of breath mired by exhaustion. The courage found him, as did his grandfather's comfort.

"And you want me to take it easy on him. No more."

"This can be over. Just give us the girl," Gregor said.

"Leave us." Davey repeated, focusing on his nemesis. He'd never challenged a man, let alone a boy, and won. This day might change his fortune. Gone were the butterflies responsible for making his knees weak and stomach sour. They were replaced by a confidence. He rolled his shoulders back and held onto his grandfather's sword as a true knight would. "And give us Gwen back."

"You want the girl but she would not come. Time to end this."

Malent sprung without a hint, his fluid strike by the ocean breeze as he leveled his sword – a brilliant light against his black façade. Their swords met again, but this time the impact bent Davey's fingers backwards, too weak to maintain proper grip.

The sword fell to the ground with a quiet thud, half-buried in the sand. The impact reverberated through Davey, causing him to fall backwards, emptying his lungs from impact.

Everything flashed before Davey as he scrambled, the outlines of the Finfolk heads swirling around him, waiting for him to fall back down until his world went black. Everything tingled right down to his toes, left helpless to Malent's wishes.

"No," Davey whispered, waiting for Malent to end it much in the same way his father punished him during a drunken bender. And as Davey held his hands in front of him, he realized his world had turned to shadow, no color, no ocean, only blackness melding with deep crimson and blues, a mosaic of colors with no form. "No."

From the disturbance of water where sea bird plucked its meal, from Kraken's stamping of feet, to the sound of Malent's blood seeping from his wound, Davey's surroundings amplified in an orchestra of sounds he never heard before.

"The Keeper has chosen this trial, and he has lost, paying for it with his sight," Malent's voice dug into Davey's chest and down to his heart, removing the false hope he experienced a few minutes prior. He should've known better. He wasn't a winner, more lucky than skilled.

"He has chosen nothing," Gregor said.

"The Tide belongs to me. You all belong to me, servants to my empire where you will join my court. He will be happy to learn the Keeper has fallen, his light never to enter this world again." Malent's threats echoed like a voice in a tin can.

Through his blinded world, Davey heard Malent's gloves crinkle as he hoisted his sword through the air, parting it with his blade. It came for him. It meant to silence Davey forever.

Before Malent could levy his sentence, something shifted behind Davey, disturbing the stagnant world around the alabaster prison. Its hair fluttered, each strand brushing against Davey. Sand shifted next to him with each footstep, though light and quick. Foreign calls spoken in a language unknown to Davey followed.

The blow never came; rather, Malent cursed in his foreign tongue as two forces collided. Struggle followed as flesh met flesh, pounding on each other in a wild manner.

"Let her go," Gregor demanded.

"Monster," Kraken struggled to Davey's right, maybe ten or so feet away, spraying sand with his feet.

"No, she deserves it for breaking the rules." With a pop and a snap, followed by a chorus of remorseful cries, a body fell in front of Davey, one he could not see but whose warmth he could feel.

"Davey," she said, a whisper lost in the tension, her last breath bearing his name. With the final exhale, the curtains of blindness pulled back from Davey, revealing a terrible scene: a Selkie curled at Malent's feet.

"No." Davey picked up his sword, his movements not his but those of rage. She was the one who reached out for him, the one he swore to protect. Her porcelain face retreated behind her hair, her golden eyes still open, facing Davey. She knew something he did not.

"Hold it." Gregor wrapped his arms around a defiant Davey. Davey didn't realize it, but his jaws locked up from teeth gnashing hard against each other.

"Best you let that whelp of yours behave. He has broken the rules and must pay. You know the punishment," Malent stabbed his sword into the ground and dropped to one knee, using it for support. Even through his anger, Davey noticed Malent holding fast to his wound.

"He did no such thing." The voice, strong in its presence, emerged from the Selkie's refuge. Another Selkie revealed herself, royal in demeanor with blonde hair contrasting against a layer of blackened sand masking her face. She would appear regal if not being famished near starvation. "She challenged you of her own free will."

"Means nothing."

"You unjustly enslave us out of fear of a creature that does not belong here. The sacrifice is hers to make, and she made, so the Keeper holds no duty to you. This contest was a draw."

"Who are you to make the rules on my island?" Malent scoffed. "What do rules mean when you are outnumbered."

"You break them, fine. But you will give the boy strength in doing so," the Selkie answered, placing a gentle hand on Davey's shoulder.

"The Code mean nothing," Malent said. "And she is dead by her own choosing. Not mine. I am not to be punished for this."

"Then place your fate in the Sirens' hands. I dare to you." She smiled a knowing grin, which prompted Malent to sheath his sword.

"Funny, you would think they still hold power. Nevertheless, that passage remains lost to me. I would hold court in my own kingdom, to make sure a punishment is carried out. I would—"

"Then the Keeper would summon the light." The Selkie's grip squeezed a little tighter. "And it *would* find your kingdom."

"Would it?" Malent hissed. "This is not the world it once was. His arrival has changed everything, and I intend to take full advantage of it and make it mine. Do you not see the Endless Ocean, how it no longer glows. Yes, the Dark Guardian is here, but so am I. This is my kingdom to rule."

"By capturing my kind? Making us slaves? Did we not coexist at one time?"

"My purpose is the truth. I merely separate you from man. That's my goal, and shall remain my goal." Malent looked at his fellow Finmen, all of whom remained steadfast in their guard despite the coming high tide washing up and over their feet.

"That is our choice to make."

"Then it's an awful one."

"You speak of madness." The Selkie, her hair clinging to her naked torso, stepped forward absent weaponry.

"Madness to you is sanity to me. Is man not the reason why we're here, subject to the Dark Guardian's rule? They poisoned these waters with their greed. They've brought us closer than we should." Malent's face twisted into an almost inhuman visage. "They do not deserve your kind as a wife. Humanity is wretched, evil beings, which is why we take them as slaves."

"Again, you do not decide," she said. Even in her tepid state, Davey saw her true beauty: a glorious creature who stood up to Malent.

"The Selkies are free," Gregor spoke up, breaking the tension.

"No," Malent answered. "This is my island. They took refuge on it, and for it they owe me."

"Fine, then you set them free, you set Kraken free, and I'll go with you." Gregor held his arms out, signaling surrender.

"The Beast of the Black Forest would sacrifice himself in place of those sea rats?" Malent's smile couldn't get any bigger.

"You give them back your skin and free my companions, and I will go with you willingly."

"Well, then that's a proposal I would very much be interested in accepting," Malent, a jester for a being, cackled in delight. "Because without you to protect him, this world will surely fall to his will, and I will be left to pick up the pieces. We have an accord."

Malent extended his gloved hand to a somber Gregor, who glanced back at Davey, paying a debt he would never owe.

Malent's guardsmen circled around and bound Gregor's arms in a chain of seashells and starfish. Gregor winced a little as the coral dug into his wrists.

"This isn't right," Davey said. "This isn't right. I made the duel."

"His light grows dark already." Gregor stared at the Selkie, keeping whatever underlying intentions he held hidden from Davey. "You can see it in his eyes. Guard him. See to it he continues."

"Of course," The Selkie answered. One by one, the other Selkies emerged from their former prison, each one looking at Gregor with reverence. The big man was immediately ushered away, disappearing into the sea of black forms.

"Let the Kraken go. We have our accord. A much stronger deal we will follow," Malent said, his ghastly veneer narrowing to reveal his malcontent.

"What about Gwen?" Kraken growled at his former guards, who retreated to the docks.

"The mermaid is not with us."

"What?" Davey asked. "You said she was."

"I lied," Malent answered in a matter-of-fact tone.

"Why?"

"Because I can, and because I know you care for her already. Makes me happy to see you so upset." He shrugged. "Regardless, one of you is much more valuable than a barn full of sea wenches. I have the Keeper's first mate, and with it, the Keeper's guard. The deal stands until high moon next night, and with it, your protection from our bargain."

"Leave us. Allow the rules of the trial to play out," the Selkie said.

"Fine, then. I would have you return to the Endless Ocean to be hunted for sport. What good are houses full of smelly sea rats to me?" Malent turned in his stance without muttering another word, disappearing into his army.

"Where are they taking him?" Davey's throat contracted as the thought of sacrificing someone innocent, someone who wanted to protect him. He wanted to charge forward, sword high in the air, and bring them all down.

"Do you want to break the bargain?"

"Do not leg anger take you." The Selkie knelt beside him. "That is what he wants. We're in no place to challenge what he did for you. None of us are."

"You ok?" Kraken joined them. Meanwhile in the distance, the Finmen procession dove into the ocean in a flurry of activity.

"No, no I'm not. I should be the one to go," Davey responded.

"Impossible," the Selkie said. "Melinda knowingly gave herself to protect you, knowing what you are, knowing what you can do."

"Melinda?" Davey's lower lip trembled, learning the fallen Selkie's name. It made her passing more personal to him. He caused the last of her breathes, the images of her fall engrained in his mind even through his temporary blindness. "I need to make things right."

"And we will make things right." Kraken massaged his wrists and back, his gaze locked on Melinda.

"Where are they taking her?" Davey looked past Melinda's body as the other Selkies circled around her, gaunt faces bowed in a sign of respect. They lifted Melinda's listless frame, her slender arms swinging underneath, a red stain marring her torso. The first words of a hymn, both magical and serene in its own right, left their lips as they walked Melinda, her body now masked by a blanket of Selkie hair.

"To peace." She closed her eyes and cupped her hands over her face. Davey listened as she sung in the unknown hymn, their words weaving a tapestry of both sadness and hope.

Another of the Selkies dropped a familiar sac on the beach. Tails spilled out onto the sands, and as the Selkies walked towards the Endless Ocean, the tails sprung to life, slapping against the beach before finding their mate. Flesh melded into scales. Legs morphed to seal tails as they took to the waters, until the last of the tails wrapped around Melinda's form, taking her back to what she was intended, their song reverberating underwater.

"I'd be lying if I didn't say it was the most beautiful thing I think I've ever seen," Davey said.

"Beauty still exists. It's just a lot harder to find it." Kraken kicked at the empty sack and looked up at the Selkie's leader." Where's yours...whatever your name is?"

"Galendra, and I gave mine to Melinda so she may return to her family. She deserves as much." Galendra removed her face from her hands.

"Awfully nice of you, if I may say so myself," Kraken stood at the ocean's edge, allowing the water to rush up over his toes. He sighed with as much relief.

"You may," Galendra's stoic expression, her eyes shaped almond like those of Asian descent, relaxed as she looked away.

"What does that mean for you?"

"It means...something." Her last word retreated behind true intentions.

The last of Malent's guard plunged in the ocean, save the last few who guarded Gregor's hulking frame. Even though they were basked in shadows, the moonlight stricken from their position, he felt Gregor look back at him.

"They didn't touch the Tide," Davey said.

"They couldn't. It's not the way of things." Galendra soft words massaged Davey.

"Why not?"

"The Code. We got a code here," Kraken said. "A code Gregor knows about. A code we all know about."

"Rules?" Davey asked.

"You can call it rules. Call it what you will." Kraken folded his arms together. "Reason why I'm not taking to the sea and taking care of those fellas. I follow the Code. Not sure if it'll change."

"You struck a bargain summoning the trial, and even Malent's corrupted soul dare not challenge the laws," Galendra said. "Which is why Melinda put herself in your position, and why Gregor exchanged himself for our freedom. Each choice independent of each other, but a fate that is intertwined."

Gregor was an enigma, a piece of the giant jigsaw puzzle leaving more questions than answers. Davey needed to repay his debt. And what did Gregor mean by referencing a betrayal?

With the Finmen and Selkie gone, Davey found himself alone with Kraken and Galendra, two creatures who were born from the pages of his mother's picture book, now serving as his guardians.

"We're going to go after him. We're going to find Gwen. That's what we're going to do." Kraken's green eyes flared with emotion. The semblance of a tear even appeared on his cheek, much to Davey's surprise.

"Yes, yes we are." Davey watched as Gregor's guards dove into the shimmering ocean, disappearing below to an unknown destination. "But there may not be enough time for both. We must decide which one we rescue."

"I'll gather the wood. We can make the repairs rather quickly before the tempest approaches," Kraken said, running off to where they left the trees.

"Wait, how? With the two...or three of us wouldn't it take long?"

"You haven't learned yet." Kraken stopped and half turned towards him. "You need to let the boundaries down. This is a new world for you, one where imagination can play a part. Harness that power, the magic."

"O…k." Davey drifted back to the ocean where a thunderclap resounded in the blackest of the black.

"A tempest gathers," Galendra said, her attention shifting to his father's storm in the distant horizon. The crashing of the ocean waves were more amplified. The dock-structure creaked and swayed with the ocean breeze, stronger as his father's storm crawled forward. It was a dream to Davey, one he thought he once had. "Are you afraid?"

"You know?" Davey asked.

"Yes, all Keepers are tested in various ways. You would face your past in order to open up the future for others." Every time she spoke, it tugged at Davey's spirit, relaxing any tension building within. "So, I ask you again, are you afraid?"

"Part of me is, yes."

"As you should be." Her hands, soft and silk-like, grabbed his own. She looked right into his eyes with a spell he could not resist. "Did you not see?"

"See what?"

"Melinda's fall?"

"I…I don't…how did you know?"

"If you go blind, the light will extinguish. Its poison has already touched your soul. We must be aware of this. Be strong. Be forceful. Promise me that."

"Ok…ok, I think I can do that."

"You will find the strength in this, and if you will have me, I would accompany you on your journey."

"It's my choice?"

"Yes it is, Keeper. Your story in this is about to begin."

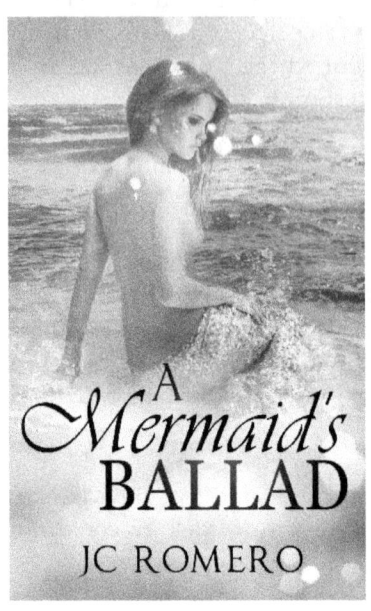

A MERMAID'S BALLAD

Davey McCrary sat on top of the captain's desk and stared through the gold-appointed windows of The Mermaid's Tide. The vessel harkened back to the pirate days Davey often dreamed about during those summer nights spent alone when his father was at the bar. Now he was a stranger in a strange land known as the Nether, where two suns, not one, warmed the Endless Ocean.

This was different. *He* was different. Davey didn't feel like a captain, nor did he think he possessed the demeanor to act as such. Less than three days earlier, he was pedaling as fast as his legs could carry him away from the neighborhood bullies who made a weekly game out of scaring the daylights out of him. He ran while his grandfather would've fought. He didn't belong at the helm of The Mermaid's Tide.

Then there was the matter of his two crewmates: Kraken and Galendra, the former brash, the latter soft spoken. He couldn't square why the two creatures birthed from man's imagination believed in this grand idea that he was some fabled hero known as the Lighthouse Keeper. He could never imagine himself a hero, let alone a captain of a ship.

Galendra claimed he could rescue the others, to bring them back home. Who the "others" were remained a mystery. Then again, nothing made sense anymore, not the platinum waters undulating outside the window, not the hand-drawn seafarer's map depicting different mythical islands, and not the way his vision faded to a palette of red and black every so often. He knew one thing: he didn't belong in the Nether.

Maybe he deserved this fate for abandoning his father, for not telling his mother how much he loved her before she took her own life. The man in the brown corduroy suit who wanted to prescribe him a cocktail of pills for depression, his office smelling of mint and flatulence, said Davey shouldn't blame himself. That was another life, though, a life Davey never thought he'd return to after he followed his mother's lead and threw himself from the top of the lighthouse.

The more his mind raced about the events bringing him to The Nether, the more his body slipped closer to sleep, fighting the fatigue from his disaster of a swordfight with the Finman known as Malent.

Despite Galendra's warning, they set a course for the Finfolk's underwater kingdom, a dangerous endeavor by any stretch of the imagination. That's where Malent held Gregor, the man who saved his soul, hostage. Davey intended to repay his debt, but it would not be without struggle. Malent had an army. Davey had two companions.

To make matters worse, there was also the specter of his father's tempest following their course. The ghost ship remained a tiny inkblot in the distance, shadowed by the blackest of skies, blacker than the deepest night. But it sailed closer. It would only be a matter of time until he caught up.

He needed to fight it, if not for himself, for the friends who he hoped to see again. Then again, that would be hoping against hope.

Davey rested back on the table and exhaled, folding his hands atop his stomach. He imagined himself back at home, fishing rod in hand, his feet dangling off his pier where the occasional spit of water would nip his toes as waves rolled into the break wall.

He smelled the Chesapeake in his mind. He heard the sound of seagull caws, of hammers cracking open crab legs, and the occasional toll of the harbor bell. He let his mind drift, racing, thinking of good things he would want if he could help his father.

II.

Davey's eyes sprung open as the candelabra toppled to the floor, its flames bursting before sputtering out. His mind still muddled from sleep, he awoke to a darkened cabin with only the pearl light of the three moons to light his way.

The ship's hull shuddered, causing Davey to slide along the desk. He curled his fingers around the desk's lips in time to prevent his fall. However, a flurry of papers and other trinkets slid to the ground, joining the extinguished candelabra. They must've hit rough waters, or maybe worse.

"Kraken," Davey yelled, somersaulting off of the desk.

A machine gun bevy of rain hammered all five windows. The thin panes rattled to the point Davey thought they would shatter.

"Kraken," Davey yelled again, stumbling forward.

The ship canted back to the right with a groan, sending Davey sliding along the floor, his arms flailing to his sides until he crashed into an errant chest.

"Anybody out there?" Davey coughed up, clutching his ribs. It was worse than thought.

The double doors exiting to the deck flew open from the power of a banshee's wail. A gust of wind stronger than any hurricane Davey experienced circled around the cabin, attempting to pull Davey into its grasp.

With every ounce of his energy, Davey fought against the pull by latching onto the chest, his feet sliding along the wooden boards until the wind dissipated.

"Galendra." Davey yelled, closing his eyes, wishing it all away. This time somebody answered, the same being he wished away from the Nether.

"Davey," his father's voice filtered through the torrent of wind.

It was his storm, his father's storm.

"Dad, no." Davey couldn't look, he didn't want to, but he couldn't find the deep down love for his father.

He pulled his eyes upwards to meet his father's spectral form, an outline carved by the three moon's light. Unlike his father's previous incarnation – the dark cloud that nearly engulfed The Tide – he appeared more human, more familiar to him.

"You need to come back home. You need to come back to your mother and me," Davey's father didn't sound his usual demanding self, having lost all semblance of anger, replaced by genuine remorse. Davey knew it well, for it was in those few lucid times when his father didn't surrender to the will of the bottle, allowing his former caring and family-oriented self to surface.

"What do you mean? Mom ain't around anymore," Davey responded, his words nearly lost in the downpour.

"You're wrong. She came back to me. She said she's sorry for what she did. Said she wants to be a family again."

"But...but." Davey's imagination whirled. She was dead, wasn't she?

"I'm telling you. You need to come back with me. I can get us back home. We can be a family. You just need to believe in me." His father held out his arm, waving Davey forward with the curl of a translucent finger.

"I don't understand."

"There's nothing to understand. She came back for you."

Davey's world tilted to the right, his visions swirling as the boat swayed. He bowed his head, marred with confusion, his gaze stopping on the comic figure of Thor printed on his shirt. His mother always called him Thor. It all had to do with a plastic hammer he received for Christmas. He hadn't heard her call him that in quite some time.

"She's dead." He wanted to believe, but Davey knew better. "She's dead, pa. And we both know it."

"You're wrong." His father answered, shaded by anger.

"Why are you acting like this?"

"She...she can't be." His father's ghostly visage twisted to one of remorse, almost bewilderment, before he retreated, hiding behind his hands.

Davey felt the unmistakable sadness of a husband having lost his wife. He remembered his father wearing that black suit at his mom's funeral, a lily – his mother's favorite flower – affixed to his breast pocket. It was one of the few displays of remorse from the broken man.

"Dad." Davey reached out. The double doors slammed shut then opened from the power of the storm. His father remained motionless, the power of the storm leaving him unfazed.

"Dad," Davey called again. He wanted to comfort his father, to tell him it would be ok.

"It was all your fault." His father flew backwards, revealing a twisted expression of the drunkard Davey knew. His father's words stabbed as deep as the first time he accused Davey of causing his mother's suicide.

"Don't say those things."

"I'll say whatever I please."

Thunder cracked overheard, mirroring his father's temperament and igniting the air surrounding Davey with enough energy to make his flesh pimple and hair to stand. It couldn't last for long. It never could with his dad.

"It was all your doing. You're just like your mom." His father's specter billowed in an out as if made of elastic. White faded to gray. His smile turned down. "You caused her to jump."

"I didn't...I didn't." Davey begged off, holding his hands up, trying to fight back the tears.

"Yes, yes you did." His father's form grew in height, his arms and legs elongating then spread out like fans until his entire form went black. It was him – his father's anger manifested into physical form. "We would still be together. We would still be one."

"She left...she left because of you." Davey dared challenge his father. His heart sank, giving birth to those familiar butterflies of self-doubt.

The wind whistled back into the quarters, accompanied by the splinter of wood, the snap of shudders against the windows. The lone candle atop the desk shot up in a pillar of fire until dissipating into nothingness, leaving behind the scent of coal.

"Why don't you listen to me?" his father' voice boomed, shattering the wall of windows. The sea poured into the cabin in an angry waterfall, flooding the floor within seconds.

"It's not you. It can't be you. I was just sleeping." The ship rocked again, causing Davey to reposition his feet to maintain his stance.

"Don't be a fool. You know what is real."

"No." Davey snapped his eyes shut, thinking about his mom, her emerald eyes, the way her hands massaged his temples lulling him to sleep.

"Oh, I see everything. You can't escape inside your mind."

Davey closed his eyes tighter, his ears popping from the force of the storm, the cold water biting his ankles.

"Try to hide boy and you will only find nothingness. You will find me. We are, after all, blood."

"Blood?" Davey repeated. His grandfather. His sword. Could it be? He opened his eyes and searched for the weapon handed to him by Gregor. Instead, the blade was lost to the rushing waters.

"Poor, poor, Davey. He's looking for his crutch, an instrument to somehow protect himself." His father held out the silver blade, and with a snap of the wrist, the sword shattered into a million pieces of crystal dust, raining down to the black tide.

"No." Davey swallowed. He lost it.

"Your grandfather was always a wretched man. You know he hated you. He looked at you as a spoiled little nothing of a person, especially after you allowed his daughter to die."

"Please, don't."

"I told him to watch it. I told him you were just like me, and because of that, your tainted blood would surely bring you around to me. We are the same person. You are my son, no Keeper."

"I'm not...your son." Davey's knees weakened, his fingertips tingling from his father's warning. He couldn't be speaking the truth. He would never hurt his mother.

"Think differently and you're only lying to yourself." A black form replaced his father's spectral being, its outer edges morphing in and out, capturing the anger of the tempest.

"Look into me, boy," his father's voice became soft, almost tantalizing to Davey's senses. "Look into the heart of who you are. You are no hero. You are a villain born from my blood, a monster meant to make sure those who would stand against the Dark Guardian would fail."

Something pulled at Davey's mind, reaching back to the base of his neck, massaging his mind into a numbed state. He couldn't fight anymore.

Then he saw it: the first images manifested within the swirling black mass of his father.

It was that of a baby swaddled in white cloth, no bigger than six months, maybe younger. He watched as the baby opened its perfect blue eyes, as majestic as the first snowfall in Maryland when white blanketed his backyard all the way up to the fringes of the Chesapeake.

"This baby would be the cure for everything wrong with the world, its nexus allowing those children like you to fight against the Dark Guardian's rule. But you will betray her. You will see that this baby and her companions fail." His father's voice echoed in Davey's mind as the image switched.

He noticed three or four children accompanied by a bigger beast, their details muffled by a thin layer of fog. They marched up the side of a mountain, torches in hand, possibly swords in the other. Whatever their cause, they appeared determined.

"Look," his father demanded. Davey wanted to pull way, but he couldn't find the strength. "Watch as you betray them."

The scene zoomed out, revealing their location along the shores of some foreign land where a castle sat, its windows dancing with flame. The fortress was built on a peninsula much akin to Davey's lighthouse.

Then Davey noticed a ship – The Mermaid's Tide – buttress against the shoreline.

"I don't understand."

"Betrayal. You are the beast."

Suddenly, three long scale-covered tentacles rocked out from the sea, assailing the small band of children. Then there was shout, a voice very familiar to Davey. It couldn't be. Davey watched his doppelganger emerge from the ship's bowels, sword in hand, an emotionless expression marring his normally placid features. With a wave of his sword, a volley of cannons boomed, joining Kraken's attack on the innocents.

More smoke swirled. Screams followed. The massacre faded.

"It's can't be," Davey paused. He swallowed, losing all fight he had left in him. "I would never—"

"Then abandon your journey. Command them to take down the sails and turn around. Allow this play to run its course."

"Stop calling me that."

"Come home. Leave these people to your imagination."

"I can't." The scene replayed in his mind. He didn't know the Dark Guardian. He didn't know who those children were or the beast that followed. Were they the ones he was meant to save? To bring back to shore of their home? And what about the baby? He imagined her as his little sister who would never take a breath.

"Surrender to your desires. You are no different than me. You will grow up a drunk, a wretched, vile creature who only hates."

The boat jarred backwards, as another board splintered, causing more water to fill the cabin up to his knees. The coldness bit deeper into his legs, begging him to surrender.

"I—" Before Davey could finish his thoughts, the first notes, a hymn permeated the destruction. The song took on a life of its own, beating back the fear creeping into Davey's being, keeping the doubt at bay.

"No," his father's rage growled. "No."

The black mass of nothingness circled around, contracting with the most vicious cries Davey ever heard, a scream knowing the deepest of pains: betrayal. The ballad continued, joined by a voice – her voice – so gentle, so beautiful, that Davey surrendered to its majesty, ignoring the destruction, the imminent sinking of The Mermaid's Tide.

"I will find you. You will not escape me. Never." With one final cry, his father's voice pulsated into nothingness, the black mass contracting into its own form, and with a boom. Davey opened his eyes.

III.

Davey jumped up from the desk, welcomed by the orange rays of the first sun, his gray Captain America shirt faded black from the amount of perspiration. He looked around, his breath short and anxious, realizing within moments it was all a dream.

"You ok, mate?" Kraken's cockney tone broke the unwelcome silence.

"Krak...Kraken," Davey answered. He didn't know what to think, backing into the galley windows that were supposed to be broken. The last vision of Kraken was that of destruction and not of kindness.

"What happened in here? Bad dream got to you?" Kraken cocked his head to the right, his slits for green eyes studying Davey as if he was some weird science experiment.

"It's nothing. Nothing at all."

"Ok, then." Kraken slowly nodded.

Davey knew better. The boy-creature didn't believe him.

"What was that noise all about?" Galendra entered, her nourished frame more majestic in the red and orange hues of the two suns – very different from the decrepit state she suffered when they discovered her on Malent's island.

"He said it was nothing. Bad dream." Kraken folded his arms over his chest. "Regardless, think we all need to have a talk, if you know what I mean."

"Right now?" Davey asked, still unsure of what he just experienced and if it foretold of Kraken's true nature.

"No better time. Got a little bit of a problem. Hoping we can deal with it before nightfall." Kraken propped his leg up on the stool like the black-bearded pirate with the fancy hat on his dad's favorite liquor bottle.

"Does it relate to that map…wherever that is?"

"You could say that," Kraken answered with a hint of agitation. "Fact is, we ain't shaking your father's specter, and we're about to, at least supposed to, head into dangerous waters."

"How can you tell?" Davey retrieved the map, brushing off the particles of spent wax. As expected, the drawings of the islands once again shifted their location, a Gordian Knot if there ever was one.

"Easy. Can tell by listening. They're already out there…somewhere."

"Who?" Davey asked, twisting the map around, still not able to make heads or tails of it.

"The three of them," Galendra looked at the ground, a somber expression crossing her downturned lips. "We must meet them, though. There's no other way."

"You guys going to tell me who you're talking about?" Davey asked, still unsure of their words.

"Relax. It's inevitable." Kraken said.

"Then can we just go around them?"

"Not if were going to rescue Gregor."

"You're not thinking of leaving him? He helped us."

"Aye. We knew the risk when we set the course. It's just that, well, you'll be tested."

"Most men are unable to resist their charm. Some legends have fallen to their call," Galendra added.

"Perfect. That makes me shark soup." Davey turned away. The deeper he trekked into the Nether, the more he felt himself lose a bit of himself. Maybe his father was right. Maybe he was doomed.

"Enough of that. It's high time you start believing in yourself. You remember our discussion from earlier?" Kraken asked.

"Yeah, and you weren't so sure of me just yesterday morning. Said I wasn't strong enough," Davey answered, his words unlike himself.

"That's the thing. I don't have time to be picky. You either meet this challenge head on, or the Tide will find her way to the bottom of the Endless Ocean. No other choice in that matter. We sink or swim."

"Can you at least tell me who we're dealing with?"

"The Sirens." Galendra backed away with a rare look of concern. In his short time of knowing her, she remained poised, almost impervious to emotion.

"Wait." The name rang a bell. "Are you talking about—"

"I'm afraid so." Galendra's words drifted along with the confidence. "Which is why we must prepare, and with that, I would see to the preparation." She excused herself without another word.

"You ok?" Kraken asked. Unlike Galendra, he didn't appear quite as frazzled.

"As good as I can be."

"You got that look about you. Like you're broken." Kraken circled around and fixated on the galley windows, peering out to the golden tide of the Endless Ocean. Davey saw the yearning in Kraken's eyes, the desire to be set free. There was something else to him, a reason for him staying.

"What else you would expect? You're talking like I'm supposed to brave and all."

"You were. You stood up to Malent."

"I got lucky. He should've, you know, beat me." He didn't want to speak of death, if death even existed in this world.

"That's where you're wrong. You showed bravery. You nearly sacrificed yourself for those Selkies."

"I told you, I got lucky. Bravery had nothing to do with it." Davey sighed, knowing the truth.

"If bravery had nothing to do with it, then why did you stand up to Malent? You challenged him were others wouldn't. Proves to me you have what it takes to face the Sirens. Proves to me you can beat that fear of yours."

"What if I told you I was more afraid than you think?"

"I'd say you're right. No arguing there." Kraken laughed. "I was the same way once. All I knew was fear."

"Then how did you get past it?"

"I never did. Just learned to control it." Kraken fixed his attention on the double doors. "But Galendra is right. We should prepare. Can smell them."

"Hold up."

"There's nothing to hold up," Kraken said without stopping. "We need to prepare."

"I don't understand how you were every afraid. I mean, you're this great big beast. You're a legend."

"Exactly," Kraken looked back at Davey, his eyes narrowed, his body rigid.

"Why are you looking at me like that?"

"Because you're finding every excuse to deny it. You think that just because I can transform into this…beast, that I'm invincible, that I don't know fear."

"I didn't mean to make you mad."

"Anger has nothing to do with it. You know that. I mean, I've been trying to make amends with my parents, even after they've been gone for several thousand years. Wanted to make them proud of me, just like you want to make your father proud of you."

"How did you know?"

"Because." A glint of a tear welled at the bottom of Kraken's eye. "Because I live it. Even though I was too young when the gods bestowed this curse on me, I still feel the pain, the rejection. Makes you weak. Makes you think you're a failure."

"Yeah. It does."

Kraken hit the mark.

"Which is why I like you, mate. It's why Gwen put her trust in you. Because you're something special." Kraken pointed back at the galley windows where his father's ship tailed them. The ominous vessel sent a wave of illness over Davey. "I hate to be like this, I really do, but you don't have the right to be afraid right now. Not with where Gregor is. Not with where Gwen went off to. They believed in you. Now it's time you start believing in yourself. You may call it luck, I call it bravery."

Kraken grunted and turned to leave.

"Wait," Davey said. He didn't mean to offend. After all, Kraken had a point.

"Have work to do. Get ready for those…girls."

"How did you get past it?"

"Past what?" Kraken furrowed his brow.

"Past the fear. You know, how did you deal with it…feeling abandoned. Feeling, I don't know, all alone. You said you compartmentalized it."

"Good question." Kraken's eyes lingered over the circumference of the formerly lavish decorum of the captain's quarters. "One that I don't like to talk about."

"I know it's bad, painful, but it would help me out here. I mean, heck, I'm all alone. Feel like I'm trapped in my imagination."

"You ain't trapped, and I understand where you're coming from." Kraken wiped his jaw then adjusted his doo rag. "Remembered when I washed up on that shore still a baby. I should've drowned in the Aegean." As he spoke, Kraken's eyes took on a deeper shade of green. "No way I should've been alive."

"Was this in my world or the Nether?"

"Our world. It was said they called me a blight, a mistake." Kraken sauntered over to the windows, his movements deliberate, the weight of his story pressing down on Davey. "Nobody knows a greater pain than that of an unwanted child. It's….terrible. You feel alone, unappreciated. The small fishing community that raised me let me know what happened. Wasn't until I was much older, maybe in my teens, when I let the rage get the best of me." Kraken leaned on the desk and hunched over, hiding his face from Davey.

"What is it?" Davey wasn't sure if he should press further.

"I hurt a lot of people because of my anger. A lot of people. After they told me, they wouldn't say where my parents were. I got so angry. I just wanted to know why they abandoned me. That's when I lashed out, punished those poor people who I called family. Then the beast came out. This." Kraken held out his arms and shook them with emphasis. "Didn't know what to think. I burned their homes, destroyed their livestock. That's when the rest of them came for me, pushed me back to the Aegean like my parents did. But something saved me, something harnessed that anger inside. Turned me into this. That's when the Kraken emerged. That's when anger took its toll on any sea faring vessel that crossed my path."

With each word, Kraken's head hung a little lower, his grip on the desk slipping.

"I didn't mean to bring anything bad up."

"Not your fault. Nobody's fault but my own. And you know what? It wasn't anger that made me into the beast I am today, this animal of legend you see in that picture book of yours. It was fear. Fear that something might be wrong with me because my parents didn't want me."

"And that's why you don't like fear."

"Nope." Kraken looked up, his irises wide enough to mask the white of his eyes. "Fear leads to bad decisions. It rules you. Can't let it take you like it took me." Kraken cleared his throat and wiped his cheeks. "My family, my real family, paid for my fear. We can't afford to have your fear put our world in jeopardy." Kraken walked away without another word.

"Sorry," Davey said, watching as Kraken disappeared through the captain's quarter doors.

IV.

Davey emerged into a wall of humidity. The stagnant air reminded Davey of late August, the unabated rays strong enough to burn his already tortured skin within five minutes. Only the cool breeze of a late summer storm could wash away the heaviness in the air.

Whitecaps sloshed on either side of the Mermaid's Tide, high enough that the Endless Ocean's waves spilled over the edges of the repaired galley.

Meanwhile, trailing several knots behind, the darkened skies of his father's specter reminded him of their need for haste. It also pulled Davey back to his nightmare.

"Up ahead. Looks like we've made some progress," Kraken said as he wrestled with an armful of rope.

Davey searched the platinum horizon for the genesis of Kraken's alarm, and there they were – two islands no bigger than Smith's Island back home.

From their current course, Davey estimated they would sail in-between the two. Hopefully, they were getting closer to the underwater kingdom of the Finfolk. That's if they could somehow conquered the obstacles known as the Sirens.

"Of course there's a problem. We always have a problem." Kraken threw up his arms in obvious disgust, allowing some of the rigging to fall to the ground.

"Keep yourself. There's no need to let it get the best of you," Galendra answered.

"Easier said than done," Kraken parried with his comment, hands on hips and muttering something under his nose. "I don't understand how this broke right again. It just ripped in half, like something ate through it."

"Let's have a look."

"What about you? You want to have a look at it to?" Kraken looked up, causing Davey to freeze.

"No, I'm ok."

"What's gotten into you?" Galendra dropped the rigging and peered into Kraken's broken visage like a mother to a child.

"Stomach's grumbling. That's for sure." He pulled his gaze away from Davey, towards the sea. Part of Davey wanted to hug him, knowing their conversation five minutes earlier played some part in the sudden downtrodden attitude.

"He's ok. Just going through some hard times." Davey hoped his words would cover for Kraken's.

"Whatever the cause, we need to fix this. It won't hold the sail. I doubt we want to risk veering off course," Galendra said.

"Maybe we're meant to," Kraken said, his spirit more broken than Davey first thought.

"No we won't. We can fix it." Davey studied the severed rope using his mariner's eye he picked up from living on the Chesapeake. Both of them were right. They wouldn't make it far. He traced his fingers along the fibers of the cord, feeling something sticky.

"Tar?" Davey rubbed his thumb and index finger together, the substance growing warm.

"Perhaps oil. There's a trail of this stuff leading over there." Galendra answered, walking over to the edge of the Tide. "This can't be good."

"What is it?" Kraken asked. "Can't be oil." Kraken leaned further down. A black substance painted the hull on both sides, dripping down to the ocean where dark element blanketed the waves surrounding the Mermaid's Tide, its origins tracing back to the direction of his father's specter. The very idea of his father trying to find another way to thwart his maneuvers caused Davey to think back to his daydream, to wonder if it was all a game for the old man.

"It looks like it's moving," Davey said.

"Maybe I should take a look. Never seen anything like it," Kraken said, removing his shirt.

"Don't." Galenda grabbed Kraken by the arm.

"Why?"

"We stick together. There." The Selkie pointed to the emerald island on the right – one with silver shores harkening back to Malent's land, but with a verdant plateau instead of a rocky spiral in the middle. "We anchor there. Wait for this to pass."

"We don't have time. Gwen could be—"

"She'll be fine. Mermaids have made it through far worse through their history."

Kraken's defeated look lingered, his reptilian eyes softer, almost surrendering to Galendra's suggestion. He replaced his shirt just as fast, not saying a word, and sauntered off towards the wheel.

"He'll be fine in good time. Like you, he cares deeply for someone," she said.

"He reminds me of one of my friends back home."

"He reminds you of you." Galendra smiled. "That's why you make good companions. Now, let us prepare to dock. Wait for this plague to pass."

V.

Unlike the island where they discovered the Selkies, the shoreline didn't appear to be inhabited. Rather, unfettered silver sands stretched across the circumference until overtaken by lush vegetation, tempering Davey's nerves. Hopefully, none of those Finfolk would make a surprise appearance.

Kraken remained silent for the most part, perhaps lost in his thoughts, likely those resurfacing after their conversation. Davey avoided the boy-creature, not wanting to cause any more strife. Galendra, on the other hand, fixated on the slick of black water trailing back several miles to his father's tempest. It split between the two islands – the one they approached and the other, maybe ten miles or so to their right.

"What do we do now?" Davey asked.

"I tell you what we do." Kraken hoped down from the captain's perch, his demeanor back to what Davey remembered. "I take a look at the ship, make a few bindings, then get off as soon as possible."

"After the waters clear," Galendra insisted.

"Maybe a while if my father is causing his. He doesn't want me to go any further," Davey said.

"That much is obvious, mate." Kraken smirked. Davey wasn't sure how Kraken was able to compartmentalize the emotional pain, even after his short breakdown. Davey wished for the same strength. "We'll let him have his fun, yes, but his power isn't that strong. His little trick won't last forever."

"How do you know?"

"He suffered the lighthouse's light. That's how I know." Kraken slapped Davey on the shoulder, again retreating to his playful side.

"See we're back in good spirits," Galendra said.

"Just needed a bit of a respite. That's it. Had to get my mind clear." Kraken emphasized by gently tapping the mast with a fist.

"Good to hear." Davey said.

"Tell you what. Why don't you go onto shore? See if you can scout about for some of them golden palms. Have a feeling we might be needing some." Kraken motioned Davey towards the shore.

"By myself?"

"No need to be afraid. Not a soul in site. It'll do you good to get some alone time. Trust me." Kraken flashed a knowing smile. Davey couldn't deny the wisdom, having spent the majority of his adolescence as a loner. He welcomed it as much, and with the island seemingly abandoned, he would have time to put the pieces of the puzzle together.

"I suppose so. You both going to be ok? Not going to leave me here, are you?"

"Wouldn't even think about it. You get along now before we sail into more tumultuous waters," Kraken answered.

"Suppose I don't have an argument," Davey said before preparing the rowboat. It wasn't worth protesting.

Lucky for Davey, the water was shallow enough for him to swim only a short distance, no less than the length of a swimming pool, until he waded in the bath-like waters of the Endless Ocean. The shimmering gold tide held a variety of alien sea life, from three-pronged crabs with a purple shell, to a school of minnows pulsating with unknown energy.

He staggered up the beach and over unblemished silver dunes carved by the ocean wind. There was something regal, almost magical about the beach's appearance, a sea unto the land, rolling its sandy tide towards the jungle reminiscent of *Where the Wild Things Are*. The beach abutted a plateau reaching up a hundred or so yards and caked with more unfettered jungle, some of the vegetation spilling over the cliffs.

"Going to take me forever to find some golden palms," Davey asked, smacking his hands clean of wet sand against his tattered shorts, only to discover they were as dry as the last sun above.

"Place keeps on getting weirder and weirder." He laughed with nerves in his throat, one echoing against the jagged cliffs, where he heard another specter, another lost boy in the midst of a foreign world where tales of the past came to life. "Too many doubts."

The jungle grew thicker upon his approach, hiding any semblance of a trail. He felt the thousand tiny bugs staring back at him, ready to feast upon his rich blood. Somewhere deep within its heart, the golden palms grew, but he needed to find them first.

A rustle of branches followed by the distinct sound of footfalls came from within the growth.

"What?" Davey whispered, pulling away from the jungle, his feet sinking into the cold sand.

Again, another rustle, this one more purposeful. Then a voice broke the silence.

"Davey," his mother's distinct voice called.

"Mom?"

It couldn't be. No here. Not on this island.

"Davey," she called again, her words as tempered as those nights when the house reeked of his father's spilled two-dollar beer.

"Mom, why don't you come out?" He asked, hoping beyond hope his mother would emerge. Instead, silence answered.

"Should've known better," he said, inching forward, stretching his head up in an effort to see past the broad-leafed plant masking the entrance – or what resembled the entrance.

"Davey," she resurfaced, this time her voice more forceful, calling from atop the plateau. Davey looked up in time to see the last hints of the orange orb dip below the plateau's edge, casting the beach into shadows. His exposed skin suddenly felt cool, the sands between his toes a little cooler.

"Mo-Mom?" He hesitated at first, studying the dense landscape above. Climbing the plateau would be an adventure like no other back home. The Nether would be a different story.

"Davey, please. You must come help," she called, again from her perch. Then he saw the silhouette, a lone figure standing atop the island's highland. Though she remained hidden within the brush, her figure was as clear as ever, just as Davey remembered. It had to be her.

"Mom," Davey called. His breathing escalated as he ran into the jungle where fuzz-covered leaves whipped against face, accompanied by the melon-collie chorus of unknown insects – some as large as mice with big murderous bug eyes.

Seconds later, Davey rushed up a makeshift path, over broken and crinkled undergrowth, nearly tripping over exposed roots and holding up his arms to shield his body from the branches relentless assault. His legs churned like they were on his bicycle, climbing up the incline towards the island plateau and into the heart of the jungle. It was darker, much darker the deeper he ran.

Taking a quick breath, he looked up to find his mother, but the trees – more mature and wider than the growth on outskirts – blocked his view.

"Mom," he called. Nothing. He needed to run.

His muscles ached as he climbed higher, his toes kicking back loose dirt, his footing slipping several times before reaching the zenith.

Davey immediately fell to his knees, sucking in a lungful of air.

"Mom." He tried to speak, but found himself absent of energy, his words barely audible over the sound of his breathing. Once his world stopped spinning, he looked around to see that the beach had disappeared along with The Mermaid's Tide from his muted vantage point. He didn't like it, any of it.

Davey, the voice called, this time more menacing in its purpose, matching the sudden wickedness of the jungle. You should have listened to your father.

"What?" Half-panicked with a racing heart, Davey whipped his head from side to side, the vegetation squeezing around, suffocating him in a green swath. It all looked the same.

"We said, welcome to your end."

Then the jungle herself opened to his right as leaves pushed aside, young saplings bowing towards the ground, as three slender figures emerged with hot coals for eyes – craters devoid of happiness, only knowing pain against a shroud of blackness. Their fingers extended down like scythes, tearing through strands of broad leaves as they moved forward, flanking Davey with ill-begotten intentions.

"What...what are you?" He closed his eyes, hiding behind the false safety, listening to feet crush undergrowth, feeling the air shift around him, growing heavier and smelling of charred firewood. He prayed for the safety of the beach, to be in the confines of The Mermaid's Tide quarters.

"This one would fetch quite the prize. Didn't think you would have it to venture up these parts. Friends might've betrayed your undoing." It spoke with a slow cadence. Nothing ever good came from one speaking in a slow cadence. It was like being in front of the firing squad known as the principal's office. "We will be rewarded as such."

"What did I do?"

"It's not what you did. It's what you can do."

"I won't do anything." They somehow knew.

"But you will. You and your friends down there would see you taken to a forbidden place where you would stop his endeavors."

"Whose?" Davey asked, searching for anyway to delay the inevitable. What would happen if they cut him down? Would he wake up from this sordid dream? Would he join his mother?

"Oh, I think you know that." The creature's voice stayed the same – constant, prying, a false cherub seeking to lure the young Davey to his quiet fate.

"I don't. I swear."

"Surely, those who follow you will. And when you find the Guardian, you would see the others succeed. And we can't allow that to happen."

Davey whimpered, trying to stay strong. He heard their breathing, his senses elevated as they closed in around him. Dark became darker against his eyelids as fear prepared to claim its next victim.

Then he remembered Kraken's words. He needed to compartmentalize fear. He needed to find his bravery, to make sure those who believed in him did so with good cause. And despite the odds, his right hand slipped to his belt, poking around in hopes of finding his grandfather's sword.

Kraken's words betrayed him. He found nothing, an empty scabbard when he remembered the blade's fate in his nightmare, his father having shattered it, then waking up with it being gone.

He was helpless, or so he thought.

He heard her words again, her magical voice reaching across the alien sky and filtering down from the treetops, until her ballad became strong.

Davey heard them stumble back, their retreat joined with ungodly shrieks, more panicked and deathly than a fox within the wood at night.

If there were a chance he could escape, this would be it.

Davey opened his eyes to find a world shrouded with darkness. He went blind again, the only color that of crimson ribbons pulsating in and out, highlighting the jungle.

With no other thought, Davey jumped up and ran, throwing caution to the wind in the name of survival

Trees snapped around, unknown plants tried to thwart his efforts. He didn't care. He listened to the ballad, her comforting hymns willing him forward in spite of fear, in spite of the numerous times he laid down to let people like the Schoolyard Four take pot shots at him during recess.

He'd never fought back, not yet at least.

And like all great escapes in the movies, this one seemed to last forever, but Davey knew he couldn't surrender. His lungs burned. His throat ached. His legs felt like jelly as he shouldered past a tree trunk, still blind in his sight.

Please, don't take me, he thought, clinging on to her song, to her ballad.

Their distinct footfalls trailed behind, their shrieks of pain turning to those of hunger as the creatures tailed him. They were moving faster than him, slicing through the jungle with their gazelle-like legs. He imagined they would make a delicacy out of him when they caught, pushing him to use the last of his energy.

When he thought he ran out of time, listening to them nearly ten feet behind, a rush of wind, of spring-smelling air washed over him as the dirt floor gave way to the soft texture of grass below.

His body slipped out from under him on the slick grass, causing Davey's world to go weightless, his body slamming against the ground in spread eagle fashion. He emptied his lungs but his vision returned, revealing a blue sky above, an endless clearing surrounded by the jungle.

"Hello?" Davey gasped. He made it out, but didn't make it away from them, or so he thought.

"A visitor," an unknown answered from above.

VI.

"Quickly now. We must make haste," the stranger said, reaching down with a velvet-gloved hand. As Davey's vision cleared, he noticed his would-be savior– a man by all accounts – clad in plate mail with various nicks and scratches marring the once regal armor

A trimmed beard framed his brown eyes, telling of a man both of valor and conviction, but also a tortured soul, a kindred spirit.

"Wait, I was being followed."

"By whom?"

"They were these things, black creatures almost like scarecrows," Davey spun around, his world still suffering from his brush with temporary blindness. Jungle stared back at him with no sign of the creatures.

"What are scarecrows?"

"You know, to scare away birds and such."

"I apologize, but I'm not aware of these scarecrows."

"Doesn't matter." Davey studied the man, his stoic features revealing no fear, only quiet contemplation. "Whatever they were, they were right there. Had these red eyes, long fingers, like talons."

"And you said they were black?"

"Yes."

"They should know better." He answered as a man would who knew his enemy. "This jungle is known to hide its most dangerous of predators. They rely on the element of surprise. But it looks like they've left us."

"Who…what are they?" Davey swallowed but could produce no spit.

"A nemesis as old as the island herself. We call them Formians, one of the many banes I struck down in my time."

"What…what are Formians?"

"Nothing to be trifled with. And if they found you, they will most return."

"For me?"

"Come now, no need to fear right now. They would dare not approach this holy land, especially if they know of my presence. "

"Good." Davey collapsed back down to his knees.

"Tell me, how did you happen upon this place?"

"We were on the Endless Ocean." Davey tried to swallow again, thinking of what he should tell the stranger and what he shouldn't. "Had to make a pit stop. Fix the boat."

"You sailed with others?" The man knelt beside Davey, his descent joined by the sound of clanging armor. If the Formians had lost track of Davey through the brush, they would certainly find him now.

"Yes. Others. But, and I hope you understand, I don't know you, so I'd rather not say."

"Even for a man who just saved your life?" He smiled a genuine smile, one warm, nurturing. "You are wise for your age."

"Thanks, I guess."

"Go on with your story. You took up to shore, then you discovered this place."

"Yes. Thought I heard…someone up here, someone important to me. Then that's when they ambushed me."

"The Formians?"

"Yes, those things."

"They are known to use trickery." The man nodded as if he knew more to Davey's story than he even did.

"Well, it was trickery that saved me. I heard this song, something I think I heard before. It was beautiful. And it caused the creatures pain, so I took my chance and—"

"She called you?" The knight spoke a little faster, his eyes a little wider.

"You know her, the woman behind the voice?"

"Quite well."

"And she saved me."

"If you heard her, she would want to see you. Come." He groaned as he stood, his armor clanging and scratching again, serving as a beacon for every creature in the jungle. Davey wished the knight would be a little quieter.

"But, wait. Before we go." Davey peered into the depths of the overgrown foliage. It appeared to go on forever, blotting out any sign of the beach.

"There's no need to worry, Lord…" The man allowed his question to trail.

"McCrary." Davey saw no use in keeping the truth.

"Lord McCrary. I would see no use in lying to you, knowing I could cut you down on a whim. No offense, of course." He brushed his fingers past his own sword, a large pommel fashioned to that of a dragon's edge. "But it would be best we move to meet your savior."

"I suppose. Not like I could survive in there." Davey thought Kraken and Galendra would be looking for him soon, especially after nightfall. He only had to stay alive until then. "But first."

"Yes?"

"What is your name?"

"Oh, yes. How rude of me. You can call me Arthur."

VII.

The trek towards the lake didn't take long, about the time it took for the second sun to dip below the crystal lake the two stumbled upon. The scenery – unblemished and possessing a hint of magic – harkened back to a movie Davey watched in grade school, something about a journey and the center of the earth.

Unlike the golden hue of the Endless Ocean, the lake's clear waters were reminiscent of home. The dying sun reflected of its body, creating an illusion of a blanket of diamonds covering the placid lake. Davey spotted a rainbow of fish dart back and forth close to the shallow shore before disappearing into its heart.

His new companion Arthur remained quiet, more focused on the outskirts of the jungle surrounding the lake. Davey felt them within the feral confines – the Formian's crimson red eyes burn with hatred, waiting for their opportunity.

"Wait here," Arthur said, his stoic expression commanding obedience but projecting compassion.

"Think that's a good idea. I mean, they're right there." Davey stared long enough into the jungle until one branch became two.

"Would be foolish to approach us. They would perish as soon as they step on the land." Arthur removed his helmet, its metal capturing a kaleidoscope of colors from the dying sun, and dropped it to the ground with a clank. Brown hair flowed down to his shoulders, edging his tired face, a man who had seen one too many battles where his brothers had fallen.

"If you say so."

"I would say so?" Arthur canted his head to the side, his eyebrows arched up in curiosity.

"Yeah, if you say there's no danger, then it's so."

"You're full of odd statements. Such is the exuberance of youth." Arthur nodded his head, and then reached around his breastplate, removing it, revealing a chain shirt underneath.

"Why are you doing that?'

"What's that?"

"Removing all your armor. Don't we have to go back through the jungle?" Davey prepared for another panic attack, given his deteriorated state and Arthur's decision to abandon his armor.

"Not a choice to be had in the matter. She doesn't like for me to be on guard when I hold court with her."

"Who's that?" Davey asked.

"The one who called you." Arthur dropped his breastplate beside his helmet with another resounding clank.

Then, as if on command, her song filtered across the lake, causing its waters to ripple to its shores like water in a disturbed glass. Unlike when he was lost in the jungle, her words were clearer, almost pure. Her song tickled his ear, massaging his lobe, putting him at ease. His world faded. His eyes fluttered. Numbness took his body.

"Davey," her words spoke in different frequencies, causing the lake to ripple once again.

"She calls you." Arthur bowed.

"She…does?" Davey followed suit, bowing as well to the unknown.

"That is a good thing."

"Why?"

"Maybe she would seek to replace something. Something you lost." Arthur's voice drifted as he refocused to the lake's center. Then, as if waiting for Davey, the waters lapping onto the beach inverted to form a circular bowl, the center bubbling then swirling around until a waterspout emerged as the singing came to a crescendo.

"And she would see you."

A figure doused in pearl radiance shielded by a white curtain rose from the lake. Davey didn't want to look, feeling like he would spoil the woman if he stared at her for too long, but he couldn't fight curiosity. He didn't know how, but he knew the song belonged to her.

"Davey McCrary," again, she spoke with etherealness.

"Yes," Davey swallowed, looking back to Arthur for any semblance of guidance. Arthur kept to silent prayer, saying nothing.

"It is not often a lighthouse keeper would visit my shores. Only when the other world's sky would turn forever black would one make an appearance."

"I suppose not.".

"This would cause worry."

"I've…been told that several times since I got here," Davey said, once again looking at Arthur for reassurance. This time Arthur spoke up.

"This is not my message to hear, if that's what you're wondering. It is up to you to make the right decision." Arthur gave one reassuring nod then positioned himself behind Davey.

"You heard me calling?" She asked.

"Your song, yes, if that's what you're asking."

"That…is troubling." Her white curtain shimmered, flashing with a powerful light that caused Davey to look away.

"I didn't mean to upset you."

"You didn't, child. You're only fulfilling your duties, for you are one of the few who are privy to my song. But it is troubling. The void is in imbalance."

"I think I've heard a lot of that lately, about us being in trouble."

"And the others would know." Her light faded back to one more bearable, allowing Davey to look back at her beauty. When he looked back, he didn't see a white curtain veiling her details, instead saw her – his mother – reaching out for him, her red hair cupping her soft cheeks, her emerald eyes wanting him to be happy.

"Mom." No sooner than he spoke the words than the image reverted to one of the unknown woman.

"I'm afraid I'm not your mother. But you would see her soon if you are to follow your path."

"They told me that too." Davey slumped back, wanting to hold on to the illusion in his mind. "I just want to see her again."

"And you will. First, tell me how you came upon the Nether. This is of utmost importance."

"I don't know. They came for me after I tried to—" Davey looked away, embarrassed about his attempt at taking his own life.

"You're ashamed of something?"

"It's just that." He thought back to watching her image fade as he plummeted towards the Chesapeake.

"There is no shame in love. It is love that gives us strength. It is love that will make you succeed in your task. I can assure you that."

"She speaks the truth," Arthur's baritone voice followed up on the mysterious women's remark.

"Then why am I here? What is this place?"

"The void between your reality and ours you will close. This is where the final war will be fought, where innocence and anger, where love and fear, where good and evil meet to purge one from the other." Her curtain pulsated with each word. "And it would be you who will help protect the innocent from the Dark Guardian, to return those who fight our battle back home."

"As the Keeper?" Davey remembered the words. The reality of everything fell upon him. Kraken and Gwen alluded to their place in the Nether.

"Yes, as the Keeper. It would not be your first choice, I realize that, but sometimes our choices are made from birth. It is up to you, like your brothers and sisters, those you know, and those who you don't know, to save our worlds. But you must put aside your fear, embrace your destiny."

"Everybody keeps on telling me that. They say I have the strength. I don't see it." Davey closed his eyes and exhaled, knowing he didn't have the fortitude to stick through it all, this grand endeavor.

"We all have the strength inside. She only means for you to understand this. Embrace it and you will help save the Nether from the poison of humanity," Arthur said. "A poison I know well."

"Know your grandfather came to me when he walked this land. He didn't know strength, but he believed in goodness, and that's what allowed him to succeed," she said.

"Succeed in what? Did he defeat the Dark Guardian?" Davey asked.

"No. He merely delayed his arrival. He is…was a good man," her words showed the first hints of remorse, of sadness. "He was like you, young and naïve when I first happened upon him. But as he grew, he found bravery, the love to protect those he missed back in his world."

"I'm not like him. Never was. Mom always wanted me to follow in his footsteps."

"Your mother wanted for you to be your own person. Always. And that, Davey McCrary, is what I feel is missing. The love for yourself, the confidence."

Davey's throat tightened. His eyes burned with tears as the figure spoke of his mother. He knew she spoke the truth. His mother never pushed him to be anyone, only to be the best he could be by reading, by writing, by knowing everything she taught him was for him.

"I know," his voice cracked.

"It is time for you to start finding out who you are. If not for your sake, for your companions." Her image twinkled, revealing an image Davey knew well: The Mermaid's Tide. He watched as Kraken and Galendra cleaned the black tar from the sides of the hull. "They believe in you."

"Hope so."

"I know both quite well. They will serve you l as you cross the precipice into his kingdom. The shadow that haunts, the shadow of a former life, will meet you eventually. And if you don't find the strength by then, humanity will suffer. Such a terrible tragedy, Keeper, but one you will prevent."

"There's a couple others that were with me."

"Gwen, my kin."

"Your kin? You mean you're a mermaid?"

"One of the last. My sisters have been hunted to near extinction in your realm and the Nether. Gwen is…the youngest." Her sadness radiated over Davey.

"Do you know where she is?"

"Unfortunately, I cannot tell. Her sight is lost to me because of the Dark Guardian's presence. But I have faith in her reappearance."

"I don't know. I have some…weird connection with her."

"As you should. All Keepers are drawn to the mermaids, as we are drawn to you."

"Provides a little comfort…I guess."

"The boy knows his humor," Arthur said.

"If only you understood how much power you wield. Maybe your light would help show others the way. Our worlds need more humility."

"I'm sort of flattered you have all this confidence in me," Davey answered, unsure of what she meant.

"This other you speak of, this Beast of the Black Forest, Gregor is his name."

"Yes. You know his nickname?"

"He is quite…notorious, one who has a sordid history. I dare to trust such a beast."

"He knew my grandfather. Said he was his first mate."

"Arthur, do you know of this?" She asked.

"This is a revelation to me as well," Arthur answered.

"Interesting."

"He saved me from Malent," Davey said.

"Malent? You speak his name," she said.

"More unwelcome news." Arthur's breeches grinded against each other as he folded his arms over his chest, obviously agitated at the mention of the Finman's name.

"He…" Davey hesitated.

"Is very dangerous. It's a miracle you survived." She said with haste, again her luminescent shield pulsating with energy.

"I told you, Gregor saved me. He sacrificed himself."

"Then maybe I was wrong. Maybe anyone can find redemption."

"I would know," Arthur said.

"Yes you would." She withdrew a little more. "Malent's reappearance worries me," she said, the waters turning two shades darker, mirroring her demeanor. "Perhaps the Dark Guardian has more allies than first thought."

"If you are indeed the Keeper as she says, then you have it within you. Lest, you wouldn't hold the mantle of your grandfather," Arthur added. "And I would fight beside you along with your companions."

"But no good soldier can meet his test without a reminder of who he is meant to become," she said. "If he survived Malent and the shadow that stalks him, he will find his strength."

Suddenly, the water surrounding the mermaid bubbled and foamed, swirling around in an inverted water vortex. The tip of a sword pierced the waters, until his grandfather's blade levitated free from the lake, its metal more polished, almost translucent.

"Is this not your sword?" She asked.

"It…is." Davey watched as the sword hovered towards him, his reflection long in its blade. He reached out for it, its hilt cool to the touch. "How did you find this?"

"In a world possessed by magic and imagination, when the Dark Guardian seeks to break the rules, I would see to it that you're capable of challenging him."

"And I would see that you're taught how to wield it…properly," Arthur said.

"You would teach me?" Davey sheathed the sword, its weight even

111

lighter than before.

"Arthur is a righteous man who…has faced his fears as well," she said.

"At your service."

"We must—" Before she could finish her sentence, the sky cracked with a whip-like sound. A bolt of electricity stretched across the vista, exploding into another thunderous roar.

"Lady, he's here," Arthur shouted as the blades of knee high grass shriveled and curled in a wave of death.

"My father," Davey shouted.

Wind swept across the jungle, tearing leaves off limbs. Gray clouds raced above like a time-elapsed movie.

"Not your father. It's much worse." Arthur fetched his armor, volleying his attention between his suit and their surroundings. Trees cracked from another gust of wind as day became dusk.

"You have no time," she said. "The Guardian is here. His power has grown too strong. The lake grows warm with his discontent. You must remain steadfast. Find your bravery."

Greens became black. Black became nothingness as the red eyes glowed brighter within the undergrowth, almost doubling in size. Then came the clicking noise, a distinct sound announcing their attack.

"Stay behind me." Arthur abandoned his armor and unsheathed his sword. In spite of the darkness, the blade itself glowed white, defying the black magic taking the area. "And do not run. We stay together."

"I will do what I can," Davey answered, following suit with his weapon. He fought against Malent and survived with no help. He would do the same for Arthur.

"Just like your grandfather. Stubborn to the last draw," Arthur twirled his sword around in a halo, displaying his mastery of the weapon. Davey though he would be lucky to show a tenth of the prowess.

"Tend to the Keeper, Arthur. I depend on you to show him the way." The crash of a wave behind Davey signaled the mermaid's departure, leaving Davey and Arthur alone.

"Watch. Become disciplined. Allow your mind and not fear to control your movements. And summon the light." Arthur smiled at the same time the first of the black figures leapt from the confines of the jungle, hands and talons spread out like the spokes of a metal rake, a face hiding corruption coming down on them from above. It reminded Davey of the Finfolk all over again.

But it wouldn't last as long.

Arthur swept his sword in front of him. The air sparked from its energy as it tore through skin as tough as sandpaper, summoning a scream from the attacker, its existence disappearing into a puff of black smoke. Meanwhile, the sky ignited again with the Dark Guardian's fury.

Davey's ears whistled, his footing loose against the disintegrated grass, almost knocking him down.

Another crack as two more of the Formians emerged, tongues clicking, eyes blazing as they fixated on Davey.

"Strike with confidence. Strike with truth." Arthur clashed with the second, then kneeled down and connecting with the third. Their screams echoed before becoming lost to their oblivion.

It was the fourth Arthur didn't see, surprising Davey from the outcropping of trees to their right. The demonic being grew in size as it struck Davey, its talons slicing deep into Davey's off-weapon shoulder. Every muscle fiber burned down to his arm. His legs feeling of a thousand bee stings, Davey tried to reach up to defend himself, but his arm would not move, paralyzed from whatever poison the Formian injected.

His vision spiraled, locking on to his executioner. Though he couldn't see past the faceless void, he felt the Formian smile in delight. Davey thought of his end, watching as his life – visions of his mother, of his good times in school – flash before his young existence.

"No," Arthur said, his words cut down by two more charging Formians, their shadow movements blending in with the almost night sky. Arthur parried their attacks, but remained too far away. "Use the light."

"Light," Davey looked at his sword, and for a moment he thought he heard the mermaid's ballad again, a vision of the woman, one resembling his mother, captured within the blade. "Light," he said again, feeling the weight of the Formian above.

Could he defend himself? He remembered fighting his father's specter during the crossover. He remembered fending off Malent with a strike of his own, but that was different with encouragement from the others.

The figure curled down, its talons bearing down on him, ready to end it all. Davey clenched his teeth, fighting against self-doubt and raised the blade in rebuttal, but he wouldn't need to answer.

The Formian's guttural scream silenced the attack before exploding into an ashen cloud. Coated in the black dust, Arthur stood, blade at his side, heavy breaths denoting his exhaustion.

Arthur managed to save him. And no sooner did his guardian deal the final blow, did the black clouds above, alive with misdeeds, dissipate, giving way to the burnt orange of dusk.

"You have much to learn." With a purposeful exhale, Arthur pulled Davey to his feet. "And we both have much work to do."

"Thank you." Davey shook his once-paralyzed arm as feeling returned to his fingers. "And I'm sorry."

"No need to be sorry." Arthur brushed his velvet sleeves free of the Formian's remains. "Only time to learn and gain the confidence."

"I can't help it. I'm not much with a blade. I mean, I'm just a kid.

"I would expect as much. But what you lack in wisdom, you make up with fight. Your grandfather learned. You will too." Arthur didn't seem fazed, sheathing his sword and toeing the ground where six black dust piles remained. "We all learn in due time."

"Still say I'm sorry. I put you in this position."

"You?" Arthur harrumphed, gathering his armor. "You have nothing to do with his presence. Our forefathers are guilty. Sins of the past will always catch up with us. Always."

"If you say so." Davey looked back over at the lake. Her absence played heavy on him, particularly after seeing an image of his mother. "Where do you think she went?"

"To protect what she can. And not to worry, she is much stronger than you think. Our focus should be on him. His power is growing stronger, which puts us in the difficult position at getting you trained."

"I'll do what I can." Davey stared at the ash at his feet. He was mere moments from meeting his end. He only hoped he could repay the favor, another one to add to the long list of IOUs.

"You'll do what you must. It is a duty that only few will have, and those who possess don't want it. Quite the quandary."

"Yes," Davey agreed, not even knowing what the word quandary met.

"We must move quickly. More Formians will arrive soon when they realize the holy ground is defiled." Arthur plucked a blade of grass and crumpled it between his fingers. "You said you sailed here, correct?"

"Yes."

"Then we should hurrty for your ship. It is not safe here as his power grows. Do you remember the way?"

"Through the jungle." Davey pointed forward, not knowing if his words held truth.

"Then we go. Hopefully, your companions are quick to accept my presence."

VIII.

Davey didn't know if it was dumb luck or intuition, but the two managed to navigate through the forlorn jungle to the beach. The walk itself proved disturbing, Arthur pointing out the various claw marks on the trees and the wilted undergrowth trampled over by their nemesis. The place must've been crawling with Formians —creatures from the Emerald Isle who brought their prisoners to the great demon known as Balor, an entity associated with the Dark Guardian, or so Arthur informed him.

Even the silver sands of the beach didn't glisten with its normal royalty, having been tainted from evil's presence. Davey found it odd that Malent's beach wasn't tainted in the same manner.

"That your ship?" Arthur pointed to The Mermaid's Tide, its hull glowing with the last hints of the golden sun.

"Yeah." Davey looked at the waters surrounding the boat. Thankfully, there wasn't any sign of the black substance that marred their passage to the Finfolk home.

"Was wondering when you would show back up," Kraken said, his boyish figure emerging from another part of the jungle.

"Man, why do you have to scare us like that?" Davey jumped back.

"Sorry. Didn't mean to."

"Were you looking for me?" Davey asked.

"Nah, figured you'd be ok by yourself. Was just searching for more golden palms since you hadn't come back yet. Only ones I found were already destroyed. Nothing but rot." Kraken nodded at Arthur, who nodded back but said no words. "See you ran into a friend."

"Yeah, met him up there along the lake. Oh, there's a lake up there. But didn't see any golden palms."

"There were some, but the Guardian's presence destroyed them," Arthur said.

"Well that explains all the thunder and the like." Kraken grunted, hands on hips. "At least we cleaned the Tide."

"Got all that black gunk off?"

"Aye. Took us a bit, but we got it. Water's clear of it. Was hoping we could find us some wood, though." Kraken squinted as he looked towards the sun. "We better be off. Galendra is waiting for us. And you see that storm on the horizon. Your father is making some headway."

"Can we bring on another crew member?"

"The captain asks permission to bring on another crew member?" Kraken rubbed his chin, looking Arthur up and down. Kraken stood in tattered clothing with a door rag for a hat. Arthur remained in his armor, though stripped down to chain. They couldn't have been more worlds apart.

"I've been tasked to protect him, and I would see my duty fulfilled," Arthur said.

"Tasked by whom?" Kraken tilted his chin up in a small gesture of defiance.

"A mutual friend." Arthur didn't smile, not one to be used to being challenged.

"Something tells me we don't have mutual friends. Can't see it happening."

"In this regard, we do."

"What's your name anyway?" Kraken kept on point.

"Arthur...Arthur Pendragon."

"Pendragon." Kraken half-muttered, half-chuckled, his face turning from confidence to a blank awe in front of Davey. "Here? All the time I thought you were the stuff of legends."

"Aren't we all."

"Yes, we are."

"Only here to provide aid to the Keeper, teach him the ways of the Light. Mean no harm."

"It'll take a lot more than talk with this one." Kraken pointed at Davey.

"I expect nothing less. It's said the meek will save humanity from itself. Now, will you have me aboard, or would you have me return?"

"Not up to me, chum. Up to the captain. What he says goes."

"He can come aboard. Absolutely." Davey smiled at Arthur, who again didn't show any emotion.

"You sure you want to do that, given who you are and all? Think it's safe?" Kraken asked.

"I make my own decisions. I stand by them and whatever punishment that might come with it," Arthur answered.

"And I take it you know what you're going up against. Rough waters ahead. And who knows when they might pop up."

"So we're going to the Finfolk home?"

"To rescue the Beast of the Black Forest. Captain's orders."

"Then it is the captain I would follow."

"Looks like he has another friend. Stay here and I'll get the rowboat to bring Pendragon with us." Kraken ran off, diving into the waters lapping up into the shore.

"Quite the charmer. Reminds me of a friend of mine," Arthur said.

"He's harmless." Davey watched as Kraken swam towards the Mermaid's Tide with the speed of a torpedo. And as Davey watched, the dull rumble of thunder pulled his attention. His father's specter made headway, and no sooner would they get to the Tide than his father would be that much closer. He knew in his heart greater dangers lied ahead.

IX.

The three-moon night came quick, and with it, the quiet sereneness of it all. Unlike daytime in the Nether with its sweltering heat reminiscent of August on Ocean City's boardwalk, night was cooler, much cooler. Even after a sweat-inducing training regime with Arthur, one lasting well after the second moon rose over the now black waters, Davey wrapped himself in a woolen blanket, learning a whole new meaning to muscle soreness.

Davey watched from his perch along stern, his chest resting along the wooden rail, at the remnants of his past. His father's tempest – the gathering nothingness with the silhouette of large mast flanked by two smaller ones – grew larger with each passing minute. He could never escape his father.

"Quite the beautiful night," Galendra joined him, casting the area in a blue light with whatever magic she brought.

"I guess." Davey didn't bother to look, allowing the railing to take on more weight. Normally, he'd be two feet out of his shoes.

"How goes your arm? Is it healing properly?" She nestled up next to him, standing nearly a foot and a half taller like most adults did back home. She possessed a sculpted beauty marred by parallel scars running the length of her right cheek. He'd never noticed before.

"Feels heavy. Like after I get my shots." He winced as he prodded the three jagged claw marks torn into his t-shirt above his shoulder. "But Arthur insisted I train. So, I don't know, may have something to do with it."

"Give it time. The tonic should help, though it is not as strong as I would like. The plants were quite old."

"It's ok. Thanks again."

"As all things will be." She exhaled, not in a way of understanding, but in a way to signal she was about to lecture or give advice. He'd been there before. Many times. "Your thoughts are not with us right now. They are of your father."

"No."

"There's no need to lie, no need to hide."

She knew better.

"It's not that I'm lying, it's just that I'm trying not to think about it."

"Then you shouldn't be standing here."

"Just making sure he doesn't sneak up on us. That's all." He glanced up at her, her attention fixed forward.

"I know the pain you experience. It is the loss of someone comforting, the loss of a parent regardless of intention. They are blankets to keep us safe from the unknown."

"You mean evil."

"No, the unknown. It's the unknown that scares humanity the most. I've seen it in their eyes when a man would look upon me as my true self for the first time." Her voice lowered as she spoke, masking something Davey couldn't reach.

"When you showed yourself as… you know." Davey thought about the sealskin wrapping around the Selkies as they marched to the ocean.

"Yes."

"Sorry. Didn't mean to bring it up." Davey shied away, catching the first notes of a sweet aroma, a scent taking him back to a time he couldn't place.

"No." She chuckled. "I'm quite used to it."

"I shouldn't have brought it up. It's ignorant of me."

"What would be ignorant of you is holding onto something you can't control. It's why the Dark Guardian is here."

"Because of the unknown?" The smell grew stronger, overpowering the scent of salted water itself.

"Quite right. Men do foolish things because of what they can't control, only what the see in front of them. You're much too young to understand, but lust, jealousy, greed, are all born from man's desire to control what they can. And it's why men commit sins, why they're so evil. Because they fear. But kids like you haven't been spoiled by man's desires yet."

"You sound like Pastor Manning. He preaches about that stuff all the time." Davey couldn't help but sniff his shirt, its fabric tainted from sweat and foulness with a hint of jungle mint. Yet, he still smelled the flowers, this time recalling its genesis – his mother's funeral.

"He's a wise man, then."

"Yeah, used to get on me about wearing my hat in church." Davey shrugged. "But, anyway, guess he's not the type you're talking about." Davey glanced over his shoulder, trying to mask his curiosity towards the aroma.

"No, the men I speak of are known to me, one in particular. Like your parents, I was in love once. When he discovered my nature, he cast me out, beat me, which is where these came from." She ran her fingers down her scars, yet remained strong, poised in telling her story. "I still can't deny my love for him. He merely fell victim to the unknown. It's the reason why fairy tales like me don't exist in your world anymore."

"I never knew fairy tales existed, at least in my family." Davey tried to forget the smell, but it lingered, stronger, as if the entire boat carried a florist.

"In time you will learn that they do. Just know this, don't fear the unknown. It is the acceptance of what you can't' control that will free you from the chains of worry. That's where you find your bravery."

"Is that why you gave up your skin? Because you're not afraid of what will happen?"

"She deserved to see her family as she walked."

"What about you?"

"I believe in something far greater in the unknown." As she placed her hand on Davey's head, the first words of another chorus plucked his ears, a melody much stronger than the mermaid from Arthur's island.

He couldn't place it: a violin, a harp, maybe even a piano, mixed with the most pleasant voices he'd heard. It had to be her again. It had to be the mermaid's ballad.

"Do you hear that?" he asked, searching the ocean where he noticed the rounded silhouette of another island, this one taken by darkness save a miniature fire aflame in what appeared to be a cove.

"What?"

"That noise."

"You hear her again?"

"No. This is different."

"What is that?" Kraken called opposite the deck.

"I hear it. It's…beautiful," Arthur said, whose constant drone of a sharpening stone against blade stopped.

"Sounds like singing, Whatever it is, it's…magical." Kraken scampered across the deck. "It's coming from over there. Right there. I think…I think they're calling for us. Maybe it's Gwen."

"Gwen?" Galendra asked.

"Maybe they would know the way to Finfolk." Arthur joined Kraken.

As the melody continued, Davey picked out three distinct voices – all females, all pouring honey into his ears. In an instant, he felt his will give way, break to their suggestion. Then he heard her voice: his mother's voice.

"I'll be. It has to be her. I say we go," Kraken hopped up on the second railing.

"Go? Now? We…no," Galendra stopped short. "Davey, stop them."

Davey's mind drifted as logic surrendered to emotion. First, there was the splash of Kraken's form entering the water, followed by Arthur as the two silhouettes disappeared into the Endless Ocean.

"I want to go…too," Davey stumbled forward. "We can direct the ship."

"We can't."

"Why?" His mind if a fog, tingling, prisoner to the women's voices, barely heard Galendra's words, but they were too late.

"The Sirens."

THE SIREN'S SONG

An ethereal chorus, one without a beginning and knowing no end, poured honey into his ears, lulling Davey McCrary closer to the edge of the vessel. Their voices beckoned him to join his companions – Kraken and Arthur – in the Endless Ocean, and swim towards the Sirens Isle where a bonfire reached towards the darkened heavens.

Davey wanted to serve the Sirens, to protect the fabled beauties from others who would cause them harm. Kraken and Arthur would certainly fail in their duties. They didn't deserve to wash the Siren's feet, let alone guard them from eager men who would claim them as a prize.

Just a couple more feet and he would feel the surge of the water bubble around. He would cast fate aside and swim through the overpowering current.

"Davey, no." The Siren's songs drowned out Galendra's pleas. It didn't matter. Davey would find a way to them – or so he thought.

The sudden blow to his neck caused him to spiral to the floor in a sea of artificial stars. His knees slammed against the wooden planks, sending a shockwave of pain up his hips.

In spite of the pain, they continued to call, their words stronger, hungrier for his presence. He had to get up. He had to meet them, to see their beautiful faces.

Maybe they looked like just Charlene Davis, the one wealthy girl in school who always had the nicest of clothes purchased from across the Bay. Maybe they were like one of those supermodels his dad fawned over on TV, the ones he wasn't allowed to watch.

"I'm not going to let you go," Galendra said.

"You need to let me," Davey groaned, trying to let his vision clear.

Davey planted his right leg in front of him and pushed up, only to be met with another blow to the back of his head, this time stronger, more forceful, sending his world spinning back to the deck.

"What are you doing?" Davey held his throbbing elbow and pushed his face off the grim-riddled floor. Nothing would stop him. Galendra was jealous, Davey thought, jealous of him wanting to be with the Sirens.

"Saving you from your self."

"They won't treat them like I will." As Davey rolled to his back, he saw a different figure straddle him, one blanketed with a brilliant blue light.

"They're taking your mind, but we won't play the game."

Before Davey could react, Galendra cupped her hands around his face, spreading warmness over his scalp. The Siren's words faded, replaced by a numbness making his eyelids heavy, sending him to slumber.

II.

"What...what?" Davey's eyes bolted open, waking from his dreamless sleep. Silence doused the ship deck, save the waves crashing in the distance, spitting up and raining down on the rocks of Sirens' Isle. They didn't go far, but how long was he out?

"Where are they?" Davey tripped while attempting to stand, burdened with a heavy rope fastened around feet tight enough to chaff his ankles.

"The more you struggle, the harder it will hurt," Galendra said absent sympathy. She stood alongside the railing, apparently keeping watch on Sirens' Isle.

"Why did you do this?" Davey struggled with the rope, only to find them constricting as if it had a mind of its own, cutting off circulation to his fingers and toes.

"To keep you grounded."

"But I have to go. They're calling me."

"Are they?"

"Yes...they are. Aren't they?"

Again, silence.

"What do you hear?"

"I don't...don't hear anything. They're gone."

"Then it's working, and I've played my part in this." Galendra looked up to the moon.

"What...what do you mean it's working? What's working? How come I don't her them?" With each second, he felt less captivated with the idea of jumping overboard and swimming to shore. What type of maddened idea was that anyway?

"Magic." Her clear blue eyes focused on him.

"Magic?" Davey stopped struggling as the Sirens' pull faded. His bindings loosened until they slipped from his hands, but he didn't jump up.

"It exists here, but the closer we get to the mainland, the weaker I become. It is magic that prevented you from heading their call."

"I suppose." Davey's muscles tightened as he stood, looking over the boat known as The Mermaid's Tide.

"They weren't so lucky."

"Who?"

"Kraken and our new friend. I fear for their safety."

"Can you see them?" Davey joined her at the edge of the boat, looking across two hundred or so yards of black waters towards the island. The bonfire still burned, and as he squinted, he could make out three figures standing around the fire's circumference, unwavering in their movements, but menacing by their presence.

"No, they are lost to me. And I am...unable to take to the waters anymore."

"I forgot. It's because you gave..."

"Yes." She looked down, the sacrifice of her sealskin forbidding her from ever entering the water again.

"Then I can go. They're there because of me."

"They're not. They made a choice to join us."

"Then what do we do? We can't just leave them here."

"Then what would you have? Rescue?"

"Wait, what?" He backed away, surprised at the open-ended question. Could she really have faith in him to rescue Arthur and Kraken?

"I asked if you could make it. If you think you can, then we will go."

"Well," Davey thought back to the memories of his trials with the Schoolyard Four. He could either abandon Kraken and Arthur or face his fears: the unknown of what waited for him on Sirens' Isle. There was only one choice to be had. "We'll take the rowboat."

"I was hoping you'd say that." A wry grin spread across her lips. "Let's face the danger together."

III.

Davey's shoulders burned with every stroke, struggling against the whitecaps which grew in height the closer they rowed to shore. An outcropping of rocks abutting proved his savior, allowing them to disembark and for Davey to catch his breath.

Latching onto a patch of slick grass, he pulled himself forward. Jagged rocks poked and prodded his ribs until he felt the welcome touch of sand.

He curled into a fetal position from exhaustion, coughing up mouthfuls of water. They somehow made it. The short journey from The Mermaid's Tide to Sirens' Isle was as tumultuous as any, even worse than being stuck in the middle of a summer storm on the Chesapeake Bay.

How am I going to make it? Davey thought, looking back at the Endless Ocean. The Mermaid's Tide seemed distant – a miniature ship stuck in a bottle.

"Are you ok?" Galendra asked, appearing unscathed next to him.

"I think…I think I am," he answered, unsure of his words as his diaphragm tightened again, expelling more water from his mouth.

"Can you hear them?"

"Who?" Davey pushed himself up in spite of his trembling shoulders.

"Them." She nodded towards the bonfire lighting up the midnight sky.

"I don't know. Water in my ears." Davey struggled up, his feet wobbling until he righted himself.

He looked over the untamed field of bay grass that bowed with the constant ocean breeze. Fireflies of ash spiraled up from the bonfire, towards the shifting gray and purple clouds. He couldn't see the Sirens, but he knew they were there. And if they were, he would have to fight, which meant he needed something to fight with.

Davey reached for his grandfather's sword, at first discovering an empty scabbard only to find relief as his fingers curled around the sword's pommel, a cruel trick played by an wearied mind.

"My magic should hold, but I'm not sure long. This is their land. Not mine."

"Then we should hurry." The knot of doubt in his stomach tightened.

"But know if my magic fails and you are able to hear their words again—"

"Doesn't matter. I can't go any further without Kraken and Arthur."

"Stay below the grass. Know their song might resurface again."

"I'll take the chance. We have to. It's only right." He would be lying to himself if a part of him begged him to turn the other way and row back to The Tide.

Davey followed Galendra's suggestion, kneeling below the vegetation's height. The muffled sound of bay grass crunched underneath with each deliberate footstep. Three football fields became two, and two football became one, until they reached the outskirts of the clearing where he spotted one of the Sirens.

The lone Siren remained silent, clad in a black robe with hair reaching below shoulder height. Her green eyes, as green as any emerald, captured the bonfire's hypnotic dance.

Davey noticed another figure, but it wasn't a Siren. He wiped his eyes for a better view and observed that the figure remained fastened to the makings of a stake or small tree. The unknown's is chin drooped to his chest as lifeless as a ragdoll.

"Arthur?" He pointed to signal Galendra. "It's him."

He massaged his sword and closed his eyes, thinking about his grandfather, his mother. Arthur saved him from the Formians, and unlike Gregor, Davey would repay the favor. With the Siren mesmerized by some unseen force, he needed to move.

"Hold on," Galendra tugged at his shorts. "All is not as it seems."

"Why?" Davey frowned. "There's only one of them. He's right there."

"What about Kraken?"

"I don't see him, but Arthur's there." His whispers grew louder and faster with each word as adrenaline pumped through his body.

"Control your emotions. It won't do us any good rushing in headfirst. We need to be careful and not wake her." Galendra shook her head once in the negative.

"Will your magic protect me?"

"As I said, best it can be. No guarantees."

"Ok, then I'll be careful. We need to do this." Davey focused his attention back to the Siren. He didn't know how, but he felt confidence about his plan. Maybe it was because of sword lesson, or maybe it was the need to repay the favor to Arthur, but the Siren appeared preoccupied and Davey already survived Malent. "Maybe we can sneak around, untie Arthur before she notices."

"What if he doesn't wake?"

"He'll wake." Davey formulated the plan much in the same hastened way he did when playing in the backyard with his friends.

"Then what?"

"We find out where Kraken is."

"And what if he doesn't know?"

"Then I don't. I don't know. Was always told to be like Babe Ruth, to swing for the fences." He repeated his grandfather's oft-used words of wisdom. "If you don't swing, then you strike out."

"I don't know this Babe Ruth that you speak of, but I would trust he is a man of great wisdom."

"He played baseball."

"Baseball?"

"Yeah, just a game. Hit a ball with a stick. Was never good at it. Anyway, we should move."

"Ok."

"Then we go." Davey swallowed his doubt, watching as the Siren's midnight hair flowed in the persistent ocean breeze. She appeared like a sleeping bird: upright and swaying to some unknown harmony.

There was no use in waiting, With a fresh lungful of oxygen, his body caked in sweat and sand, Davey stepped forward.

He made sure to keep below the bay grass, using it as camouflage, his attention volleying between the transfixed Siren and Arthur. No matter how slowly he moved, there was a snap of a blade or a footstep too loud. With each mishap, Davey held his breath, waiting for the Siren to wake. But the Siren remained quiet as he entered the clearing.

The warmth from the fire, its logs cracking and snapping, casting more fireflies of ash to the sky, captured him. He saw how the fire's hypnotic beauty mesmerized the Siren. It was as if some unseen force spoke from its core and commanded her movements.

Counting one, then two, then three in his head, Davey crept up behind the wooden stake holding Arthur. With a simple cut from his blade, Arthur's seaweed bindings slipped off, exposing chaffed and blistered wrists.

"Arthur," Davey whispered, keeping an eye on the Siren. Arthur remained silent. "Arthur."

"We need to go," Galendra said with the bite of urgency.

"I'm trying."

A laughter like no other – vile and corrupt – echoed around him.

Davey slipped to the ground, his eyes growing wide as he looked over at the now aware Siren.

Arthur staggered towards the Siren, his movements as rigid as the board that once bound him, his arms locked by his side, pale skin with eyes devoid of emotion. He was the one laughing.

"He's lost," Galendra said, pulling on Davey's shirt.

"He can't be."

"Very well done, my love." The Siren turned and reached her arm around the spellbound Arthur.

The blaze captured her flawless skin, the orange hue highlighting her ethereal nature, a specter like his father's manifestation. Then her words, a mystical tune with a diabolical composer, followed.

She could've been a member of a church choir, an angelic voice matched by her magnificence. She sang the same words that transfixed Davey when he was on The Mermaid's Tide.

Davey looked deep into the emerald void behind her lying eyes. They beckoned him forward, tempting him to cross the line. He was at once lost, wanting to feel her comforting embrace, one his mom could only provide.

"Do not let her take you," Galendra pulled again, this time snapping Davey from his semi-hypnotic state.

"Wha...what?" Davey shook his head clear. He remembered her tune, the way he lost himself. "No," he said, regaining his senses. In an act of defiance, Davey raised sword, its blade trembling slightly.

"Oh, a strong one?" The Siren smiled in a way Davey imagined Ray Bradbury's Mr. Dark would. "I would be a fool if I didn't offer you the same end as Arthur."

"Let him go." Davey fought against her will, blinking several times in an effort to snap himself from her pull. He couldn't give in, not now, not with his companion's lives on the line.

"Pity. Why would do that to me, young man? Would you really want to cause me harm?"

"Let him go from whatever you've done."

"Do you really want to leave?" She smiled, revealing a perfect row of ivory teeth more suitable for a vampire bat. "Is the bottom feeder...convincing you that you should go against my word?"

Her presence played on Davey's senses, like massaging his back after a day spent out in the sun raking the yard or shoveling mulch.

"Your days are numbered, witch," Galendra demanded.

"A scorned woman knows not when to surrender." The Siren rolled her head to the right, her expression still empty of emotion. "I feel it in you. Yes I do. Such is the pain of a woman whose lover has rejected her."

"Quiet."

"Why should I be quiet? I'm merely trying to help. But it seems I cannot join you in your pain, for I have never shared your rejection. Men find me irresistible. They seem...smitten by a certain talent." She tapped her fingers on Arthur's shoulder.

"Don't speak to me as if you know me."

"I don't you. I just revel in your pain, your sadness. It must be such a burden to carry the guilt of tearing a family apart, an abandoned mistress left to the waters of the Endless Ocean." The Siren's lips curled from ear to ear.

"Pity," another voice matching the Siren's sung with a gust of wind. Two more slender figures manifested behind the bonfire, the light capturing their wanton forms. The Sirens were twins, triplets to be exact, all sharing the same wicked energy, a forbidden apple not to be eaten

"Truly a shame she would cause such a crime," one of the other Sirens answered.

"She should not be allowed to leave this place in the Keeper's company. She would misguide him, to use him. For it is his light, not hers, that should show him the path." They spoke in unison, a spellbinding chorale making Davey's knees weak, prompting him to relax his grip on his sword.

"You know nothing of my pain, you harpies," Galendra said, her voice cracking. "We need to go."

"What?" Davey moaned, his thoughts broken into snippets of an unedited movie. "What do I do?"

"We need to go. Please," Galendra's voice cracked.

"We should put the adulteress out of her misery. She should be pardoned from such a broken state." Each of their words weaved an entrancing melody. "My dear brave knight, maybe you should prove your worth, your last duty to our cause. Find the seal-woman to the bottom of the Endless Ocean, and you will be rewarded...properly."

"My...ladies," Arthur answered with a robotic tone. He staggered forward, his steps slow and deliberate, his arms reaching up to attack.

"I won't leave you here." Galendra remained defiant. "You will find out what power I possess."

"Your sorcery holds no power here. How else could the Keeper fall to our words?" The Sirens smiled at once, each one mirroring the other, an unbroken chain of movements.

"We'll get the boat. We'll get others." Galendra hugged Davey, pulling with more force. He knew he should leave, but he couldn't. Their deceitful gaze captured him. He was nothing more than a prisoner to their will.

"He is ours. Not yours."

"No."

Galendra pried Davey's sword from his hand and raced towards the Sirens. Before Galendra could attack, Arthur seized the Selkie by the hair and pulled back, releasing the sword. Her head whipped against the ground, her body contorting to an unnatural position as she rolled over with a whimper. Arthur was upon her, straddling her while applying all his weight.

The entire display snapped Davey from his stupor, causing him to remember the most terrible night of his life. Flashbacks to his parents, the one night his father threw his mother to the ground during his drunken madness. Davey remembered running up the stairs to his mother's pleas of telling him to run. He was too afraid to intervene after suffering his father's wrath. Davey shouted for his father to stop, but it fell on deaf ears, his father possessed by something unexplainable.

It only lasted a minute, but to Davey it felt like an hour, watching as his mother slipped into unconsciousness. The next morning would be her last. Davey woke up to feel his mother's hands stroking his hair, her fingernails massaging his scalp. She looked down with a swollen lip, a purple circle under her right eye, but she was still beautiful. There wasn't even a hint that she would take her life later that evening. Maybe he should've known. Maybe he should've been proactive.

As the hypnotized Arthur raised his arm to attack Galendra, Davey remembered. He needed to stop it all.

"Please," Galendra's broken words matched those of his mother begging his father to stop.

"No." Fueled by remorse for failing to protect his mother, Davey rolled forward, picked up his sword, and slashed at Arthur. The sword bit deep into the knight's arm, causing him to recoil long enough for Galendra to escape. "Get up." Davey pulled up Galendra.

"Run," Galendra said. "We need to run."

"Not a wise move. We were going to offer you his kingdom in exchange for your light." Their words plucked his lobes, but he resisted, closing his eyes and remembering their crime.

"Davey," another called, this time it was Arthur. "What...where am I?"

"He's up," Davey said through the chaotic scene.

"Summon him. Summon him. Summon him," the Sirens repeated in unison, their words hitting a crescendo when the pop of a wave slammed against the rocks. Sea form bubbled up onto the cove, raining down on them.

Then Davey saw them – two monolithic shadows towering above them in the shadows. Two become three, then four, each one independently moving from each other, spreading as far as the cove was wide.

Davey remembered the tentacles from before. It had to be him, and if it was, Kraken fell to their whim.

"What happened?" Arthur rushed over to join the two, clutching his arm. Galendra backed away, her battered face already taken to swell from Arthur's actions. Regret took Arthur's defeated eyes in streams of tears.

"Kraken," Galendra said, raising her arms and closing her eyes, chanting something in an unknown language. "He's under their spell."

"My lady, I must apologize," Arthur said. Galendra ignored him, continuing her chant.

"We don't have time," Davey said. He didn't want to abandon Kraken, but he saw no choice.

"You have plenty of time, our love. And you will fetch a prize more worthy than the Dark Guardian could provide," the Sirens said. "Bring it to its watery grave."

With the rush of water and a deafening crack, Kraken's monstrous form disappeared below the surface, silencing the area, save the back and forth chanting.

"I can't. They've got too much control." Galendra slumped back into Arthur's awaiting arms.

"I didn't mean to," Arthur said.

"Don't blame yourself," Davey said. "Need to focus now on how we get Kraken back."

"You won't," the Sirens cackled together, levitating into the air.

The pop of wood echoed through the sky, drawing Davey's attention upward and out towards the Endless Ocean where The Mermaid's Tide remained anchored. In a matter of seconds, four tentacles extended up from the black waters and surrounded the boat before crashing down over its hull and wrapping around its mass.

"No," Davey shouted, watching as one of the masts tumbled to the ocean. Another crack followed, and then another, until The Mermaid's Tide splintered in two. With one final pull, The Mermaid's Tide surrendered to Kraken's onslaught, allowing the Endless Ocean to overtake it and bring it to the unseen floor.

"We're...trapped." Hope escaped Davey in a desperate breath. They were captives on the Siren's Isle, and with no other vessel, they would have to fight to survive.

"Stay with me now," Arthur said. "There is always a way."

"Is there? She needs help." Davey cupped her head in his arms around Galendra an attempt provide the same comfort she provided him. Her eyes rolled back as she let out a sigh.

"All the more reason to fight...to make things right." Arthur's repentant, yet defiant gaze lingered. "I...must make things right."

"Bring him to us. Fetch the others. Take them to the bottom," the Sirens commanded, levitating higher into the sky, their forms igniting with the bonfire's flames reaching around their legs. Their song captured the approaching storm's essence, the weather a slave to its master.

The ocean swelled around the cove then burst, giving birth to Kraken's monstrous form once again. The tentacles twisted, joined by a dire caw from the Sirens.

Davey fixated on the impossible spectacle of the three sirens and the fabled Kraken. Never in a million years would he think himself in such a position, but he was, and he had no choice but to survive. There was no option to cower.

"We need to fight." The hilt slipped in Davey's hand where a nervous sweat stung his palm. "That's the only way."

"And I'll stand by your side," Arthur said.

"Summon the light. You are the Keeper, are you not?" Galendra choked out the words through blistered lips, fading in and out of consciousness.

"I am." Davey remembered his confrontation with his father, the way the lighthouse's light came upon him, but how? "And I'll try."

If there was ever a time in his life where he thought himself backed against the wall, this was it; even when the Schoolyard Four flushed his head in a toilet or made him eat the grimy soap in the bathroom, he never feared for his life. Not once. This, however, was different. He was responsible for others, those who followed him, and those unseen.

"Kraken," Davey shouted, hoping beyond hope he could break the Siren's spell. "Kraken, listen to me. This isn't you."

"It will not be. It will not come to pass." The Sirens raised their arms then swung them down. Kraken's tentacles mimicked their command, whipping down on the beach cove. The ground shuddered from the impact, sending Davey sprawling to the ground and his sword clattering to the side. The Sirens cackled between their terrible chorus.

"We will fight," Galendra groaned. Davey tilted his head to see her spit out a wad of grass then float to her feet. Galendra chanted once more, this time more forceful, taken by confidence.

The air shimmered in front of her like that of a frozen windowpane in the throws of winter. With a push of her arms, the wraithlike sheet flew forward, tearing across the clearing.

The Sirens were helpless to avoid the spell. Galendra's shield slammed into the three, shattering into a million pieces of frost, capturing the three in a web. They shrieked as loud as any bird Davey heard along the Chesapeake.

Gone were their melodies, the wretched song, replaced by the vile nature of their true selves.

"Why didn't you do that before?" Arthur asked, but his words would betray him. Kraken's tentacle swung down once more, curling around a preoccupied Galendra and pulling back. Before Davey or Arthur could react, Kraken's appendage recoiled and took with it the Selkie known as Galendra.

"No," Davey stumbled forward, but it was too late. Galendra disappeared into the midnight horizon, a victim to the depths of the ocean.

"Dear God," Arthur said.

The Sirens shrieked again, the harpy's call causing Davey to double over and gag. His vision swirled, his footing collapsed to the ground, but he held fast to his grandfather's sword.

"She would not make a fool of us. She would not take what is rightfully ours," they cried, their shadows growing large in the bonfires light, reaching up like the bell towers of a gothic cathedral.

Davey didn't have time to be afraid. With his ship gone and Galendra taken, there was no other choice. He closed his eyes, but unlike his past, he opened them and squeezed the sword's hilt tight enough to cut off blood to his hands.

"Harpies, I would send you to the abyss," Arthur yelled in the background. The knight rushed forward, his fortitude unquestioned.

"No," Davey swallowed through dry mouth, planting one foot then his left, fighting through the waves of nausea and vertigo. He kept focused, turning around to see the three Sirens nearly doubled in height, their visage hiding behind locks of black hair stretching down to their feet where Arthur choked and rolled to his stomach.

Davey ran, fighting through the confusion of a swirling world. The Sirens did not move. They didn't have to.

The smell of lilies permeated Davey's nostrils, his senses overcome with their presence, causing him to enter oblivion once again.

IV.

"Where is the light? We need the light. Would he tell us?" The Sirens bickering woke Davey, his neck barely able to support the weight of his head. His tried to see where he was, but his vision was distorted by a dank foulness, a shroud of nothingness, save the rhythmic pluck of trickling water.

He remembered the fight, charging towards the Sirens with his sword held high. He remembered watching Kraken pull Galendra to the depths, her act of bravery ending as a sacrifice for their cause.

As he regained his senses, Davey attempted to step forward, only to find his legs and arms bound together and fastened to something unseen. Misfortune had found him once again.

"Davey, is that you?"

"Arthur?" Davey asked, his attention pull towards the voice to his right. "I can't see."

"Neither can I," Arthur whispered.

"Where are…we?"

"I don't know. Must be close to them because I can hear them. A cave perhaps?"

A cave? It made sense. He remembered seeing an opening to the far right of the cove when they were fighting the Sirens.

"Galendra?" he asked.

"I don't know." Davey imagined Arthur shaking his head in the negative. "This is my fault. I should've been true to my faith. They broke me…like I've been broken before."

"What do you mean?"

"Nothing of importance right now. One I will rectify in the future. But for my part, I am sorry."

"It wasn't…your fault. They had you. Had Kraken. Had me, too."

"But she's gone because of me. My penance will be a harsh when we escape. I would've never touched a woman in such a way."

"I believe you." Davey tried to rip his hands free to no avail.

"I will never stop asking for your forgiveness. I let you down as a mentor." His voice echoed with each word. "But we must focus on escaping this place."

"Were you awake when they took us?"

"I remember few things since their song…entranced me. Very few things."

"Me too."

"Why do they hold us captive? The Sirens should've ended us."

"Listen to them. They're repeating something about the light."

"If it's your light they speak of, it wouldn't make sense. It serves to end dark creatures and open the gateway to your world. It makes no sense for them to possess it."

"So how do we to escape?"

"Patience," Arthur said. "Even in my darkest of hours, I held to patience, and patience guided me right."

"Bring us the light," their words reverberated once again gain, emanating from a pinprick of light at the cavern's entrance.

"We can do it. We can form a plan," Davey said.

"I wouldn't try, gents," a familiar, but unwelcome voice broke the Sirens' song.

"Kraken," Davey said, balling his hands into fists, ready to lash out if given the opportunity.

"Traitorous fool." Arthur seized.

"Such harsh words. Would think you would be wiser after what happened." Kraken toyed with them.

"What did happen?" Arthur demanded, the struggle in his voice not lost upon Davey.

"Wouldn't you like to know?" Though Kraken hid within the shadows, Davey saw his silhouette bounce back and forth.

"Whatever they've done to you, you need to forget. You need to help us," Davey pleaded, hoping the other Kraken he knew still existed.

"And why would I go on and do that?" Kraken's figure skipped to the next rock.

"Because, this isn't you. You took Galendra."

"She meant nothing to us, a mother to weak to protect her flock." Kraken's harsh words betrayed his true self, one viler than Davey remembered. Maybe he was a traitor all along.

"You're under their spell," Arthur said.

"A spell?" Kraken laughed. "How about a promise?"

"What sort of promise?" Davey asked, focusing past the darkened form, listening to the lulls and notes of the Sirens as they took to song.

"To reunite me with my parents. To promise me their love I never received."

"That's...that's not going to happen. You should know better," Davey wrenched his right hand, peeling skin from wrist. "They're gone. You told me."

"No, I don't think so. You're jealous because of the way your parents treated you." Kraken's rebuttal punched Davey in the heart. "My parents want me back. I've been assured."

"And what are you to do in return for this...promise," Arthur's tone grew angry.

"Simple." Kraken's eyes flashed green, highlighting his diabolical glare. "I am to retrieve something that belongs to them."

"And what is that?" Davey said.

"Oh, Davey. There was always something about you I hated, that innocence, the way Gwen spoke of you. The way you were so important and I was nothing." Each word served as a stake, driving deeper into Davey's will to continue.

"You will never see the light," Arthur said.

"And you are to rot, to be a slave to the Sirens as they claim their dominion over this land and the next." Kraken hissed between words.

"Witches. Foul witches," Arthur yelled as the sound of rope scratching against stake betrayed his fruitless attempt at escape.

"Careful, wouldn't want to hurt yourself." Kraken's cackle echoed in the cave. "Tire yourself out. You might drown."

"You will be a slave to them."

"Much more. Much, much more." Kraken cackled again with all the delight of a madman. "But first, I need to claim their prize before the tide rises again, and you are forever buried at sea."

"No," Davey said. "I'll never, not like my grandfather—"

"Was a coward."

"He wasn't."

"Why do you think he never ended the Dark Guardian?"

"It wasn't time."

"Wrong again. It was because he was afraid of crossing the Siren's path. That's why. You think we would've had these issues if your grandfather found bravery? When given the opportunity, he slinked away just like every pathetic human."

"He fought in the war."

"Keep on listening to those fairy tales of yours. Keep thinking he's some type of hero. He's not, just as spineless as you, if not more."

"Don't listen to him," Arthur said. "His mind isn't right."

"As if your mind hasn't been right in the past, dear knight. It poisons us all. Just like Davey's grandfather knew pride, you knew lust, having sentenced your wife to die because of an affair. Or should we ask your best friend?" Kraken harsh words fiddled a sordid ballad like Pan.

"Enough," Arthur snapped back. "You know nothing."

"Yes, that's what we want to see now. We want to see that anger. Let it consume you once more."

Arthur struggled through his grunts, the crack of the stake and a whimper. Davey couldn't afford to lose Arthur again, his only crutch in a time of crisis. And like the dream of his father earlier in the day, the slow trickle of water grew steadier, its cold bit nipping at his exposed feet. It appeared high tide had discovered the cove.

"Don't do it," Davey said, again back to struggling with his bindings.

"He says don't do it?" Kraken laughed, pulling close enough for Davey to smell the foulness of rotten fish in his breath. "Look at you. Do you really think you have a chance?"

"Better than you." Davey defied him.

"Better than me?" Kraken harrumphed. "Keep on believing that happy ending kind of stuff, mate. Because you ask me, I don't see how you get out of this situation."

"Easy," a voice called that Davey hadn't heard since they landed on Malent's Island. It's whimsical nature warmed the natural coolness of the cave, allowing Davey to relax his grip on his bindings.

"Who?" Kraken couldn't finish his sentence before something dull and solid shattered. A groan followed, as Davey watched Kraken's silhouette collapse to the bed of rocks with a thud.

"We need to go," the still unseen Gwen said.

"Gwen?" Davey answered.

"Who is this?" Arthur said.

"A friend," Gwen said. "One you should listen to." Though he still couldn't see her, Davey felt her tepid body heat brush against the side, followed by the prodding of fingers against his wrist as she wrestled with his bindings.

"A friend she says. I've been told that many of times," Arthur answered.

"She's a friend. We can trust her," Davey said, though unsure of the truth behind his words.

"Are we sure it's not another trick? Perhaps a deception on the Sirens part?"

"Neither of you have much choice, especially you, Pendragon. You have nothing they want. It leaves you with only two choices. You either stay down here with the beast, who will most certainly wake up with a bad attitude and an even worse headache, or you trust me to get you out of here."

"She does bring up an excellent point. Can't say there's much wrong with her wisdom," Arthur said.

"Now that we have that settled, let's get out of here." No sooner did she speak when an eruption of sea foam crashed against the cave's entrance and surged over the rocks. Ocean water flowed down to Davey's feet, the force of the rush snapping his spine against the stake.

"Give us the light. Give us the light." Their chants surfaced again, accompanying the strengthening waters.

"Stay with me," Gwen whispered

Cold water nipped at his hips, then rushed up to his chest, causing his lungs to seize.

"I must insist your hurry." Arthur's words trembled.

"You need to hold onto once I let go. The undertow will take you, and I don't know where it goes," Gwen said.

"I'll hold on." Water sloshed up to Davey's chin, causing most of his body to go numb. He dug what was left of his chewed off fingernails into the stake, reciting a prayer his mother once taught him.

A burst of water rushed into his ears, drowning out the world around him in a chilling wave. With a last gasp of oxygen, darkness followed, the same darkness he remembered after diving off the lighthouse. He survived too many dangers before, how could he survive again?

"You're with me. Always." Her words came upon him like a swift sunrise, basking him in courage, sweeping away the worry. Though he did not see her, he felt the tug around his waist, pulling him free of the stake and against the torrent of the undertow.

He felt himself rocket through the water, faster than he could ever swim on his own.

"Stay with me. Stay with us all."

The current grew stronger, pulling him harder, nearly ripping his t-shirt off as they fought through its power.

His lungs burned, searching for air. His throat expanded. He needed to breath, his adrenaline burning too much oxygen. With every stroke, with every kick of his feet, his world faded.

A dull roar.

A pop of his ears.

He couldn't hold it.

Suddenly, the riptide subsided. Moonbeams cascaded down through the ocean in an orchestra of light. Rage surrendered to serenity. Clear water – as clear as Davey had ever seen – reached out as far and as deep as infinity.

There was no anger. No hatred. Not even a sense of fear about it all, just peacefulness he'd yearned for since she left him.

"Do not surrender to it again. You are brave. You will succeed. It is time to grow into the man you are."

"Mom?" He asked as water filled his lungs. He didn't choke, not even convulse. "I can breath."

"Come with me," Gwen appeared from around his right shoulder.

"Where is everyone else?" He asked.

"You'll see. Now follow," she answered, smiling back at him. The two were off, swimming through the water, heading to the roundness of shoreline.

He reached out, fingers touching the porous surface of rock and immediately pulled up, once again fighting through his fatigued muscles. He held onto his mother's words, breaching the water's surface and meeting the orange glow of the bonfire again.

He was back, back in the Sirens' Cove.

"Why did you bring me back?" Davey looked back to see only the tide lap against the shore. Gwen was gone.

He had half a mind to jump back in, and as he prepared to perform such an act, he stopped. Fear moved him, not courage, and it was courage his mother wanted him to have, courage in the face of madness.

"I can't," he whispered, his frosted breath forming dragons in front of his nose. "I won't."

The crackling of fire brought him back to face the Sirens' Cove, its warmness wiping away his gooseflesh.

There was no sign of the Sirens, only the flames reaching up where the same three moons hovered high above. A distant howl followed by the fire crackling was the only life the cove held.

Davey staggered forward, his legs burning, struggling through the deep sand and collapsed to all fours.

"Where is everyone?" He asked, followed by emptying his lungs of water in three heaves, creating a small river in front of him. Even at his sickest point with chicken pox, he didn't throw up as much. "How did I do that?"

"Davey?" Arthur groaned, his footfalls heavy and kicking up sand. He collapsed as well, his chain armor clanging even louder in the silence.

"Yeah?" Davey spit out again.

"We made it. Somehow." Arthur rocked back on his heels and gasped.

"We did. But we lost…them." Davey looked back at the three trails of moonlight stretching across horizon. Whatever the fate they met, he shared. "Gwen. Kraken. Galendra. Gone."

"Who was that? The one who rescued us?"

"A friend…of sorts. Thought she was gone." Davey's throat tightened as his lungs filling with oxygen, but unlike any breath before, he could detect the smell of oxygen and the unique scents it carried, one being the strong sense of floral. He immediately darted up. "They're here."

"Who?"

"The creatures return to us," the Sirens' deceitful voices sang out, the bonfire subsiding to a low flicker of dying flame, exposing the three witches. "The beast failed in his task, one we should end ourselves."

"Never," Arthur charged forward.

"Arthur," Davey shouted.

"You'll need this." Her voice came from the sky.

The patch of bay grass next to Davey exploded into a cloud of sand and tattered vegetation. In the middle of the burst, his grandfather's sword stood tall among the debris and as brilliant as ever. It returned to him.

"Back to hell with you," Arthur shouted from opposite the dying flames.

Davey withdrew his sword, watching as Arthur plucked another sword from the ground and swiped at the first of the Sirens.

The Sirens cloak swirled as she screamed, her form flailing to the ground. But unlike fairy tales blessed with happy endings, her sister Sirens sang out in a melon-collie chorus. Arthur grabbed his ears just as fast, falling back to his knees.

"Arthur." Davey charged forward, sword high and with purpose. He leapt over the fire, its hot coals lost on him below.

He would show his strength. He would defeat fear.

Davey's fast blade sliced through the Siren's bat-like cloak, exposing pasted flesh. For once he would be a hero of sorts, finding retribution for Galendra and the others. It felt as if the blade itself had a mind of its own, filling Davey with renewed purpose, with an unmatched skill measured against the finest of swordsmen in his imagination.

Davey swiped again as the Siren reeled back, her cries of mercy muted in his fervor.

His vision turned from blue tones then to red. Her face – a former visage of beauty – warped to one of horror, exposing fangs longing to taste the suffering of an innocent. But there would be no others, not anymore.

"Stop it. Stop it at once," the other two sang out, their lyrical chains attempting to seize Davey.

His arms went heavy like stone. He could barely fill his lungs with air.

"Seize him. Seize him now."

Air shifted around Davey as the cove bulged with three tentacles once again, each one extending high into the air.

"Please no," Davey collapsed to one knee propping his elbow up on the sword, his energy spent. Kraken survived, and he would want retribution.

"Stay with me." Arthur crawled next to Davey. "Remember what I say. We do this together."

"Seize him if he will not give us the light," they sang. "We shall pry it out of him. Have it for ourselves."

"Are you prepared?" Arthur looked down at him. His unwavering resolve even in the face of their demise prompted Davey to study his sword. This would be it. This would be his end. He would make his grandfather proud.

"Yes, I'm ready," Davey repeated, readjusting his grip, feeling every crevice and carving within the hilt. Unlike before, there would be no retreat.

"Attack him, beast." The Siren's voices escalated to a flourish of cries as Kraken's tentacles reached higher and higher until Davey noticed a bulbous shape doused in shade surface, its form almost filling the cove.

"Kraken," Davey exhaled. "I don't want to do this."

"Follow me." Arthur nodded, a wry grin barely visible along his face.

"Yes, sir."

The two raised their swords as one in an act of defiance – two Davids against one Goliath.

"End this." The Sirens cackled, hyenas ready to feast upon a carcass. They threw their arms forward, prompting Kraken to swing his tentacles towards Arthur and Davey – or so Davey thought.

The first tentacle slapped one of the Sirens, her cry of surprise so powerful that it caused the smoldering flames to reignite.

The large tentacle, as big as any anaconda in the picture books, wrapped around the Siren then pulled back, catapulting the witch into the sky and over the Endless Ocean.

Her screams were heard during her unwelcome flight, until her body dwindled to that of a speck, then vanished. The other three tentacles retreated to the ocean just as fast, leaving Arthur, Davey, and the two Sirens alone.

"It appears righteousness knows his name," Arthur said.

"No. Impossible. We've been betrayed," the Sirens bemoaned. Their once contorted faces, eyes as big and as red as the Formians, revealed surprise. No longer did they seem invincible, rather more like kindergartners waiting for their bus to arrive.

"Betrayal? More like justice," Arthur said.

"You know nothing of betrayal. Nothing. We will end this," the Siren hissed.

"Then this shall be your end."

Arthur charged forward. The Sirens fell to their knees, holding their hands up in surrender. Their red eyes faded emerald, recapturing their former beauty.

"We relent. We ask for forgiveness. Please" Their tune changed just as fast.

"They say they would seek forgiveness." Arthur leveled his sword across the back of one of the Siren's necks, who in turn sniveled in regret. "What say you, Keeper?"

"They took Galendra. They took Kraken." Davey positioned himself next to the other Siren, mimicking Arthur's guard.

"The knight asks another of what to do. Perhaps a true chink in the armor." The two Sirens said, their lying tones summoning another stiff breeze.

"Enough of your sorcery. We won't fall for your honey twice." Arthur forced the Siren's head up with his blade. "Understand?"

"He says we won't cross him. Perhaps the brave knight would rekindle an old lust, a desire to quench his earthly yearning." The Siren grabbed the shoulders of her robe and pulled down, exposing just a hint of her pale skin. Unwavering in his poise, Arthur pressed his sword harder, causing the Siren to stop her act.

"You know not of what you speak of, witch. Memories not forgotten, but forgiven."

"So it would seem," the Siren sneered.

"Davey, are you ok?" Arthur asked.

"I'm…fine." Davey swallowed. The Siren Davey guarded smiled at his sign of nervousness, reaching out, her fingers crawling along the length of the sword like a spider. Davey looked deeper in the Siren's emerald glare, the reflection opening an endless cavern of visions complete with his mother and father hugging, a new home, and a little sister. His entire body grew weak from such impossible thoughts.

"I would have the two of you." Kraken's harsh words broke the daydream.

Kraken pushed Davey's Siren to the ground, causing her to relinquish her hypnotic grip on Davey's mind.

Having reverted to human form, Kraken's tattered clothes dripped with water, his hair slicked back, eyes taken by rage.

"Sing again and I'll rip that tongue out for you," he demanded. Unlike Arthur, Kraken was more forceful, pressing his foot into the Siren's ribcage.

"Kraken," Davey said, unsure of Kraken's intentions.

"We show no mercy to the demon spawn or their little songs. Have a better idea." Kraken ripped a piece of his shirt and fastened it around her mouth like a gag and pulling back. "I suggest you do the same, hero."

"Would rather my sword be in hand," Arthur said.

"You talk of a real weapon while theirs is forged by a sharp tongue. Or haven't you learned your lesson?"

"I've learned many lessons in my past. Showing restraint is one of them."

"Fine. If you won't do it, guess I will." Kraken didn't hesitate, manhandling the other Siren. Her eyes bulged as he tightened the gag around her head. "I've already had my fill of their tricks for the evening. As weak as they appear now, trust me, they're powerful."

"And how do we know this is not some sort of trick by you?" Arthur raised his sword, this time at Kraken's throat, narrowing his eyes on the boy-creature. "They don't swear allegiance to the Dark Guardian. What about you?"

"I would expect as much given what happened." Kraken let go of the bindings around the Siren's throat, who in turn clawed at it. He seemed lost for a moment, his lost stare lingering over the clearing then to the Endless Ocean. "I suggest you keep to silencing her. Who knows? They hypnotize me again, it might be you taking a trip across the ocean."

"There won't be a second time," Arthur said.

"Not now," Davey interrupted.

"Then he must explain his intentions." Arthur said. "How are we to know this isn't all a trap?"

"I don't remember much," Kraken sighed, displaying more hints of regret. "Wasn't even me. Whatever I did… was these two." He kicked the closest Siren, summoning another whimper.

"The brute shows his true self," Arthur added.

"You took Galendra," Davey said, biting his lips as soon as he spoke.

"I what?" Kraken's head snapped up. His eyes rolled to the right, then to his left as if his thoughts turned the page to the terrible ending of a story. "I remember," he whispered. "It wasn't me."

"A reason to silence the Sirens, right?" Davey wanted some reassurance. Maybe Arthur was right. Maybe Kraken was a monster deep down inside.

"I don't know." Kraken squatted and traced his fingers through the sand. "She was beautiful. Innocent, unlike myself."

One of the Siren's attempted to speak, but only muffled nonsense followed, words restricted by Kraken's bandage.

"She's gone. I took her," Kraken cracked. Unrestrained tears ran down his green-scale cheeks. He tried to stand, but staggered to his right knee, then to his left, sobbing uncontrollably. "I've gone back to who I was, the animal."

"You did no such thing." Gwen's voice ushered in her impromptu entrance.

"Gwen," Kraken bolted upright. "I'm sorry. I didn't know. I didn't know."

"Whatever foulness overcame you is not your fault." Gwen touched the back of Kraken's neck, her soft words acting as a sedative, causing Kraken's eyes to close halfway.

"So my savior makes her entrance." Arthur bowed his head.

"You knew about her? About Galendra?" Davey asked, not surprised by Gwen's sudden reemergence. It was part for the course with her.

"I've had much to deal with, but I've been watching." Gwen scuffed Kraken's hair, ignoring Davey's question. "I assumed you could take care of yourself. And I was right."

"Take care of myself? What's that supposed to mean?" Davey asked.

"I was called elsewhere. Abandoning you was never my intention." Gwen snatched the first Siren by the throat and lifted her up. Energy matching the brilliance of the three moons coursed through Gwen's fingers and down to the Siren's throat, illuminating the area with its power.

Spittle bubbled at the corners of the Siren's lips as a beam of light shot out of her mouth. Her body shook as her sister Siren watched with wide eyes and agape mouth.

Gwen released her grip, causing the energy to subside. The Siren collapsed to the ground in a listless heap.

"This should put an end to their charade." Gwen approached the last Siren, who attempted to crawl backwards, but Gwen was too quick, snapping the Siren by the throat and hoisting her up with the strength of a ten men. The Siren's legs dangled, helpless to Gwen's power.

There was something different about Gwen, a different demeanor Davey recognized in adults. Even Gwen's body appeared more mature, a little taller and filled out. Perhaps, there was something more to the mermaid.

"What are you doing?" Davey asked.

"She's making things right," Kraken said.

Gwen stared daggers into the harpy, removing the bindings that imprisoned her speech.

"You silence my sister. You took our voices," the Siren struggled to speak.

"No, you silenced your sisters, and I would silence you if you do not show us the way," Gwen said.

"And what way am I supposed to show?"

"Finfolkaheem." As soon Gwen spoke the words, the Siren's feet stopped moving. Her face went flaccid, her defeated gaze no longer poised and defiant.

"Why?"

"The Keeper would seek passage there, and I have yet discovered how to navigate to the Finfolk kingdom…until now. It makes sense."

"They would have me. They would have the three of us."

"Do we look concerned about the three of you?" Gwen released her grip. The Siren collapsed to the ground, but made no motion to escape as Arthur brandished his sword back at the Siren's throat.

"You cannot ask me to open the portal. They would see me burned."

"No worse of a punishment if you refuse our offer," Gwen answered, still unwavering in her demeanor.

"Your offer?"

"You open the portal, silence will not leave you. You reject our offer, you share your sister's fate."

"Why? Why would you risk traveling there?"

"Malent is a means to an end."

The Siren gasped, her expression changing from that of fear to understanding to awe.

"You…you are going to challenge him, aren't you? The Dark Guardian?"

"Yes, he is." Gwen smiled.

"We're very serious," Arthur added.

"Impossible. He is everything, everywhere since his arrival."

"Not yet." Gwen leaned over, extending her hand, which hummed with energy. "He is still weak, not strong enough to learn about your betrayal if you open that portal."

Gwen's fingers came within inches of the Siren's throat. The energy reflected in the Siren's lost gaze.

"Ok, ok I'll open it. But you need to promise me something."

"You ask me to promise me something when you took an innocent. There will be no promises, just bargains. Understand?" Gwen's fingers swirled with purple and white tones, reaching out for the Siren.

"I'll open the gateway," she stuttered, keeping fixed on the energy.

"Good."

"Up with you now." Arthur hoisted the Siren to her feet.

The Siren cleared her throat, looking back at her distressed sister.

"If he learns of this, we will burn either by Malent's hands…or the Dark Guardian's."

"It'll be too late when either of them learn," Gwen said.

"So be it." The Siren released the first octaves of a chorus. At first, nothing happened, only the words of the Siren's song – one different than before.

A flurry of nocturnal birds cawed along the skyline. The cave where Davey and Arthur almost met their watery grave shuddered along with the ground. With each verse, rocks broke free from the cavern opening. A surge of water rushed out into the black cove from the cavern.

"Impossible," Davey said, but it wasn't. Nothing was impossible after watching the Nether transform the world around him. The earth itself cracked as the cave's mouth widened to nearly triple its original size – big enough for a ship.

"And the Nether reveals and of her secrets," Arthur said.

"Trust in our purpose. We will succeed," Gwen said.

The Siren's chorus faded to the sound of the surf.

"It is done," The Siren said, collapsing back to the ground. "Now what is to become of me?"

"I regret I cannot allow you to sing another song." Gwen's hand once again captured the moon's power, swirling in hues of a rainbow.

"You dare silence me forever?" Siren looked up, panting, attempting to lift an arm. "We had a deal."

"Why should I let you retain your song when you've taken so many innocents, many of them my kin?" Gwen held her hand close to the Siren's throat.

The Siren struggled, her emerald eyes nearly clear as she confronted the end of her purpose.

"Because…because we were not always like this. We weren't."

"Speak up or the mermaid will take it from you," Arthur said with as cool of a demeanor as any of Davey's favorite action movie stars.

"We were left here, abandoned."

"By who?" Gwen didn't relent.

"The three of us were his ward, the Dark Guardian's ward."

"How?" Arthur asked.

"Long before other lands were settled, both in this world and the next, he came to us, a man clad in black with reddened skin. We were born to an Assyrian woman in the slave pits. He promised us riches and freedom. We were young. No other choice. We wanted to escape, to taste freedom."

"So the Dark Guardian saved you out of the kindness of his heart? Doubtful." Arthur joined Gwen in her skepticism.

"We would sing for the other slaves to calm them, and he heard us. He said we would be useful in his endeavor and offered to purchase our freedom. We did not realize our place in this grand bargain. He used us for wealth, for influencing the kings of kingdoms. We could...lure men to his bidding with our song. We saw terrible things, awful things that only men could create. When we refused to follow him any longer, he banished us to this island, one caught between the world and The Nether."

"So you decided to sing, to lure others?" Gwen asked.

"It was our...hatred. When we realized we would not age and were forever cursed to leave this island, we wanted others to share in our misery, particularly men who held sordid desires. Then when the Dark Guardian arrived, we struck a bargain with the Finfolk, who hated men as much as we did. We agreed to guard their kingdom in exchange for an opportunity. Malent would help us fight against the Dark Guardian."

"Hence you want the Keeper's light," Arthur said.

"Yes," the Siren said. "We would use it against him."

"There is no excuse to cause harm to innocents." Gwen pressed her hand to the Siren's throat, her face infused with light.

The Siren answered in a garbled mess.

"What'd she say?" Davey asked.

"Mercy," the Siren cried again as Gwen's light enveloped the Siren's throat.

"Wait." Davey grabbed Gwen's arm.

"What is it?"

"She said mercy. Shouldn't we...show mercy?" Davey looked to Arthur.

"Then what would you have me do?" Gwen asked. "I know her, her vengeance. She would rule the Nether as her own kingdom after we defeat the Dark Guardian."

"Not without my sisters," the Siren said. "Our magic is in each other's voices. Not alone."

"Then it would be a much harsher punishment if your sister is not able to join you in song," Davey said.

"The Keeper has a point," Arthur said.

"But they took advantage of me. They made me—" Kraken interrupted Arthur, scowling at the Siren. "You made me a monster."

"Enough," Arthur held Kraken back. "And it is not our choice, but the

Keeper's, and his alone. For it is his journey we follow."

"We're all vested in this. Not just the boy." Kraken's lips formed a thin line of disdain.

Davey looked at his three companions, each scorned in their own way during the journey, then back down at the Siren's pathetic form, the way her mouth trembled like a little child afraid of opening the closet. He couldn't help but see a reflection of the fear in himself.

"Let her sing." Davey swallowed.

"What?" Kraken shook his head, the corner of his mouth turned down in betrayal.

"I said let her sing. Her sister is gone. The other is helpless. She said it herself. Her magic is broken without their words."

"This isn't right. This isn't right at all." Kraken stormed off, uttering words lost to the wind.

"Kraken," Davey said.

"Relax. He's been through a lot." Arthur shook his head. "Perhaps we may still find her."

"Let us not retain false hope." Gwen sighed and released the Siren.

The Siren whimpered and rolled to her side, her attention shifting to the Endless Ocean's horizon, likely yearning to see her lost sister once more.

"Your retain her voice, but do not play games with the Keeper's mercy. Do you understand?" Arthur said.

"Yes," the Siren choked out. Her sister scampered up and cradled her. Both looked up at Davey, their hair a little less black, a tinge of blue – of rediscovered humanity – in their eyes.

"Do not make me regret this," Davey said, manufacturing strength. "It may not happen next time."

"We understand." The Siren said, both standing in unison. "Thank you for your forgiveness."

The other Siren bowed following her sister's words. They were not long for the world, the two giving one last glance at the horizon before retreating into the bay grass surrounding the cove.

"Why did you do that?" Arthur asked, sheathing his sword.

"Because." Davey attempted to watch their silhouettes escape to the unknown, but saw nothing. It was if they were apparitions and never real. "Because I want to believe in something good here. All I've seen is, you know, bad things."

"We should all be as strong as you." Arthur adjusted his chainmail then patted Davey's shoulder like a proud father. At least it was better than Kraken slapping his shoulder.

"A brave decision, but one I'm not surprised with." Gwen's smile relaxed Davey, who already questioned his decision. "For now, we can only pray Kraken forgives himself before he becomes a danger to us all, including himself."

"Are we to be worried?" Arthur asked. The three of them watched Kraken, who stood lost in his thoughts along the beach, tossing pebbles into the surf.

"Not yet at least."

"Why should we worry when we can't even sail to the kingdom?" Davey asked, realizing their dilemma: There was a gateway to the Finfolk kingdom, a fresh body of water to leading through a tunnel to use as a roadway, but no vessel to take them below.

"Not to worry." With the snap of Gwen's finger, Davey watched as the water within the cove surged upwards into three waters spouts. One by one, the spouts exposed wooden masts all too familiar to Davey – that of the Mermaid's Tide – until his ship rocked before them, untouched and perfect in every way. Even Kraken backed away upon seeing the ship.

"How did you do that?"

"As long as you are here The Tide cannot sink. It is only when you leave us will it return to the depths for when you would arrive again."

"And we take it…to their kingdom?"

"Yes, to a place I've never been before, that none of us have been before." Her gaze hovered to the large cavern where the water ran.

"And you think it's down there."

"There's only one way to find out." Gwen stepped forward.

"Then…we will be off, I think." Davey studied Kraken. "All of us, I hope."

FINFOLKAHEEM AND THE KEEPER'S END

Looking back from his perch on the frigate, Sirens' Isle appeared desolate, lifeless in its purpose, a mausoleum for the evils the Sirens committed. Only the broken caw of seagulls provided any sense of life. They were gone now, leaving the island abandoned, a haven to be rebuilt. Even the constant breeze sweeping across the cove's black waters felt less angry, but still held fast to the scent of spent bonfire and lilies.

Davey felt a tinge of pity, remembering the Sirens' tale about their enslavement to the Dark Guardian. He knew very little about this enemy of all enemies who wanted to rule over The Nether, only that he wanted to destroy his home – his mother's home – along the Chesapeake.

The idea of fighting this great evil sent a shudder up his spine and through his shoulders. Since his arrival in a land where fantastical creatures ruled, he didn't have time to ask any questions about the Dark Guardian's origin, too preoccupied with wanting to find his mother, and he wasn't even sure if Gwen's promise to make that happen would stand true.

Then again, what was real anymore?

He looked to the stern of the The Mermaid's Tide where a fugitive lightning bolt arced across the distant skyline. *He* was getting closer. What once felt like a day's lead dwindled to a half, possibly a quarter. The time spent on Sirens' Isle allowed him to catch up, and he was certain he would once again confront the spectral manifestation of his father's rage.

"Are you quite alright?" Gwen asked.

At first Davey didn't answer, too engrossed with the punishment he would receive by his father's hand.

"Davey, you in there?" Gwen's muddled face appeared in his line of vision, jarring Davey from his semi-comatose state.

"What? What was that?"

"I asked if you were quite alright?"

"I guess. Just…thinking."

"About?" Her eyebrows peaked in curiosity.

"Galendra." Davey eyed the ropes Galendra the Selkie used to bind him – to save him – from the pull of the Sirens' Song. "She's gone because of me."

"Why would you say such a thing?"

"Because." His voice cracked, but he hid the sadness. "Because if I fought back, if I was able to, she wouldn't be gone."

"You can't know that for sure."

"I do know." He looked into Gwen's knowing stare. "She sacrificed herself for me. It's not fair. She's gone, and there's nothing I can do about it."

"Is she now?" Gwen stood with a wry grin on her face. "Then you still have much to learn on your journey."

"How can you be like that?" Davey questioned, disturbed at Gwen's indifference. It reminded him of his father's hardened nature.

"Because, I know."

"Know what?"

"Know that she would want it this way. We all have a purpose. You and I, even Kraken are born for a reason, though he might need another talking to." She shifted her attention to the forlorn heap of Kraken, who secluded himself since they arrived back on The Tide. "Lives intertwine then fray. Most people cut off loose ends, memorializing them in pictures. I'm glad you want to hold onto something more. That's good of you."

"How can you be like that?"

"Be like what?"

"So…confident. I've never been that confident."

"It's not confidence. It's more like…faith that everything will be ok. We're all strong, including you."

"I don't know." Davey thought about his duel with Malent then to the confrontation with the Sirens. "I haven't contributed anything close to strength."

"We are a team. Are we not?"

"Don't teams stick together?" He focused on the cove where Galendra met her end. "Shouldn't we try to at least find her?"

"In time you'll learn. We all have an end. What markers we chose to leave on our path for others to discover are up to us."

"Funny."

"What's that?"

"Mom used to say something like that. She used to tell me I could do whatever I wanted. If I wanted to climb Mount Everest, I could. If I wanted to become a lawyer or even write a novel, I could." His eyes stung with her memory. He didn't want to cry, not in front of Gwen and the others. "I just wish she could've stuck around. Now I'm here, and I'm...lost."

"And what happens right before we're found?"

"Well, I guess, I mean, we're lo—?"

"Everything looks good." Arthur interrupted with the clang of his chain mail and labored breath. "She's held together. Not even the sign of a leak. It's...up to you how we take this next step."

"Yes." Gwen's forgiving gaze lingered on Davey before her attention shifted to the cavern on the opposite side of the cove, which echoed with the sound of rushing waters. "Finfolkaheem would be our destination," she said, referring to the Finfolk's kingdom.

"It is what you want, is it not?" Arthur asked, his taut cheeks emotionless but the void in his eyes displaying weakness for the first time.

There were things Davey wanted to know about Arthur Pendragon, things the knight alluded to while they were under the Sirens' spell. Yet, there was another who carried an even bigger burden, one who he needed to trust, a kindred spirit who caused the fall of Galendra. Davey peered between Gwen and Arthur to Kraken.

"Should we talk to him first?" Davey nodded to Kraken.

"Kraken?" Gwen sighed. "He'll recover in time. As I said, we all follow our own path. He'll have to find his before we can follow."

"Can it be found?"

"That'll be up to him, but for now you need to be sure about this. Do you want to go to Finfolkaheem?"

"Gregor said he was my grandfather's first mate. I mean, he must know things. He saved us," Davey kept fixed on Kraken. There was no other choice. If they abandoned Gregor's rescue and headed for Gwen's initial destination – this land across the Endless Ocean – then Galendra's fall would be for nothing, and Kraken's guilt would be a sentence he carried for eternity. "We go."

"And we go where the Keeper leads." Arthur smiled. "Can't say that I'm much of a sailor. My legs are best used on land, but I will most certainly follow anything you say. What would you have of me, my lady?" He looked to Gwen.

"Tend to Kraken. We need all four of us if we intend to take on an entire kingdom."

"I can talk to him," Davey interjected.

"You sure?" Arthur asked.

"I think I owe it to him. I'm the reason why he's in the situation."

"While I admire your sympathy, you must man the wheel. Only the Keeper can steer his ship from this point on." Gwen pointed to the ship's steering mechanism. As large as any tractor-trailer wheel, the ten spokes blanketed with seaweed loomed at the stern of The Tide.

"I don't know...how." The warm rush of embarrassment flooded his cheeks.

"And why should that stop you?"

"It shouldn't. It's just that I never sailed a boat before. Was too young when my grandfather had a boat. Mom sold it after he passed, and we didn't have the money to buy another one."

"Again, why should that stop you?"

"I don't...know."

"You won't know until you try. I'll watch, make sure you don't veer off course." Gwen's words flowed as naturally as a mother would to a child.

"Ok," Davey looked back at the cavern. He hadn't noticed, but The Tide drifted closer to the entrance. His fingers and toes tingled at the thought of maneuvering the large vessel through the cavern's narrow opening and towards an unknown destination.

"What if she lied? What if the Siren wasn't telling us the truth?" He stuttered.

"Under threat of losing song? I doubt it," Gwen said. Seconds later, Davey felt her arm nudge him towards the wheel.

He imagined entering the cavern, the sides of boat rubbing against rock and stalactite, peeling wood from hull, then sending them to a watery grave amidst a chorus of their cries. The wheel grew in size as they walked up the short flight of stairs to the captain's deck. Doubt dug its claws into his already fatigued state, scratching away at any confidence he held from facing the Sirens and Malent.

As he took the wheel by the two spokes, his fingers went numb with a thin film of sweat formed on his nose and lips. He needed to stall. He noticed Arthur and Kraken conversing on the deck, wishing he'd been assigned to mend the fences with Kraken rather than steer The Tide to certain doom.

"I've always wondered what it was like," Gwen said, the confidence in her tone far removed from Davey's inner-reservations.

"What's that?" Davey asked.

The frigate jarred to the left like a water flume ride. His arms shook as he fought to keep the wheel steady, holding his breath as the masthead entered first. So far, so good.

"Finfolkaheem. I've never been there, though I've never had reason to go."

"Then how do you know we're going the right way?"

"Because, I can feel it. It's there. And with it, Malent and the Finfolk."

Their voices echoed as The Tide breached the cavern's entrance, dousing the ship in shadow. A wall of humidity settled on the deck as she sailed deeper into the unknown. The sound of the ship scrapping, but not breaking, along the walls reverberated within the rock walls.

"Malent," Davey whispered and closed his eyes, keeping his arms locked on the wheel in a last ditch effort to prevent a shipwreck.

The Endless Ocean roared as the Mermaid's Tide rocked forward like a seesaw. Weightlessness pulled on Davey's legs. He gripped the steering wheel tighter as they picked up speed, wind blowing fast through his hair.

Part of him wanted to let go, for it all to be over. But what use was in meeting that end? He couldn't be afraid, not now, not this close. He owed them, all of them.

The roar of the current faded, replaced by a sound so tranquil, so relaxing, Davey nearly loosened his iron clad grip. It brass sound of a church handbell choir, of innocent echoes massaging his worries. With each chime, a rainbow of pastel lights pulsated around him as if he was navigating the ship through space.

Davey no longer felt gravity's pull attempt to rip The Mermaid's Tide apart. Rather, he floated upward as the chorus of blinking lights cascaded across the deck.

He reached out, watching the silhouette of his fingers spread wide in an effort to grab one of the lights – this one pastel blue – as it pulsated with enough intensity to blind him.

"What is it?" Davey asked, unsure of why he even proposed such a question.

"Those long forgotten. Those who would you see free," they answered in the voices of a thousand children of all dialects. Somehow, he was able to decipher their words.

"What?"

A green light shimmered to his right, lighting up the entire ship. He expected to see Gwen, Arthur, or Kraken, but they were gone.

"You are getting closer, Keeper. Trust in yourself." The green light pulsated with each word, followed by another short chorus of handbells. "See to it that his prophecy will go unfulfilled, and with it, freeing us"

"Who are you?"

"You have followed your instincts. Do not look back now."

"I won't." A frosted plume circled around his mouth as he exhaled, a million tiny ice crystals twinkling in the glow of the lights, forming, dissipating, then reforming different shapes.

Then, as if on command, the handbell chimes stopped, along with the orchestra of lights. Davey found himself left to darkness once more.

"Hello," a whisper called. The single word echoed in the void until there were a thousand "hellos" all speaking different languages.

Then he noticed – a point of a light in no certain direction. Unlike the pastels circling The Mermaid's Tide, this one was definite, concrete in its apparition. Though he couldn't feel the boat below, he saw the skeletons of the masts rising against the light with white becoming blue – an ocean blue.

"The ocean?" He asked.

Sound returned with a pop. Another symphony of instruments melded with the most beautiful of voices – a thousand angels in his mind calling for him.

Davey blinked and discovered a fantastical sight. An aqua landscape of ridges and mountains lit up by the phosphorescent glow of the sea surrounded the Mermaid's Tide.

Overtaken by curiosity, Davey ran to the side of the vessel, discovering a spectrum of electric colors painting the sea floor. A potpourri of vegetation, from three pronged stalks, each one capturing a different hue, to alien seaweed flowed in the sea. A crab as large as buffalo, its shell blinking with fluorescent lights, scurried across the bottom, more afraid than its size should dictate.

Davey pulled his hands to his face, finding the small fuzz of his arms wavering. They were underwater.

"I can breathe." Bubbles flowed from his mouth with each word.

"Davey," Gwen said, drawing Davey's attention to the mermaid, and a mermaid she was, a creature more beautiful every time he saw her. Her red hair appeared as vibrant as ever and flowed around her natural form. Her tail shimmered with the rainbow of electric colors as if a thousand diamonds were painted across her scales.

"You're back."

"We never left."

"But." Davey looked back, expecting to see the cavern's exit only to find a great mountain blocking their way. "Impossible."

"Remember, the Nether always changes its ways."

"It does." Davey remembered the purpose of their visit, taken back by the splendor of the underwater landscape. If this was heaven, he wanted to stay. "Are we—?"

"No."

"Then where are we?"

"Look forward and you will see." She whipped her tail around and floated backwards, revealing another fantastical sight.

Davey counted eight spirals reaching upwards, each one a perfect distance from the other, circling a translucent structure – a prismatic hallway fashioned to look like a pyramid. As The Mermaid's Tide coasted between two ridges, more crystal structures appeared within the spiral circle, each one surrounded by a garden of rainbow seaweed and ocean flora glowing in the phosphorescent light. With each sparkle, Davey thought he heard one of the church handbells toll. How could something so majestic, so beautiful stay hidden?

The underwater city came alive with the sighting of humanoid creatures swimming about the spirals, some riding on the backs of large seahorses, others tending to the gardens.

"What is this place?" Arthur asked, standing on the deck next to Kraken, who remained in his human form.

"Finfolkaheem," he said, drawing back as the details of the mythological town, one lost to the annals of oral tradition, shimmered into its full existence. Davey's heart sped up a few paces when he realized their quandary: they were uninvited guests, guests who got the best of Malent. Their welcome would both be unexpected and unwanted. "We need to stop before he spots us."

He looked up to see masts holding no sails. He immediately turned the wheel, but the ship did not move, rather remained fixed on its destination. He was a prisoner to the whim of the vessel.

"Gwen, how do we stop this?"

"We can't. He knows we're here."

"What does that mean?" Arthur asked. "That he knows we're here?"

"This is his kingdom, not ours. They rule here with magic not of our creation, and with it, we remain pawns to his whim," Gwen remained relaxed as she circled around, possibly enjoying the freedom of her natural state. Perhaps she wasn't worried because she could simply swim away, Davey thought, looking back to the expanding halls of Finfolkaheem. The closer they sailed, the more Davey realized the true breadth of Finfolkaheem: massive, a kingdom surrounded by monoliths and a crystal hall that would put the White House to shame.

"Then what should we do?" Arthur asked.

"There's nothing we can do. There are only four of us and an entire army of them." Gwen pointed forward. Davey turned to find a procession of figures mounted on large seahorses – larger than the biggest of stallions – approaching. They brandished petrified stalks of seaweed fashioned to a point at the tip in hand, their black hair highlighted with gold fashioned

152

with pearls and seashells.

"You should've warned us?" Davey said. "Why didn't you?"

"You knew the risk, and trust me, this might be a way to find yourself," Gwen answered, still showing no signs of concern.

"Kraken," Davey said, but Kraken didn't answer, remaining captivated by the sentinels.

"We need to fight," Davey insisted. "Do something."

"In times of war, we must realize when courage and bravery surrender to pride," Arthur said, his never-surrender composure lost, replaced by a stone expression of one facing his execution.

The two columns of seahorse-mounted Finfolk circled The Mermaid's Tide until they cut off their means of escape.

"Think it would have been better of us to have a plan," Kraken's cockney accent broke the tense silence. Even in the midst of certain doom, the boy-creature held onto his dark humor, much to Davey's chagrin.

The Finfolk's angular faces remain rigid, fixed on the four members of The Tide's crew. Davey wondered if any of them every experienced a smile.

"Keeper, present yourself," the Finfolk riding the largest seahorse, one clad in crab shells for armor, said from the bow's direction.

Davey looked to his companions. Each one of them placed themselves in danger because of him. He couldn't ask them to do anymore by hiding his nature.

"I am...who you are looking for." Before Davey could react, Arthur said, shoulders rolled back, chest forward. Again, another would put himself in danger for Davey.

"No." Davey stepped in front of Arthur with as much confidence as he could muster. "I am...the Keeper." He kept his eyes fixed down in the crevices between the planks, refusing to look up to the Finfolk.

"So, this is the one who Malent spoke of?" The Finfolk commander's voice boomed, prompting a hushed laughter from the others. "This one is a mere pauper, not even a threat. Perhaps Malent has lost himself." The subtle innuendo of dissension silenced the others. "Tell me, Keeper, what brings you to the halls of Finfolkaheem? Our riches of silver? Or perhaps you would seek to lend your power to our cause?"

"And what is your cause?" Gwen asked.

"Our cause is one of freedom."

"If it is of freedom, then why do I see slaves tend to your gardens?"

"Because, mermaid, what other purpose would humans serve?" The Finfolk commander's lips curled to a defiant grin.

"Humans?" Kraken scoffed. "Maybe you should hold your tongue."

"Animals excluded including yourself," the commander growled. The gregarious Finfolk dismounted from his stead, its pale face wrinkled with disgust as it swam towards Kraken. "Perhaps we should send him to tend the fields before Malent makes an example of the rest of you…if he still holds such a stomach."

"No." Water rushed around Davey as Gwen darted to Kraken's side, arriving as the Finfolk commander brandished his spear to Kraken's chest. Kraken remained poised, save a smirk reaching to his right ear. If there was ever a time for Kraken to release his fury, this was it. "Hold fast. We didn't come here to make war."

"Nor should you with the size of our army. A fool's errand to come here. Perhaps we overestimated the Keeper's intelligence." The Finfolk commander drew back.

"We came to ask for our friend's release," Gwen said. In an act of defiance, she pushed the spear from Kraken's chest. Her bravery was on full display for Davey, a fact not lost upon him. He wanted to follow her example.

"You came to *ask* for something?" The Finfolk stifled a laugh. "Do you realize your current position? Perhaps you misunderstand our intentions. A welcoming committee we are not."

"The only intentions I'm misunderstanding are why they're so many of you when there's only four of us?"

Davey watched Gwen's subtle threat ripple through the Finfolk platoon, each one looking at another as if the mermaid revealed some great secret. Their foreign tongue spoke of ill will but also revealed an unspoken fear within the ranks.

"Do not mistake my reserved nature as weakness. Humans who attempt to claim freedom are not long for this realm, especially those with an animal among them." The commander's eyes narrowed towards Kraken before leaning into Gwen. "Understand fish? Or would you rather visit the gardens? Maybe find yourself a suitable job among the land walkers?"

"Maybe you would like to meet the end of the Keeper's Light?" Gwen circled around, almost toying with the commander. "Would be a pleasant end to your existence, I'm sure."

The commander's eyes shot open as he tilted his jaw up, revealing a row of jagged teeth in a downturned smile. Gone was the Finfolk's flawless complexion, his impenetrable demeanor, replaced by genuine fear.

"That's not what I hear, what I understand." He feigned knowledge. "Your little savior doesn't know what he truly possesses."

"But I do." Davey, again finding a courage he didn't know he possessed. Again, his words permeated through the Finfolk ranks in a wave of nervous banter.

"Then should we put it to the test?" The commander asked, calling Davey's bluff.

"Ornay," came a shout from the crystal hall's direction. The commander's spine stiffened like a soldier called to attention. "Bring the whelp and the others, and make sure the beast is kept in chains. We would not want him to lose himself within the Great Hall."

Davey saw the message's carrier: another Finfolk clad in shell armor standing underneath the archway leading to crystal palace, but unlike the others, he wore no lavish headdress fashioned from pearl. Rather, he kept a shaved head and a thick collar around his neck, appearing more like a barbarian than an exquisite Finfolk. With a grunt, he dismissed himself.

"Command me without respect," Ornay muttered.

"What does he mean that the beast be kept in chains?" Gwen asked.

"Don't be foolish," Ornay said, nodding to a few of his men, who in turn leveled their spears in Kraken's direction and approached at a deliberate pace. "We can't afford to allow him into the palace knowing what he's capable of."

"What is this?" Kraken's nose crumpled as he readied himself for the Finfolk. Their spears elongated and twisted like a vine receiving a fresh does of rain.

"Yes, what is this?" Arthur grabbed his sword, but stopped short as another Finfolk jabbed his spear into his spine.

"This is our territory, not yours," Ornay said. "You would be wise to understand a land dweller's limitations underwater."

"You will regret this." Arthur surrendered.

"We will regret nothing. Now bind him. Make sure they are secure," Ornay commanded. Before Kraken could react, two Finfolk seized him from behind with a collar and two cuffs, securing his appendages.

"Kraken," Gwen called out.

Davey didn't understand. Kraken possessed the strength of a thousand men. Couldn't he just break out?

"Don't worry about me," Kraken struggled with the chains, only to be struck on the back of the head with the stalk of a spear, a single blow silencing him.

"It's time we see this light of yours," Ornay said. "Bring them. Time we get this over with."

II.

After a quick procession through seaweed gardens of bright yellows, reds and oranges, Davey and the others entered through an archway – an immense architectural wonder adorned with black and white pearls– and into the Great Hall of the Finfolk.

Lavish draperies in a spectacle of colors mirroring the gardens decorated the translucent walls. Columns fashioned from glass lined the chamber, and within the narrow structures, a rainbow of fish swam in circles, unaware of the terrible nature of their keepers. Hypnotic chimes tugging at Davey's eyelids resounded throughout the chamber, whispering for him to drop his guard.

The chamber emptied out into an even larger room. Intricately carved mosaics fashioned to depict different battle scenes of underwater sea life adorned the vaulted ceilings, reminding Davey of the cathedral back home. The ocean's phosphorescent light shone through the glass artwork, lighting up the hall in a cascade of colors. A silver throne at the head of the cavernous room – at least a football field's length from their position – sat abandoned, the only piece of furniture within the hall.

"Amazing." Davey couldn't help himself, captivated by the sheer size. He then noticed the first clue of Finfolkaheem's dark underbelly. Sulking forms lined the outermost walls, their lost gazes fixed on their arrival. Each one appeared bound to a Finfolk clothed in the now typical seashells and weaved sea grass. "Humans," he whispered. And they were, all of them slaves to their Finfolk masters.

"Stop," Ornay stuck the shaft of his spear into Davey's chest, prompting him to stop.

"Don't be afraid. This is necessary," Gwen said before drawing a hush from her guardian.

The brute of a Finfolk who commanded Ornay to enter the hall appeared at the seat of the throne, balled fists at his side, a derelict expression highlighted by a slack jaw.

"Are you ready...Thorfinn?" Ornay asked, making no effort to hide his displeasure.

"One moment." Thorfinn held up his hands. The human slaves stood in unison, their heads hanging down in either shame or defeat. The Finfolk army stood at attention, spears planted into the ground at a forty-five degree angle, backs straightened in an obedient military stance.

"Pull," Thorfinn swept his arm down, prompted the slaves to grab silver ropes hanging from the ceiling and pull down. Davey waited to hear something, but nothing sounded, no bell, no whistle, nothing.

But there was something. The water shifted. The fish contained within the crystal columns swam downwards. The way the mosaics above twinkled with a little less light. The current swirled around his ankles, tugging at his legs with the force of the riptide during his youth.

"It's draining," Arthur said.

"What's that?" Davey asked.

"They're emptying the chamber of water."

"In order to keep your beast at bay," Ornay said. "We wouldn't want him to lose himself while in the company of the king. The damage he could deal to these eternal halls…irreplaceable."

"You would deserve such a travesty," Gwen said just loud enough for Davey to hear.

"What was that?"

"Silence," Thorfinn's voice boomed.

Davey remained helpless until the weight of his body returned from the absence of water. He looked down to his feet where a floor once fashioned from crystal appeared marble.

Thorfinn swept his arm across his chest, which signaled the human slaves to release the ropes. Whips cracked in the background as the Finfolk masters rewarded the slaves for their efforts.

"No," Davey cried, breathing in his first mouthful of oxygen. As soon as the chilled air filled his lungs, his throat erupted with displaced water and caused his body to shake. Unable to control himself, Davey dropped to the floor with a thud, rolled over, and threw up more water across the floor.

Arthur joined him, spitting up water and holding his chest as oxygen flooded his body. Davey couldn't help but feel the pang of responsibility. It was the second time he'd led Arthur to such a terrible position.

"Get them up," Thorfinn sneered. With little remorse, two Finfolk underlings yanked Davey to his feet. Though his vision swirled, they kept him upright, pulling on the back of his hair, forcing him to look forward.

He realized the splendor of the Finfolk palace faded to the industry of marble and earth. Gone were the crystal walls, the symphony of light and sound, replaced by something more concrete, more uncaring.

Finfolkaheem's splendid veneer vanished, a facade of tranquility replaced by the true nature of their captors.

A horn blasted through the hall, followed by another, and another, until they hit a crescendo. It could've been Medieval Times with all the pomp and circumstance.

"Keep straight so the king would have words with you," Thorfinn's baritone voice commanded as he stepped down from the throne's plateau, his purposeful strides long like a gazelle as he approached another group of Finfolk – one of which Davey immediately recognized.

"Malent," Davey uttered, his unsteady words matching his anxiety.

Malent abandoned his black cloak in favor of ornate robe hemmed with pearls in long strings dragging behind. His hair didn't hold the same night shade as the others, capturing the glint of platinum and silver, but the regal entrance couldn't hide the foulness of the creature.

"I thought our bargain complete," Malent's words beat against Davey's chest. "Yet you set foot in my kingdom, a brash endeavor for which no free man has seen in several millennial. I would question your purpose, but I believe I already know."

Malent's spider-like arm sliced through the small opening in his robe, his talons for fingers curling to his palm. The wall groaned to his far right as stone separated from foundation, revealing a hidden entryway.

Two armored Finfolk emerged, holding oblong chains fashioned from coral and rock. They grunted as they yanked on the chains, once, then twice, until their ward emerged.

"Gregor," Davey gasped at the sight of the board-shoulder man. "What's wrong with him?"

It wasn't the shackles that surprised Davey, rather the blank expression and distant void within the giant's eyes. His skin appeared pasty and raw, with several lacerations from where a whip left its mark. His beard grew in an untamed manner, as wild as the jungle on Arthur's island. Absent was the warmness the father-like figure radiated, replaced by a hollow man.

His guards prodded him, poking him with spears, but Gregor barely seemed to notice, trudging forward without a semblance of recognition.

"Is this who you came for? The Beast of the Black Forest?" Malent needled Davey with his words. "A fair reward for our duel...if I remember correctly."

"What is the meaning of treating him like that?" Arthur demanded.

"Who...is this creature addressing me?" Malent asked, not taking his eyes off the shackled Gregor.

"Tell us your name, whelp," Ornay trumpeted.

"A true king does not treat his captives like this." Again, Arthur defied him.

"I see." Malent rubbed his chin. He sized up Arthur, his cheeks twitching like a man who would soon lose his nerve. "And it would quite the foolish man to challenge a king when he is no more than a jester."

"Even my jester would beat a king like yourself."

"Enough of this," Ornay growled and seized Arthur by his locks before sending him to the floor with a kick to the back of the knee. Arthur struggled against the hold, keeping his defiant stare locked on Malent.

"Ornay," Malent yelled, holding an open palm up. "Do not treat our guest in such a way. That would be unkind of you," his voice mellowed. "I would have plans for him. But first, the Keeper is here." His heavy stare fell upon Davey.

"Yes." Davey mimicked Arthur's poise, a falseness he hoped Malent wouldn't discover.

"I would assume it was your command to bring your companions here? Am I correct?" Malent took two deliberate steps down. "Typical human foolishness."

"I would have you," Kraken growled in a reprise of clanging chains as he jumped up, casting his guards aside. Malent took a step back as his lips tightened with concern. The shackles bent and elongated, but didn't succumb to Kraken's diluted strength as two more guards wrestled him back to the floor.

"You would have nothing. You bet is to obey my commands, and I may just make good use of you yet," Malent said.

"And what use would that be?" Gwen asked.

"One of the last mermaids speaks to me as if she were on my level. Pity. You will make a nice prize in my collection after our war."

"What war?" Davey interrupted.

"The war for The Nether, of course. This is my land, not the Dark Guardians. And with an animal." Malent pointed at Gregor. "And a legend." His talon shifted to Kraken. "And the light." Then skirted to Davey. "I would be unstoppable. This is my kingdom. I am the king. I kneel to no man." His voice escalated to a crescendo. "Do you understand?"

"You think you stand a chance against him?" Gwen asked, almost mixing laughter between her words.

"Why wouldn't I?"

"Only a fool would think he could defeat the Dark Guardian, lest stop him. To even consider fighting him is," Gwen paused, her soft eyes becoming despondent, "A sacrifice."

"Then you underestimate the scope of my power. I have an entire legion at my back."

"Does that legion include the Sirens who failed you? Did you think about that, about how the four of us were able to breach your so-called power?" Gwen stepped forward, drawing no baneful spears from the guards. "Do not underestimate the Keeper."

"You're lucky you're not a Finwoman. We would whip you for such insolence," Malent growled. Davey knew she hit a nerve.

"You lay your hand on the lady, and I would remove it just as fast," Arthur removed his sword in a single swoop, fast enough that it almost hummed. It was not without risk. The surrounding Finfolk leveled their spears at him as one unified unit. "And like a supposed king, you hide behind others. A coward."

"A coward he says," Malent sneered. "Would a coward allow you to remain in possession of your weapons? Would a coward take on the Dark Guardian? I think not. Bind him. Bind the mermaid, too. We've played enough of these games."

Then Davey noticed – whether by mistake or purpose – Gregor's bewildered gaze look in his direction, acknowledging something greater, an understanding of his role. Davey had to act.

"Wait," Davey said.

"Wait?" Malent hoisted his hand. Again, the Finfolk stopped their efforts. "What would the Keeper want for us to wait?"

"There has to be another trial."

"A trial? For what purpose? You intruded on my island before, but this, this is a—"

"A crime. You said it yourself. We're trespassing, and that's a crime from where I come from. So I want another trial."

"And what trial would you want without the great Gregor to protect you?"

"The Order demands a trial. Give it to him," Gwen said.

"Fool. This is my kingdom, and with it, the Order holds no ground. Do you understand? Bind her, bind them all."

"I would summon it." Davey imitated what Arthur would do. The bold act caused Gregor to stir, his zombie-like stance wavering again. "I would bring the lighthouse's power here."

Malent froze. Davey's threat, however false and full of bravado, worked.

"You lie," Malent's black tongue flickered like a snake.

"It's true. I used it against your Sirens," he lied, again feigning strength.

"Why do I detect such fallacies?"

"Fine. Then I would prove it." Davey remembered the Lord of the Rings, how the great magician Gandalf used his staff and uttered some nonsensical words to summon his magic. He could pretend as well, just act like the magician. He raised his hands, concentrating on anything his imagination could conjure. The only thing missing was a white beard.

"Wait. Wait right there. If it is a trial you want, a trial that you get." Malent descended the stairs.

"And what are the terms?" Gwen asked.

"Simple. We play along like we did in the land of mouth-breathers."

"Pull...pull out your sword," Davey stuttered, cursing himself on the inside at his first slip up. Malent would detect his fear.

"My sword?" Malent laughed. "A king would not draw upon another in court. No, I would name a champion."

"Then Ornay." Though overmatched, Davey would take out his anger on the Finfolk commander. If anyone deserved to fall, it was the wretched Finfolk who offended Gwen.

"Not quite." Malent clapped. "I have in mind someone greater. Someone...more appropriate."

"Then who?" Gwen asked.

"The Keeper will duel my beast." Malent smiled at Gregor.

"No," Davey lost his words just as fast. "I fight you, or I would release the light. That is what I offer."

"Listen to the boy. He challenges me like an equal. Did he not learn before?" Malent's multi-colored cloak flowed behind as he approached. Fetid water and lilies filled Davey's senses. "Then again, I would cherish the opportunity for revenge."

"No," Gregor woke. "He would fight me."

"Yes, he would fight you." Malent stopped, a deliberate grin revealing his rouse worked. "To the death."

"No," Gwen said, her desperate breath lost on Davey.

"That's not what I want." Davey scattered, reaching for his grandfather's sword.

"Such a youth does not understand the ways of the world. Fairness is a false hope." Malent returned to his throne. "A deal has been struck. A broken deal holds harsher consequences."

"I shouldn't have come," Davey muttered. He'd been defeated without even taking a swing.

"Release the beast...the Beast of the Black Forest," Malent commanded.

The Finfolk guards removed Gregor's shackles, scattering upon the last one to clatter to the floor.

"Clear center court. I would enjoy this before I take his light. And why not fetch me the finest of my wines." He draped his cloak across his silver throne. "This should be amusing."

The guards ushered a now bound Arthur, Kraken, and Gwen away from the center, leaving Davey abandoned. He knew the feeling well, often being the last player in dodgeball – at least until they banned the game. But this was no dodgeball game, and the fear was real.

"You ok?" Gregor's low voice boomed.

Davey looked up to see the beast's ghost-white body stagger into the circle. Though they were meant to duel, Gregor recaptured the soft glow Davey remembered. His muscles relaxed, somehow feeling – and knowing – everything would be all right.

"I've been beter."

"Awfully brave for you to try and rescue me."

"It was the right choice. You...helped me up there. Only wanted to return the favor, something my grandpop would have wanted."

"A good man. Will always remember him." They slowly circled each other.

"You don't have to do this. I'll take on Malent."

"But I do. It's the only things to do to make things right."

"What do you mean?"

"I didn't want to say," Gregor said, shying away. "But—"

"Enough of this babble. Gregor, why don't you introduce the Keeper to your true self," Malent slid to the edge of his seat, rubbing his hands together like some greedy banker about to make a mint in a deal.

"What?" Gregor lifted his head in surprise.

"You heard what I said. Show him why they call you the Beast of the Black Forest."

"This...this was not discussed when I accepted."

"Fine, then the duel results in a draw, and a draw goes to the hosts. Guards."

"Wait, wait." Gregor raised his maw and swallowed. "That...that is not necessary. I will obey."

"What's he talking about?" Davey asked.

"Don't be afraid. Know your grandfather fashioned that sword to protect him against all enemies."

"I don't understand."

"Enough." Malent slammed his fist down on the armchair.

"It is time to find yourself." Gregor's eyes shifted, the brown tint expanding outwards, swallowing the white. His muscles rippled then contorted with a pop as coarse hairs sprouted from every pour in Gregor's skin. "Do not be afraid."

Davey stepped back, watching the wicked display unfold. It couldn't be, or could it?

"Davey," Arthur said, meeting the three spears to his stomach, forcing him back in line with the others.

"You must...defend yourself." Gregor's distorted voice matched his stance. He lurched forward, placing two hands on the floor as his spine curled up, stretching skin, exposing more fur. Within seconds, Gregor transformed into something more beastly than human, complete with an elongated snout and eyes holding a quiet rage.

"No," Davey whispered. Out of the corner of his eye, he saw a grin of satisfaction sweep across Malent's face as the Finfolk king licked his lips, ready for a fight that would surely take Davey.

"Let me go. Let me go," Kraken's chain rattled to no avail.

"Keep yourself. Don't give in," Gwen said. Unlike Kraken and Arthur, she remained coy about overwhelming odds Davey faced at Gregor's hand. Whatever the cause, there was something Davey needed to capture that only Gwen knew.

"Run," Gregor yelled, expelling the last semblance of humanity as he rocked back to his hind legs, exposing a wide chest matted with the same black fur that blanketed his entire body. He exposed jagged ivory teeth along with claws as he stepped forward with a snort.

"I can't," Davey said, paralyzed with fear. He didn't want to look back up, instead focusing on his blade, imagining the adventures it'd seen by his grandfather's hand. As the shine in the sword faded from the werewolf's shadow falling over him, Davey felt the beast's breath upon him – moist and fragrant of death.

But something was off. There was calmness to it all, a silent understanding between the two.

"What are you waiting for? Take the boy," Malent hollered, but his words sounded like a mouse. "I said take him."

"Do what you must," Davey swallowed, ready to meet his end. "Know I'm sorry. I tried…for all of us."

"No." The beast still held Gregor's voice. "The blade is silver. Know that." The werewolf known as Gregor – the Beast of the Black Forest – opened his arms, exposing his torso.

"Silver," Davey muttered, realizing its purpose. Closing his eyes and quickly reciting one of his mom's old prayers, Davey thrust the sword's into Gregor's stomach. He thought he would meet resistance, instead, the blade punctured Gregor's skin with the ease of a straw through a fruit box.

"Thank you," Gregor whispered, clutching his stomach where Davey's sword found its mark. The beast staggered back and hollered towards the crystal ceiling turned marble.

"What is this? What is the meaning of this?" Malent bolted out of his chair.

Gregor howled again, a lone wolf calling for mates that would not come. He collapsed to the floor, his eyes rolling back until his body held no breath. His dying call carried across the vaulted structures, leaping from archway to archway, until it blasted down the far end of the Great Hall. Davey couldn't be sure, but he thought he heard a subtle crack as Gregor's cry dissipated.

"No. Get up. Get up. The beast betrayed us all," Malent seethed and raced towards the beast.

"I won," Davey whispered, looking at the tip of his sword which held no blood. He traveled all the way to Finfolkaheem to save Gregor only to end him instead."He's…he's gone."

"We can leave," Gwen said. "The duel is over. The Keeper has won."

"No. This will not stand," Malent demanded.

"It doesn't matter. You agreed to the terms," Gwen said, casting her captors aside. "The Order must be kept."

"Order? Did you not hear me? There is no Order here. This is my kingdom, not yours. I decide what's final and what isn't." Malent brandished his weaponed.

Another crack, this one louder and more definite, drew their attention to the ceiling where a few drips of ocean splashed down to the floor.

"We made a deal," Davey hesitated, looking around for an escape route that wouldn't come.

"Didn't you hear me? There is no deal to be made, and that light of yours will be mine." Malent raised his blade across his shoulder, but before he could react, Davey watched a larger shadow ellipse Malent's terrible form from behind – Gregor.

"No being controls me," Gregor growled, saliva dripping from his jaws.

"Save your king," Thorfinn yelled, followed by another crack, this one exposing Gregor's purpose.

A waterfall of ocean ripped through the cracks in the ceiling, sweeping over the floor with enough power to knock Finfolk to their feet. Davey watched as more pieces of the ceiling broke free, changing from stone to crystal, shattering as it hit the floor.

Malent screamed as Gregor pounced upon him. Claws dug into a struggling Malent. Gregor howled once more before an open jaw clamped down on the king's neck, prompting the Finfolk guards to panic, some dropping their spears, others fleeing to the entrance, dodging chunks of the ceiling.

"Gregor," Davey said.

Gregor recoiled and hollered towards the ceiling, exposing Malent's sword buried deep in his stomach, before clamping down again, maintaining his grip until he silenced Malent forever. And as Davey watched Malent's eyes roll to the back of his head, Gregor's stance relaxed. The beast's fur retreated into his naked body. The beast sacrificed himself for Davey again.

"Davey, we need to go," Gwen said. The mermaid transformed back to her native self as the water in the room reached his hips.

"We take him," Davey said. "We need to take him."

"What are you talking about?"

"Gregor comes with us."

"We must go," Arthur yelled with his back turned to Davey, beating back one of the disorganized Finfolk.

"Finfolk, on the king," Thorfinn commanded, his words lofting over the disorganized Finfolk. "Sound the conch! Sound the conch!"

"Enough," Kraken yelled, throwing off his guards. "I've heard enough horns in my time."

"He's going to change," Gwen said, her arms pulling Davey's waist.

"Not without Gregor." He reached out, his fingertips barely touching Gregor's facedown corpse. He wouldn't abandon him in the cursed kingdom of the Finfolk.

"Fine, but we must hurry. We need to return to The Tide." A trumpet blast so loud that it shook the foundation drowned out Gwen's words. Davey didn't realize, but his feet no longer touched the floor.

"Finfolk, take the intruders in the name of Malent," Thorfinn hollered, causing the water to swirl – or so Davey thought.

Kraken's tentacles breached the surface and wrapped around one of the columns. The structure couldn't withstand Kraken's strength, as the myth snapped the column in two, sending another section of ceiling tumbling into the rising waters.

"Stay with me now. You know your power." Gwen whispered, pulling Davey below.

With a few blinks, Davey said a silent prayer and breathed. Water funneled into his lungs, but he felt no pain, no sense of dying. He blinked again, the water becoming clear as his heart slowed.

Davey first spotted Arthur at the bottom with Gregor's lifeless body wrangled under his arm. At least he was safe.

As Davey surveyed the rest of the Great Hall, he noticed a much more worrisome sight: Kraken's bibulous form nearly filled a third of the hall. Finfolk swarmed in from the entrance and surrounded the nautical beast in a frantic effort to fend off imminent destruction.

"He's going to bring the whole thing down," Gwen pulled Davey to the bottom where they regrouped with Arthur. The Finfolk all but abandoned their pursuit of the three, focusing their efforts on prodding Kraken with spears that snapped with each jab.

"Do we stop him?" Davey asked.

"I'm afraid not. I've seen that look before. He wants his revenge," Gwen said.

"Then what?" Arthur said.

"We need to get to The Tide. We need to find the portal," Gwen insisted, guiding them against the far wall where the invisible ropes once hung. The sight reminded Davey of others in need, those slaves who remained captive in Finfolkaheem.

"What about the slaves?" he asked.

"Slaves?" Gwen answered, her attention fixed on Kraken, who swung his tentacle around and smashed another column. A pulse vibrated in the water, sending the three of them backwards.

"We can't let them stay here."

"The boy has a point," Arthur said, shifting Gregor's body to his left arm. "Wouldn't be right to abandon them."

"How would you find them?" She asked, her words muddled with urgency.

"They went in that direction." Arthur pointed to the oblong stone from where Gregor emerged. "Behind that stone."

"We can do it," Davey insisted.

Kraken lashed out with another tentacle, sending a row of Finfolk tumbling backwards. He groaned as another flank charged and jabbed their spears all at once, causing crimson fluid to erupt from Kraken's scales.

"No," Gwen winced, her attention volleying between Davey and Kraken. He knew she cared for Kraken, and leaving him to fend for himself against the Finfolk wasn't an option for her. "You go. I'll secure The Tide."

"Nonsense," Arthur said. "You're going to try and rescue him?"

"It's…not easy for me to abandon him. I need to try.".

"I don't understand. He's big enough to fend for himself."

"Go." She released Davey. "Go rescue them. Promise I'll meet up with you."

"What if they take you?"

"They won't. Believe me." Her lips formed a defiant frown. "Go, now. I'll find you with The Tide."

"Ok." Davey nodded. He didn't know how, but comfort found him. "We'll catch up with you."

Arthur nodded, slinging Gregor over his shoulders. The pair moved as fast as they could towards the discolored rock. And as they arrived, Davey looked back to see the end of the destruction. There was no sign of Gwen, just Kraken as he wrapped three more of his tentacles around the last of the supporting columns.

The room shook.

A crack louder than the last echoed.

"We go," Arthur insisted, touching the rock, which immediately dislodged from the foundation with a groan, exposing the tunnel. Arthur ushered Davey through, and as the knight followed, another crack sounded, and with it, the first of the columns tumbled, followed by another, bringing the entire hall down on Kraken and Gwen.

III.

The two swam through the claustrophobic passageway carved from rock, listening to the last of the destruction. All Davey could think about was the last glimpse of Kraken's carnage in the Great Hall and his friends' fate.

"Up ahead, I see something," Arthur said. "Looks like this empties somewhere."

"It does?" Davey answered only to let Arthur know he was still there – physically at least. His mind remained flat, his desire to continue decreasing with each step. He failed at every turn, and to see he disappointed his grandfather would be an understatement.

"Hopefully, we can find them right quick. Would do wonders for my arm."

"Sorry," Davey looked at Gregor's closed eyes. He seemed more asleep than dead. "It's just that I owe him."

"No need to explain. We all carry burdens." Arthur smiled before carrying on, the once dimmed phosphorescent light returned. "Here we go."

The tunnel spilled into a cramped room. It appeared in sharp contrast to the splendor of the Great Hall. Vegetation sprouted between crumbling stone, its purpose obviously not meant for royalty. A hundred little lights floated around them, highlighting every corner of the space. It wasn't until closer inspection that Davey noticed the lights were not lights, rather minuscule fish twinkling with each stroke of their fins.

"Looks like this is the end. No sign of the children," Arthur said, laying Gregor's body to the floor. "What do you think?"

"Something, isn't it?" Davey said, transfixed by the light display. He imagined himself running through his front yard in June, mason car in one hand, a converted aquarium net in the other, hoping to catch his first firefly of the season.

"What's that?"

"Fact that something so small can make it, even down here."

"Oh, lad, you'd be surprised what a little effort will do in your life."

"A little effort?" The words trailed off Davey's lips as he went to poke one of the luminescent fish. The fish swirled about then resumed its endless journey.

"One never gives up when hope is involved. These little things may have hope even in this domain."

"What about the slaves? Where is their hope if they're not here?"

"Don't tell me that you've given up already? Much too soon for that" Arthur pressed his hands against the wall, prodding each crag with his fingers. "We encountered one false stone. There must be another."

Davey joined in the effort, but not before one of the small fish landed on the bridge of his nose, its fins flapping as it hovered, looking straight into Davey's eyes. Davey stared at it as if the two were two travelers passing in different directions, each with their own story to tell.

"What are you doing?" Davey asked, not realizing he spoke.

Then, as if guided by some mysterious hand, the pulsating fish hovered to the far end of the room. One by one, the lights joined each other, forming lines of illumination.

"Magic?" Davey asked, watching as Arthur continued his search.

More lines formed, parallel to each other in symmetrical bars of light, until Davey realized they had a purpose. They formed the outline of a cage, and with the final bar joining, the structure pulsed once, casting a blinding light throughout the room. Davey closed his eyes as tight as he could and shielded them with his hands. Then he heard it: whimpering.

"Children," Arthur said. "Can't be."

Davey opened his eyes to see children no older than he, all huddled in a corner, holding starved legs to chest. It reminded him of the Selkies.

"How?" Davey said. The lights faded, dissolving the cell. "They're kids."

"Hope is not lost for them. Not yet at least." Arthur said, kneeling next to the closest of child, one with dirtied blonde hair and a face too angelic to be caged.

"How wrong you are," the voice boomed from behind, followed by gagging. Davey and Arthur twisted around, revealing Ornay float into the room, his left leg a crooked debacle trailing behind. Scars and patches of dark green smeared his face. "There is no hope for any of you."

"And how would you know about hope?" Arthur stood as the children cowered closer together, shielding eyes from their personal boogeyman.

"I know that I have the both of you. And you would have—"

Before Ornay could react, Arthur seized the Finfolk by the neck and slammed him into the wall.

"I'll give you one chance, and one chance only, how do we leave this place?" Arthur leaned into Ornay, showing no sign of weakness or mercy.

"Does it matter?" Ornay asked. "There is no escape. Even now, Malent's army surrounds you."

"Perhaps you didn't hear me?" Arthur pressed even harder. "The way out, if you would be so kind."

"You…you think I would show you?"

"It's right here," a squeak of a voice came from behind. One of the children extended his finger towards the ceiling where a circular stone extended out halfway around the room's circumference.

"No," Ornay squirmed, his secret revealed.

"Enough of you," Arthur said, slamming Ornay back into the wall. The Finfolk's head ricocheted against the rock, his disdainful glare vanishing as his eyes lolled back into the oblivion of his mind, floating down to the floor. The lights discovered a new purpose, swimming towards Ornay, one by one forming a bubble around the lifeless form.

"Where did you say it was?" Davey focused on the child.

"We seen them just swim towards the stone. It'll open up to the ocean," the red-haired boy said.

"Very good. Very, very good," Arthur said. "Very brave of you."

"Can you all swim?" Davey asked.

The children looked at one another – wide eyes knowing only fear – but did not speak.

"They're all gone. Promise. You're safe with us."

"We can swim," the apparent leader of the children answered. "But where are we going? Last time one of us escaped they punished us.

Whipped us."

"There will be no more punishment. Not now. Not ever," Arthur said, shedding the anger he used against Ornay. "We'll take you to safety. Have a big ship that will take you away from this place. Ain't that right, Davey?"

"Yes, we will." Davey didn't know if he spoke the truth. The Mermaid's Tide was lost by all accounts, and if Ornay's words were true, they would certainly confront another band of Finfolk.

"The boy will lead us out. I will be the last," Arthur looked up. "You say the stone will show us the way."

The red-haired boy nodded with authority, his dirtied face exposing a yearning for freedom.

"Ok, but remember to stick together," Davey said. "All of us."

Kicking his feet, Davey swam towards the stone circle. One by one the ten children followed, some slower than others, but all holding the same anticipation for escape. They each had a home at one time. Davey wanted to help them find that home.

He didn't know what to expect, but as he ascended, the stone rippled from a solid mass to a crystal pool as if he tossed a pebble into its center. The vast ocean of rainbow colors and towering spirals manifested on the opposite side. It was indeed an escape.

"Stay close." Davey pushed through the crystal façade and out into the cooler waters. His flesh pimpled out as he helped them through, but as they escaped Davey noticed to his right several dozen silhouettes. Even though he couldn't see, he imagined their sinister grins, their hatred for the land-dwellers.

"Finfolk," Davey whispered as the children found their smiles. He couldn't let them down, not now. "Arthur," he called. Instinct took over. He would protect the children at all costs, their pain familiar to him. "Arthur."

The first of the children whimpered as he noticed, his arms and legs darting out in a wave of panic. Davey needed to think, and with no sign of Kraken or Gwen, they were on their own.

"Davey," Arthur said, pulling Gregor's limp form through the portal.

"We need to return. We need to return or they'll punish us." The red-haired kid stammered, eyes filled with fear only a beaten child would know. His companions followed suit, jaws trembling, cheeks flushed with fear. Visions of another beating surely were on their minds. And for that moment, Davey saw himself and remembered his promise: If he ever saw another child in need, treated in the same way his father treated him, he would do anything to save the child.

"No, we go. I'm not going to let you guys go back into that cell," Davey insisted, drawing his ire back to the approaching Finfolk militia. Sure they were outnumbered, outmatched, but there would be no more running. There was a purpose for his journey. The idea of being locked up in some magical cell wasn't that end. "You ready?"

"I already pledged my loyalty to you. That goes to the end." Arthur brandished his sword and looked back at the small platoon of scared children. "Stay behind us. All of you. We promise no harm will come your way."

The children huddled behind much in the same way they did while captured, exposing lash marks tattooed on their backs.

"Good." Davey's skin tingled with adrenaline. "The end. This will not be ours."

Fifty feet became forty as the approaching legion of Finfolk darted in and out of different crags, swimming through the spiral towers, their numbers filling the sea.

"Are you ready for this?"

"No, but we'll win."

Thirty feet. The first line drew up their spears with one hand and nets with the other. Nets, Davey thought. They didn't intend to harm them, rather to capture Davey and the children, possibly using them as slaves.

"Yes we will." Arthur's brown eyes grew big in both confidence and defiance.

A high-pitched wail resounded through the waters, followed by another. The first line of Finfolk stopped, released their weapons, and held their ears tight while letting out a stomach-curdling scream. Another wail, this one louder and more forceful, caused more Finfolk to cower, ivory teeth exposed as they cried out in agony.

"What...what is that?" Arthur asked, his head darting in different directions.

Something caught Davey's attention to his right. The mass darted one way then another, resembling a school of fish. The Finfolk took notice as well, some retreating, others frantically reaching for their spears.

"March...forward," a Finfolk shouted, but wasn't long for his own command as he curled backwards, clutching his head as another cry blasted over them.

"It can't be," Arthur said.

"Galendra." The Selkie leading an army of her kin was improbable as anything. But it wasn't the impromptu rescue that tugged at Davey's upturned lips, it was Galendra adorning the seal tail of her species. She found her way home.

"It's her," Arthur said, followed by a boisterous laugh. "It has to be her."

Galendra and her Selkie companions dwarfed the beleaguered clan of

Finfolk. Overwhelmed and with no ability to defend themselves, the Finfolk retreated in a chaotic scene reminiscent of the Great Hall.

The children saw this too, cheering, realizing they indeed have a chance to be set free.

"Galendra," Davey yelled and waved at their companion. With a slight smile and a wave back,

Galendra darted off into the fray without a word where another old friend introduced itself in the throng of Finfolk and Selkie. The long grain lines of the ship's masthead – a mermaid carved by Kraken – parted the fleeing Finfolk.

"Gwen," Davey said, "she must've made it."

IV.

The children were eager to leave Finfolkaheem, wearing smiles ready to rediscover happiness. As they sailed through the turquoise majesty and over the rubble of the Great Hall, under the archway adorned with pearls and flanked by rainbow gardens, Davey wondered how such beauty and grace could hold so much darkness. It would serve as a graveyard of sorts for the Finfolk. Maybe some of them would see the error of their ways. Maybe some of them wouldn't.

"You ok?" Gwen swam up next to him, her fingers tickling his neck in spite of their current situation. He glanced back over his shoulder at the crystalline destruction and the innocence it stole from the children.

"Seems like you're asking me that question a lot these days, but I'm ok. Thank you, again."

"There is no need to thank me. Not at all. How such beauty can hold such deceit. It's one of life's great mysteries."

"I've been fooled too many times. Know better now."

"That's what builds character. Struggle. Overcoming obstacles."

"Are the children...think they'll ever be ok?"

"I'm sure they will."

"What will become of them? I mean, why are they even here?"

"Life took them too early. It'll take some time to heal those wounds, but they can be mended." She sighed, apparent she held something back.

"Hope so," Davey said, bracing himself on the ship's wheel as they breached the portal, welcomed by the return of the hand bell symphony and pastel lights. Ocean water soon subsided, cascading off the ship's sides as Davey's weight returned to Davey, as did a fresh lungful of oxygen. He held fast to the ship as the undersea kingdom closed.

"Will never get used to that," Davey spit out another mouthful of water. "You ok?"

171

"Yes, though I was just getting used to being back in my natural form."

"And Kraken?"

"Recovering." The beast survived the Great Hall's destruction, secluding himself on the deck with a jigsaw puzzle of bandages covering his body. He seemed reserved, holding company not being his priority. "He's happy Galendra survived."

"So am I."

Without warning, the ship's bow rocked upwards before propelling forward. They were returning to The Nether. Davey readjusted his grip on the wheel, a last ditch effort to maintain his footing as gravity pulled at his body until the ship leveled off. The fresh scent of lilies and limestone returned.

Seconds later, the cavern ejected The Mermaid's Tide to a spray of black waters and the crack of lightning. Whitecaps splashed onto the deck, forming a thin layer of the same oil like substance from their time on Arthur's island. But they had other things to worry about. The ship wrenched right, then spun around like a merry-go-round.

"Davey," Gwen whispered, her subtle words capturing her surprise.

"Dad," he answered, focusing on the storm's genesis – the specter ship blocking their escape from the cove. With a crew of one, the ominous cloud of his father's rage manifested, its purpose deliberate to see Davey's end.

"Arthur, get Kraken up. We need to secure the sails," Gwen ordered as a smattering of rain fell from the sky. Another gust of wind blasted over The Mermaid's Tide, sending Davey crashing to the floor.

Pain jolted his ribs, but Davey wouldn't allow himself to lose consciousness, not with his father's spirit waiting for him.

"Get up," he said, rolling to his side as the pain subsided. He heard the makings of a scuffle on deck, followed by the clash of metal and a scream.

"The kids," Davey muttered, planting one wobbling foot on the ground. His vision swirled before he righted himself. He squeezed his eyes shut then opened hem to see his albatross levitating before him.

"My son," his father's voice boomed.

Davey backed away, noticing his companion's lifeless bodies drug across the deck at the wind's behest. He was alone in this fight.

"I told you to return with me. Now it looks like I'm going to have to persuade you in other ways." The storm's intensity matched his father's fevered words, tearing at the half-raised sails snapping against the masts.

Davey refused to back down. He couldn't. Against all logic, Davey peered into the precipice of his father's anger – a pulsing void commanding the storm. As he stared into the abyss, all sense of happiness, of whatever jubilation he was able to harness in the far away world, sapped from his body. There was nothing, no hope, no sanctuary, simply nothing. Only emptiness.

"Why?" Davey asked, struggling to find a reason to go on.

"Because the world will have its end, and you only stand in its way." The mass thickened and expanded before retracting. The form slowly faded to a translucent torso with arms and legs. Moments later, his father's towering spectral form loomed over him.

"I asked why," Davey repeated.

Fear should've driven him into his father's arm, cowering before the thought of receiving another beating. He didn't. Instead, he saw the rest of his dead end life flash before him.

He would return to an empty shell of a home where he hoped for his mother's impossible return. That's all that it was: a mere hope, a false expectancy. He was a fool to think he would see her again. Guilt abandoned his sub-conscious, replaced by absolution – the last notes of his mother's song lingering in the first autumn breeze along the Chesapeake. Four walls didn't make a home. It was family, and family wasn't reserved to only blood, especially his father's.

"I'm not going with you," Davey said. "There's nothing for me."

"Don't be a fool." His father's spectral form levitated forward. "You're coming home."

"And where is that?'

"You know where."

"Back where you drink all day, huh? Is it back where you come home drunk and take your anger out on me? Is that's where it's at?"

"Don't get smart with me."

"I will get smart. I'm not some punching bag for you to take your anger out since Mom left." Davey defied apprehension. "If you loved her so much, you should look in the mirror. See what you did to your son."

"The son who forced my wife to take her life." His voice thundered with the storm.

"No. Not this time. I've heard that story too many times when you're drunk. I'm not running from you any longer."

"Then I would show you what suffering really is."

A blast of wind seized the bow of the ship, lifting it up before slamming it back down, mirroring his father's anger. Davey refused to fall. Not this time.

"I think you'll leave without me." Davey couldn't believe the words that came from his mouth. The last time he stuck up to his father, he received the end of beer bottle to his temple.

"Looks like it's time for another lesson."

"Enough lessons. Enough teaching. I think it's time for you to leave."

Another sheet or rain poured down as a stretch of lightning exploded on the center mast, igniting the sky in a firework of colors. For a second, Davey saw his father's true face reflecting against the specter's translucent façade – sad, lonely, and forsaken – a rotten symbol of all that was wrong with the life Davey led. "I know you love me somewhere deep in that heart of yours, but I can't be with you anymore."

Davey closed his eyes, picturing the concrete monolith painted in red and white reaching up to a baby blue sky. An orange hue glowed down the length of the structure, a fire blazing as hot as Nebuchadnezzar's furnace.

Its energy coursed through Davey's body, a rage meant to punish the wicked. He imagined the blaze growing to a raging inferno, shooting out to every corner of the earth and beyond.

Its warmth massaged his flesh, its signal ripping the fabric between the two worlds. Below, The Mermaid's Tide shuddered, and with it, he heard his father scream.

"You need to go home." Davey opened his eyes seconds before the beam of light and fire speared his father's form, enveloping it in a wave of energy so profound that the black waters awakened to gold and silver.

"No. No." His father panicked within the light, tearing at his chest, falling to one knee as the world around him tore open, revealing a scene familiar to Davey – the Lighthouse on Mermaid Row.

"I'm sorry dad," Davey whispered, realizing he would never return home, leaving behind both good and bad memories. He pictured his grandfather rocking on the porch, his mother trying her hand at a Smith Island Cake, and his father who once knew himself asking for help to build the outside deck. It was the good memories he would hold.

"Davey," his father yelled, reaching with a hand made of flesh, not spirit.

"Go home, dad. You don't belong here." Davey turned away, giving one last glance as the curtain between the two worlds sucked his father inside.

"Please. I love you, son. I'm so sorry," his father begged, words lost to the storm's last gasp.

"I know." Davey closed his eyes again, imagining the lighthouse's fire extinguish.

"Davey," Gwen said.

Davey kept his eyes closed as the boat stopped rocking. The first caw of a seagull told him everything would be ok. The toll of a harbor bell, the rush of a wave onto shore, the fizz of ocean foam upon sand, lifted his worries.

"He's up there," Arthur said.

Davey opened his eyes to a scene familiar to him – a landscape he saw within his mother's painting, the one he kept hidden from his father. The

174

yellow morning brought upon by the sunrise bathed him with warmness, its rays shimmering in the gold waters.

Below, a procession of multi-colored fish circled about the boat. Birds as large as pterodactyls, covered in perfectly white feathers glided along the wind. They were looking over him, perhaps long lost relatives in spirit form.

"Gwen," Davey swallowed as he looked upon the mermaid.

"Davey," his mother's calming voice replaced Gwen's. His lips trembled upon watching Gwen's face age just slightly, her jaws growing a little longer, her hair a little less red. He looked into his mother's face the morning before she took her life.

"Mom," his voice cracked as he threw himself into her arms – a hug that he'd been waiting to experience. He buried his face into her stomach, basking in the smell of lilies and vanilla perfume, wishing the moment would never end. Tears sprang forth, but he wasn't ashamed.

"It's ok," she said, running her fingers through his hair. "It's good to see you, too."

"I don't understand." He pulled back, wiping his face to see Kraken and Arthur keep at a distance.

"It'll be ok. We'll all be ok."

"It was you all along, wasn't it?" He didn't know whether to feel betrayed or thankful.

"Yes, it was."

"Why?"

"I couldn't reveal myself, not until you were ready."

"Ready?"

"Yes. If I didn't allow you room to grow, you wouldn't have grown to take on your challenge." She knelt at eye level, her emerald-green eyes projecting a saddened contemplation. "And boy how much you have grown. You're a brave little one. A mother couldn't be more proud."

"So, then we're reunited. We can stay here. We can fish." Davey cracked a smile and turned towards Sirens' Isle, or what he assumed would be Siren's Isle. Instead, he saw a foreign land, a shoreline extending along the horizon as far as he could see. Though sun replaced night above the Endless Ocean, dark clouds hovered above the unknown continent, casting it into shadows. "What? I don't understand? We're right here."

"This was always your destiny. Though I love you and want nothing more to be with you, you are your own person, a person with a calling."

"What...what do you mean?" He turned to see the downturn in her mother's strawberry lips, a glaze over her eyes. Something was wrong. Something was very wrong.

"I'm sorry."

"You can't stay with me, can you?" He knew.

"That is not the way The Nether works."

"Yes, yes you can. Can't she?" He looked up to Arthur and Kraken for guidance. Both avoided eye contact.

"She can't, Davey." Another voice – one familiar yet distant – pulled Davey's attention up to a sight he didn't expect to see. Gregor stumbled up the stairs, a wearied expression marring his face. "That's not how it works."

"Gregor?" Davey stepped back, nearly tripping over a splintered board.

"At your service." He took a bow, joining Davey's mother.

"You're alive. How? None of this makes any sense."

"It will in time." He sighed. "But we need to get going."

"What?" He asked, grabbing onto his mother.

"Your task has just begun."

"No, this isn't right. I've done all the good things you told me to be, mom. How come I can't spend time with you here?"

"Because," she said, "my crime is not one I can escape."

"But I'm helping everyone." Another tear trailed down his cheek.

"I know." She embraced him again. "And I should've never left. So much more to tell."

"No, my lady, not now." Gregor interrupted as thunder rumbled over the foreign land. "I'm afraid you must let him go now."

Gregor's soft, but calloused hands pressed upon the top of Davey's head.

"No," Davey shrugged him off, only to feel it again on him. "Why?"

"I'm so sorry," she said, her face red, glistening with remorse.

"This...this isn't fair. I want to know why," he demanded, hiding behind his hands.

"Arthur, please," Gregor said. "I need to prepare to depart."

"Of course." Arthur gentle hands cupped around Davey's shoulders and pulled back, but not before another pulled at him.

"Relax, Davey. I believe in you," Kraken said.

Davey opened his fingers just enough to see Kraken's faded green skin, his reptilians eyes staring back at him. Just for a second, Davey thought he was looking into a mirror.

"What?" Davey asked.

Kraken joined Davey's mother at her side. Much to Davey's surprise, she wrapped an arm around Kraken's shoulder in a maternal way.

"We need to take you to shore before the sun sets. He can't see us in the light," Gregor said, hoisting a sack over his broad shoulders. How or what resurrected him would remain a mystery. "A little birdy tells me our party has already arrived."

"What party is that?" Arthur asked.

"Think it'll be one glad to see the little feller here. Proved himself just right today. He's a fine Keeper." Gregor threw the sack overboard. "I take it you'll be joining us?"

"Would be an honor."

Davey focused on the forested land where feral trees hugged the shoreline like witches dancing around a cauldron.

"I'm not going without them," Davey said, looking at his mother and Kraken. "They can come with us."

"They can't. They aren't allowed on the mainland."

"Then I'm staying here."

"Without you, all hope is lost," Gregor answered without a semblance of compassion, rather a bit of haste as he tossed another sack overboard. "We have no time for further discussion. Not until we arrive."

"Mom?" Davey asked. He knew. There wasn't another way.

"I'll take care of mom." Kraken brandished his trademark crooked smile. "We need to get our other passengers away from here passengers we wouldn't have if it wasn't for you."

"Do me proud, just like your grandfather." She scuffed his hair again. "Make sure you find those kids and get them back home."

"To bring them back?" Davey asked. He knew better. He came for a purpose. The reunion was not one of them.

"Yes." His mother kissed him on the forehead.

"Time to go," Gregor hoisted Davey up by the chest and brought him on his boulder-sized shoulders. The hurried exit played out faster than Davey liked. Before he knew it, Gregor rappelled down the side of the ship towards a rowboat Arthur manned.

Davey looked up as they descended, seeing his mother and Kraken watch their movements.

"Love you, mom," Davey mouthed, watching the sun swallow their silhouettes. What crime was she talking about?

Davey took the middle bench seat with Gregor helming the oars as the rope fell to the waters. He kept his eyes focused on The Mermaid's Tide. Its sails raced up the masts, the wind already finding its purpose.

"You'll find, Sir Knight," Arthur said, "All great adventures face moments of doubt. You already passed yours."

"Don't get so comfortable," Gregor said. "Pendragon is it?"

"Yes"

"Good to have you aboard." Gregor heaved as the oars churned the water. Davey noticed the once shimmering gold reflection fade to water absent of fish and skeletons of seaweed reaching up from below.

"The honor is mine," Arthur answered, adjusting his mail.

Davey studied the forested landmass where a purposeful howls welcomed them to shore.

"What is that?" Davey asked, his mind still lost in the flurry of activity.

"That, my boy, is the heart of The Nether calling. And it's up to us to make sure you get the other band of heroes to safety."

"Think we can do it?" Davey asked. "Like rescuers?"

"Yes, if we want both worlds to survive."

With one last row, the three coasted into the shore and the beginning of Davey's next great adventure.

ABOUT THE AUTHOR

JC Braswell lives on the Chesapeake in Maryland with his wife, Mika, and their daughter, Ayana.

Please visit www.jcbraswell.com for news on his other releases and to join his newsletter.

www.ingramcontent.com/pod-product-compliance
Lightning Source LLC
Chambersburg PA
CBHW060155130626

46556CB00006B/2656